D0917056

AMERICAN GIRL

BOOKS BY WENDY WALKER

All Is Not Forgotten

Emma in the Night

The Night Before

Don't Look for Me

Hold Your Breath

American Girl

What Remains

WENDY WALKER

A NOVEL

AMERICAN GIRL

BLACK
STONE
PUBLISHING

Copyright © 2023 by Wendy Walker
Published in 2023 by Blackstone Publishing
Cover design by Audible

All rights reserved. This book or any portion
thereof may not be reproduced or used in any manner
whatsoever without the express written permission
of the publisher except for the use of brief quotations
in a book review.

The characters and events in this book are fictitious.
Any similarity to real persons, living or dead, is coincidental
and not intended by the author.

Printed in the United States of America

First edition: 2023
ISBN 979-8-212-38532-9
Fiction / Thrillers / Psychological

Version 1

Blackstone Publishing
31 Mistletoe Rd.
Ashland, OR 97520

www.BlackstonePublishing.com

For Sharon Cohen

PROLOGUE

Rule Number Three: People are predictable.

Which is how I know everyone will be asleep when I get home. I take a shower and wash away the smell of the grease from the grill and the juice from the pickles. I wash my hair and put in conditioner and wait exactly two minutes, like it says on the bottle, counting the seconds in my head. I rinse it out. I reach for the faucet, but then, suddenly, I stop.

Soap, shampoo, conditioner for two minutes. Water off, reach for the towel—which is on the rack—dry body, wrap hair, put on pajamas . . .

I remember all the things that come next, but I stand still, the water pounding the top of my head, because something isn't right.

It's the bleach. The smell of the bleach that I can't wash clean. And this smell has derailed my train of thought.

My heart takes over now, and not in the emotional way, but in the *holy-shit-what-do-I-do-now* way. In the pounding-faster-and-faster way. In the blood-rushing-through-my-veins-and-then-up-to-my-head-where-it-heats-up-and-makes-me-turn-and-press-my-palms-against-the-wall-so-I-don't-fall-over way.

I am not equipped for any of this. For what's happened tonight. For what will happen tomorrow. I am just a girl with a set of stupid rules.

There's a soft knock on the door, and then my mom's voice. It comes in an irritated whisper, which is the only way she can yell at me without waking up Dusty and their boys. My mom had been sleeping too when I got home. She would have whispered her yell at me sooner if she'd been awake and heard me coming up the stairs.

"Charlie!"

I turn off the shower but don't answer. The cold grabs me in seconds as the drops of water on my skin thermoregulate the temperature of the air.

"Charlie!" The whisper is louder now.

I can't find my breath to speak. I grab the towel and wrap it around my body, which isn't the right order of things, but I do it anyway, then I open the door.

My mom steps back, crosses her arms, and looks at me, the irritation now sweeping across her face. I know every single one of her expressions.

"What are you doing? It's four in the morning!"

I start to shiver. Her face softens and she sighs, which means her irritation is turning into worry. She steps inside the steamy room and closes the door behind her.

"Here," she says. And then she finds my pajamas, unfolds them, and hands me the pieces one at a time, all with her back turned. She does not touch me or look at me while I'm naked, because the last thing she wants at four in the morning is for me to be upset. She wants me to get into bed and go to sleep so she can go back to sleep, because she's always tired from something. My mom says she would sleep for a year if God would let her.

When my pajamas are on and my hair is wrapped in the towel, I tell her I'm fine, and she leans her face in close until my eyes meet her eyes so she can tell if I'm lying. I avoid seeing her thoughts by counting her eyelashes. It's a trick I discovered when I was thirteen.

She makes her decision, then backs away.

"Okay. Now go to bed!"

I promise I will. And I do. I walk back to my room, brush my hair, and get into my bed.

Under the covers, I shiver again until I stop, and then I wait for the news to break and the texts to come, which they do a few hours later. There are no dreams and no memories of waking, and my body remains in the exact same position. But the time passes quickly, so I know I sleep for some of it.

The first text comes at seven thirty. It's from Nora, the manager of The Triple S. The others follow within seconds as the big news spreads across our small town. News that will be inside the walls of this house any second too. News I brought with me when I walked through the back door, smelling of sandwiches and bleach. And fear.

One after another they come, and I read them but don't reply. I know what to say, what to write, but I can't make my fingers move. Not yet. All I can do in this last moment before my mom is back with a louder knock and a real yell is read about how a man is dead, not just any man, but the most important man in our whole entire town, and then try to predict what each and every person in my life will do next.

Which is hard, because all rules fail under certain circumstances. Some people call those caveats—it sounds better than the word *failure*—but failure is what really happens when a rule doesn't hold true.

Rule Number Three, Caveat One: People are predictable until someone gets killed.

CHAPTER ONE
TWELVE YEARS EARLIER

I was five when my mom lifted me from my bed and into her arms. Before I was even fully awake, she whispered in my ear, "We're getting out of this place."

The fighting must have been going on for a while by then, because they had gotten to the part when one person has stopped yelling and is running away.

My mom carried me as she ran out of the house where I was born and where she was born—the only home either of us had ever had.

I wrapped my arms around her neck and my legs around her waist as tight as I could so I wouldn't fall. She was running fast.

Over her shoulder, I saw my grandmother storm after us, and then my grandfather behind her. They were both in their pajamas, and my grandmother's curlers were loose and uneven. This was how I knew it was the middle of the night and that the fight had woken them.

My mom had to put me down at the curb to open the car door, and when she did, my grandmother caught up. She grabbed my shoulders and turned me to face my mom. It was then that I saw she was wearing her going-out clothes and her going-out makeup, which meant the fight must've been about her going out after her shift at the diner. She'd been crying, so the makeup was running down her cheeks like railroad tracks, one on each side of her face.

My grandmother let go and I fell forward into my mom.

"Go ahead and take her!" she screamed. "You'll never be able to raise a child like that! No. Way. In. Hell." When screaming was not enough, she spoke with her words broken up, like each one was its own sentence. This was one of the few things I would remember about her.

My mom put me into the car and reached for the seat belt, her black tears dripping on my head as she struggled to make it click, and she told me, "Close your ears! Close your ears!" So I put one hand over each of my ears and pressed hard.

And then she shut the door and ran to the other side while my grandmother kept saying things. Even with my hands over my ears, I could still hear her, because my mom hadn't said to close my eyes and I was watching my grandmother's wrinkled mouth through the window.

"She. Needs. Help!"

When my mom didn't answer, my grandmother screamed out her name: "Eileen!"

And then, after slamming her palms on the roof of the car and peering in my window all the way through to the driver's seat where my mom was starting the ignition, she screamed to make sure we both heard her: "Whores get what whores deserve!"

The car jerked forward, almost taking my grandmother off her feet, and I couldn't help but look back at her. My grandfather had stopped at the edge of the lawn, and the two of them stood there in their pajamas, watching us drive away.

When we turned the corner, my mom pulled over to find a cigarette in her purse. Before she lit it, she took my face in both of her hands.

"You forget everything Granny said!" she cried.

She lit the cigarette and blew the smoke out the window. The car was moving again and I couldn't take my eyes off her face. I had never seen someone act like that before, and it felt important to remember it.

"There's nothing wrong with you, Charlie! Do you hear me?"

I didn't answer. My brain was busy sorting out the contradiction of her words, which said one thing, and the distinct look and sound of fear, which said something completely different. I had never been more confused about a person than I was that night.

"You're perfect and we're going to be fine! Wait and see!"

She took another drag, blew the smoke, then gasped with a giant sob.

She repeated those words as we drove around town, looking for a place to park for the night where the police wouldn't bother us, and I started to say them along with her, like we were singing a song together.

We're going to be fine . . . we're going to be fine . . . we're going to be fine.

This is when I made my first rule about people.

Rule Number One: If someone says the same thing over and over again, that means they don't believe it.

CHAPTER TWO

Four years later, my mom finally explained what made me a child *like that*.

It was Sunday, and on Sundays she took a long nap in the afternoon while I watched my shows in the kitchen. Sunday was a bad day for shows on cable, so I watched DVDs on the little silver machine she bought me for Christmas.

The day had been strange—strange in a way that made her seem happy. In a Burger-King-for-dinner way, even though it was not in our budget. And in a humming-songs-to-herself way. And in a laugh-out-loud-for-no-reason way.

It made me nervous: when my mom got happy like that, it usually meant something bad for me.

At 6:30, after her nap and after Burger King, she went to the bathroom to put on her eye lashes. Humming and perfume slipped beneath the door and into the room where I was alone on our unmade bed, having returned there as soon as we finished eating. I liked being in our bed. It smelled of her, and her smell was comforting.

My mom taught me there was no point making a bed unless we had company coming. She taught me other things too. Important things that I couldn't learn from my shows or from watching the kids at school. Like when someone asks me what I like, I should answer quickly, then ask what they like. Because people like to talk about themselves, and they don't really want to hear about me. And like when the teacher says to raise my hand if I know the answer, I shouldn't do it every single time, because that's annoying.

I was waiting for her to finish in the bathroom and kiss me on the forehead and tell me she'd be *back before I knew it* and then grab her purse and the nice wool coat that hung in the closet by the door and then turn out every light that I didn't need and say one last goodbye.

But on this night, at seven o'clock, after she'd put on her eyelashes and perfume, she'd come and sat on the bed with one leg tucked under her and one hanging off the side. She had a familiar smile on her face. It was the smile she had when she told me things I wouldn't like but that I couldn't change. Things that I wasn't allowed to be mad about.

That's when the bad thing that I knew was coming finally came.

"This is what's happening," she said. More words followed about how it might be hard for me because I've gotten used to these past four years with it just being the two of us, but there were things about the world that I didn't understand.

"Please try, Charlie. Try not to be too upset. Try to be a good girl about it."

I studied her face because being a good girl could mean different things in different situations. If she was sad, I should pinch my eyes together and tilt my head to one side. If she was happy, I should smile so big my teeth showed. I knew my mom very well. Like she said, it had always been just the two of us. But at this moment, I felt scared. I didn't know what she needed from me to stay happy. And I wanted her to stay happy. I wanted it more than anything.

"I've been seeing Dusty for over a year and a half," she said.

My mom counted time in all different increments. Years, months, weeks. Sometimes even in hours or minutes. "It's been four hours since I called Dusty . . . It's been three minutes since I texted Dusty . . . Why won't he call? Why won't he answer?" I should have known Dusty was going to ruin things.

Tonight, she counted in years, which meant she wanted it to seem like more time than it was.

She went on about how she'd been dating Dusty for *over* a year and a half, and how that was long enough, and so they were getting married. But that wasn't all. She grabbed my hands in her hands and squeezed so hard my knuckles cracked.

She was *having his baby*, she said.

My mind spun in circles with what this meant for me. I was consumed by self-interest—from being nine, but also from something else about me which I was about to learn.

She was right that I was used to sharing this small apartment with her and sleeping in the same bed and that I had liked it because I never worried about scary thoughts or bad dreams, except for the nights she went out with Dusty and I had to go to sleep before she came home.

And the baby? I decided that was good, because I liked babies. But then her words—*try not to be too upset*—snuck in and around all of my thoughts and squished them like Play-Doh, reshaping them into other thoughts.

She worried that this news would upset me, which meant there was something upsetting about it.

"Do you have any idea how lucky we are?" she asked me. Dusty was a lawyer at his own law firm. He was a good man, she said. The kind who went to church and sat on the town council. He was an important person in this town, but what mattered most was that he was going to marry her and make us his family.

Dusty was thirteen years older than my mom, thirty-eight and still not married, so people were starting to talk. He was running out of options, she explained, and I pictured us like the last turkey at the grocery store the night before Thanksgiving.

I also pictured his short, stubby body and double chin and wondered if it would be hard to look at him every day for the rest of my life. Then I told myself to keep that inside my head. That was not a nice thought to have, and I had been practicing at not letting those thoughts sneak out.

Next came her grand finale. "And we can finally leave this shitty apartment!"

It was not the first time I had heard that word, but it took on a new meaning when she used it to describe our home.

Shit is a word that would stick in my head because it's used in more ways than any other word I would ever know. Like when something unexpected happens: *shit. Oh shit! Holy shit!* Or to describe someone: *ape shit, full of shit, chicken shit, scared as shit, tough as shit, piece of shit, shit faced, shit head, up shit's creek.* Or to describe something bad: *horse shit, dog shit, bull shit, a pile of, a load of, a world of, a crock of, a shit show,* or just plain *shitty.* Then there's the caveat for when something is good: *THE shit.* And you can even be in it—*deep* or *up to your eyeballs.* Or just inside the place we put it: *the shitter.* There must be a hundred more that I collected as I got older.

But I had never thought of our apartment as shitty, and I realized then that I had missed the signs that my mom did.

Her eyes grew distant like she was seeing a script she'd written play out before her. I watched her lips move as she rambled.

No—we wouldn't have to live here anymore with the roaches and mice and creepy old man down the hall, and she probably wouldn't even have to keep working at Dusty's office, because how would that look if the receptionist and the boss were married? It could've backfired, but it didn't, and now she'd gotten us out of this disaster by the skin of her teeth. The disaster that started when love stole her dreams.

When she was done looking through me to her new perfect life with a house and a husband who was a lawyer and a new baby, her face grew reflective and serious. Her pupils narrowed inside the bright-blue circles that surrounded them, and her focus returned to me and to this moment on our unmade bed in our shitty apartment.

"Do you know how lucky we are?" she said a second time.

I noticed then how she lifted just one eyebrow, and because I knew her face better than I knew my own, I also knew that this meant I was supposed to imagine more words than the ones she was saying.

In the next moment, a dam burst in my brain and I was suddenly drowning in all of those unspoken words.

About the other boyfriends who left her after they met me.

About the endless conferences with my teachers at school.

And, of course, my grandmother's words the night we escaped—a child *like that*.

"You're old enough to understand," she said.

She spoke to me then about being *me*, and I felt my eyes ache from opening too wide and for too long without blinking, because I could not afford to miss one change in her expression.

For the first time in my life, she was describing things I already knew about myself that I thought no one else had noticed because I was so good at pretending. I watched my shows, studying every character and scene. I watched the kids and teachers at school, the people on the street and at the grocery store and in the mall and every place we ever went. And most of all, I studied my mom. I began to form rules like math equations. *When this happens, people act that way and say those things. When that happens, people act this way and say other things.* And those rules stayed in my head, each and every one. I realized I could use them to prepare for whatever was coming. To protect myself.

My mom went on to tell me I was like a lopsided seesaw, and this image gave my feelings a home inside my head. A shelf to sit on. A box to live in. I didn't know the box had a name and that the name was Autism until I was eleven. It was a relief, but also a burden I would carry forever. Like if she'd told me my nose was too big or my eyes were set too close together. I would never again be able to think that I was the same as everyone else.

I didn't like seesaws, but of course I had watched them and knew how they worked. They became lopsided when one side was heavier than the other.

My seesaw, she explained, was uneven because I was very good at some things, like math and remembering, and not as good at other things, like talking to people and playing at recess and handling situations that other kids enjoyed, like noisy places and bright lights. And how, when that weaker side of my seesaw had too much to handle, it caused my entire head to get hot.

Hot head. Lopsided seesaw. Hot head. Lopsided seesaw. These new words would stay with me like all the *shit* words, which is fitting since that was how it felt to know about them. Shitty.

"You know that thing you do with your hands?" she asked me, and I was doing it then, the second she'd let go of them, tapping my thumbs with my forefingers, right and left together, right then left. When she looked at my hands, I was tapping in a pattern, *three together, then right-left-right-left, three together, then left-right-left-right.*

"It takes a lot of concentration to do that," my mom said. "It cools off your head."

I stared at my fingers and thought about the times I tapped them, or watched my shows, or found a place to be alone and scream into my elbow so no one would hear. She was right: it was always when I felt the heat coming.

"And when you move your shoulders back and forth, you know, like a little dance? You do that when you're happy. Back and forth, like there's music playing but there's no music anyone else can hear."

This was also true. I did like to shimmy when I felt good. And when I was bored at school, I tried to cross my toes inside my shoes, which is very hard and can keep me occupied until I stop being bored. There were other things too. Movements and motions for different feelings.

I had never, ever thought about any of this before. Kids did all sorts of things, like chew their nails and twirl their hair and even pick their noses. And they said stupid stuff and made other kids cry or run to tell a teacher or start a fight. We were all just trying to figure out how to be, in our own ways.

Or that's what I'd always thought, until my mom sat on our bed.

"Mrs. Westerly explained it to me," my mom said, and I wondered when this happened and how long she'd known. Mrs. Westerly was my homeroom teacher. She thought she knew everything about all of us and said things like "Sam, you're just angry because you didn't eat enough lunch" or "Julie, you didn't do your homework because you're trying to get attention." I thought about what she might have said to my mom.

Suddenly, I saw the faces of all the men who asked her what I was doing with my hands or my shoulders and why I never looked them in the eye or why I stared at them too long. I thought they just didn't understand kids.

But right then I knew. We were lucky that I hadn't driven Dusty away, because whatever I thought about other kids and how I was just like them, I was wrong. I was a child *like that*. A child with a lopsided seesaw. I had made *us* the last turkey the night before Thanksgiving.

Hot head. Hot head. I stared at my fingers as they tapped faster.

She leaned forward and kissed my cheek. Her lips were soft and sticky from gloss, and her eyelashes tickled my skin. She smelled nice, and I still thought she was beautiful even though her words had set my head on fire.

She got up and turned out the lights throughout our shitty apartment, and grabbed her purse and pulled her nice wool coat from the closet and said she'd be back before I knew it. She left, locking the dead bolt from the outside.

I let the upset come, and then I pushed it away by watching my show in our bed, and this cooled my head and kept me distracted for a few minutes. But my thoughts quickly wandered away from the show and sneaked back to the things I had just learned.

There had been an urgency on my mom's face that told me my life would not be what I imagined it could be.

She'd opened a door to a room I didn't know existed. A room where children don't belong. She'd opened it just a crack, enough to let me see the smallest piece of what was inside, like one inch of a painting, the eye of the Mona Lisa, not the smile, not the part that I needed to see to fully understand, so I knew that there was more. Much more.

Her words and the knowledge of this room and what waited inside it would fight against my childhood, my naiveté, my ignorance, and, most of all, my lopsided seesaw. It would feel both disturbing and satisfying all at once, like I always sensed the place was out there, and now

I knew for sure. I was nine and I knew things that I shouldn't, about love killing your dreams and being the kind of person who would drive people away.

And they were things that I could never unknow.

Like that night when we ran from the house where we both were born, when I was five and she was twenty-one. When I was a child *like that* and she was a *whore*.

By the time that door swung all the way open eight years later and I saw everything that waited behind it, a man would be dead at my feet.

CHAPTER THREE
EIGHT YEARS LATER

A man is dead. This thought arrives just as I get to work. But then come the words I always recite as I turn into the parking lot.

Lettuce tomatoes pickles onions. Lettuce tomatoes pickles onions.

The instant I stop, the thought returns: *A man is dead.*

The Triple S opens at ten, so I get there at nine. It's Saturday and I'm on the schedule for morning prep through closing, which is nine a.m. to ten p.m., a thirteen-hour shift. I beg for hours on the weekends when I don't have school.

The Triple S is a sandwich shop here in Sawyer. Technically, it's called the Sawyer Sandwich Shop, but everyone calls it The Triple S, so now that's its name. It's even printed on our cups and bags. The owner, Clay Cooper, insisted on having quotation marks around the words: "The Triple S." He said the quotation marks would avoid any problems, because as long as something is in quotation marks, it can't be considered false advertising.

Everyone calls him Coop, and Coop is the most important man in our town. He owns a lot of businesses and runs the town council. No one who's ever worked for Coop will be sad he's dead, and yet everyone will be sorry about it. That's what people call irony.

I started working at The Triple S when I turned fourteen, which is the first year a person is allowed to work in Pennsylvania. I was about to start high school in the fall, but I was still young and Coop was the only person who would hire me.

I needed to work for one reason, like anyone else. Money.

I have a spreadsheet that keeps track of it. The first column has five entries. Tuition, room and board, books, clothes. These are added together. The second column has three entries. Federal loans, savings from my job, and the town scholarship (which I will win if I keep getting the highest grades). These are added together. The third column takes the difference and divides it by my net hourly wage and shows me the number of hours I still need to work before I can leave Sawyer for good. The number goes down every time I walk out the back door at the end of a shift.

My mom was right. I became very good at math and got accepted to MIT, where I plan to study data analytics. That was the good news. The bad news was that I had to pay for it myself. Dusty made too much money for me to get financial aid, even though Dusty wasn't helping me pay for college. People call that a catch-22. I call it a shit sandwich.

The point is, without Coop I wouldn't have what I have. My third column wouldn't be going down and I wouldn't be going to college. It's not easy to hate the person who's giving you the one thing you need most in the world.

When I'm not at school or work, I'm usually with Keller, my best friend who also works at The Triple S. She has a boyfriend named Levi who's a mechanic at the gas station across the parking lot. I was the one who got her the job here, and the one who covers for her when she's taking care of her sick grandmother. I'm the reason Keller met Levi. I'm the reason she met Coop, so I guess I'm also the reason for a lot of other things.

But that's another story.

Keller: Idealistic, compassionate, emotionally fragile. Vices: smoking, drinking, being in love.

My mom is the one who told me I needed to get out of Sawyer before I fell in love and had a baby. Love was like gravity, and it would grab hold of my ankles and never let go. If anyone would know about all that, it was my mom. If that ended up being true, Keller and Levi would be stuck here forever.

Grades. Scores. Money. I've been doing everything I can to get out of Sawyer. And it has all been going as planned.

Until today. Until Coop is found dead on the side of the road, just outside his own driveway and right next to his own car.

Janice is the first person I see when I walk through the back door. She works here full-time. Janice is in her forties. I don't know exactly how old she is because once someone's past thirty-nine, it's not polite to ask. I learned that from a movie my mom loves, where a younger man asks an older woman her age and she slaps him clear across the face and then tells him she's thirty-nine. My mom always laughs at that scene.

However old she is, Janice and her husband Shane have four kids and a lot of bills to pay.

Janice: Dependable, devoted, affectionate. Vices: Eating, worrying.

She's already prepping the tomatoes in the slicer, tossing them one at a time in front of the blades and slamming the handle against them until they're pushed through the other side, the slices falling into a rectangular metal pan. Her face is distant, and she's slamming the handle harder than I've ever seen her slam it, except maybe on the day Coop fired Shane from the tobacco store, which he also owns.

She's not paying attention either, which is very unlike her. Not pulling out the tomatoes that are too ripe for the slicer, so they explode when they hit the blades, spraying bright-red guts against the white wall behind the table where she works.

She stops when she hears the door close. It's heavy and makes a loud bang. She wipes her hands on a green apron and pounces before I can hang up my coat.

I wonder if I'll be able to look her in the eye today, but then I do.

"Oh, Charlie!" she says, and then she pulls me into a giant bear hug, which isn't easy for her because she's only five feet tall.

I close my arms around her back and feel her rolls of flesh press against me. Her face nuzzles into my shoulder and I let my cheek rest against the top of her head. I don't like to be touched without warning, so I always warn myself before I see Janice, because Janice always hugs me.

Lettuce tomatoes pickles . . . It's over before I can say *onions*.

"This is all so horrible!" Janice says after she lets me go.

I look beyond her to the tomato guts sliding down the wall, which ignites a sudden compulsion to clean.

Janice's eyes follow.

"Oh, jeepers . . ."

She draws a hand to her mouth and sighs, her whole body limping with defeat.

"I've got it," I tell her, and I move quickly to hang up my coat on a hook by the door. There are two people here already: Janice and Nora, the manager.

"Nora's here?" I ask, surprised. Saturday is usually her morning off, and I didn't notice her car in the parking lot.

"She's having a smoke."

I take the hook at the far end where it's less likely to be doubled up. There will be six of us here by noon. Me, Janice, Nora, and Keller make four. Plus two other part-time workers. Keller calls them Lazy Tracey and Horny Helen. Tracey goes to my school, but he's a year younger. I can make twice as many sandwiches as he can in half the time. Helen is recently divorced, so she won't work the grill because it makes you smell like grease for the rest of the entire day, and she never knows when she might get a date after work from this app called Find Love Dot Com.

"Is Nora okay?" I ask Janice.

Nora said she was quitting smoking two weeks ago. She's never lasted two weeks before. It can't be a coincidence that she's giving up the morning after Coop is found murdered.

Janice makes a face that says she doesn't know.

We both glance through to the dining room and the side door, which leads to a few outdoor tables, and I picture Nora sitting at one of them. Smoking and thinking.

Nora: Honest, loyal, disciplined. Vices: Smoking, being alone.

Janice squeezes my hand.

"Let's just get to work," I say, trying to reassure her. Her worry feels infectious.

———

I know a lot of things about people. And not just by observing them on TV and in everyday life, and from the things my mom has told me. I've learned from research as well, online and in books. Everyone, it seems, has something to say about why people do what they do. Why they have bad habits and shitty marriages and can't make their kids listen. There are psychological patterns, causal relationships, personality traits, all of which help to make human behavior predictable. I've written down just about everything I've ever learned, because in spite of what my mother likes to say about my math skills and my memory, they are not that extraordinary. I'm not a robot. And these are the types of things I can't afford to forget, because they help me make predictions about the people around me. Today, I'll need this more than ever before.

I grab a green apron from the pile on the back table where we keep things that need to stay clean from the prep. Aprons, purses, backpacks. I grab a towel to wipe up the spray from the tomatoes.

The prep isn't messy if you do it efficiently. Every machine put to proper use. Every surface covered with containers of meat, cheese, tomatoes, onions, iceberg lettuce. We shred the lettuce at The Triple S so it crinkles like confetti. This adds volume and texture and releases the sweetness that's trapped inside.

The smell of produce and meat fills the air and mixes with the bleach from the cleaning, the preservatives in the cans of red peppers, and the vinegar from the salad dressing that's poured from buckets into the pans. The smell is distinct to this place, like the smell of my mom when we shared a bed. I don't notice it until I leave and then return, and when I do, it not only enters my nose, but reaches inside my body and tells it how to feel. For me, the smell of The Triple S is the smell of freedom.

After a few months of working here, I built a model for Nora on her laptop—an Excel spreadsheet for the inventory. We track what is used for every lunch and every dinner, and the model allows us to make predictions. We know, almost to the ounce, what we need for each rush. I can think of only four times we were wrong and had to run back and stock something on the fly.

Nora is tall and thin, and she smells of cigarettes, makeup, and hairspray. She dresses in nice clothes from the outlet stores, our town's main attraction, when the rest of us wear jeans and company T-shirts. Even in her dress clothes, if she's needed, she'll throw on an apron and start taking orders, jumping into the trenches and chaos as scraps of food fall onto her nice leather shoes.

Nora is our fearless leader.

At least that's what I thought until today. The day Clay Cooper is found dead and nothing is the way it should be.

Today, Janice is exploding the tomatoes.

And Nora is smoking.

And Keller has called in sick.

The tomato guts slide from the wall to the floor as I wipe the cloth over them.

A thought comes. About blood. *Bloody blood blood.*

I close my eyes and shake my head, which is getting hot.

Hot head. Hot head.

Janice is beside me, her hands squeezing my arms. Her voice asking me, "Are you okay, Charlie?"

The smell of cigarettes and hairspray fills my nose, and a new voice fills my ears. Nora is here now, asking the same question. "Are you okay?"

And I realize that in all the years I've been studying everyone and anyone who might affect my life, I overlooked the most important person.

Lettuce tomatoes pickles onions. Lettuce tomatoes pickles onions.

A man is dead.

His head bashed in.

So much blood.

No. No. No.

I open my eyes and look at the wall, washed clean. Then I take a very deep breath.

"We need four pans of lettuce," I tell them. Janice looks confused. But Nora understands, because she knows the spreadsheets as well as I do.

"That's right," she says. "Because it's Saturday."

I nod as I feel my head cool down. Then I repeat the words as I pull the list from my memory.

"Four pans of lettuce. Because it's Saturday."

————

Tracey and Helen come in at eleven. By eleven thirty, the five of us are ready to take on the rush. Fresh green aprons tied neatly at the waist. Thin plastic gloves over scrubbed hands. Smiles glued on our faces.

The store has two sections divided by a metal counter. On one side are the customers. The line where they order. The corner where they get their napkins and straws and throw away their garbage. The tables where they eat. And the bathrooms in the back.

Behind the counter is a square work area. On one side is a giant grill. It looks like nothing, but if you put so much as a drop of water on it, it would come to life like a sleeping monster that just got a poke. Pans of freshly sliced meat and vegetables sit beside it with tongs and spatulas, all shiny and clean.

There's a center island that holds the cold cuts and salads and more vegetables, like the shredded lettuce and sliced tomatoes. There are wood carving boards on either side where we assemble each sandwich, made to order. Each one different in some way. Each one a new challenge.

It's the same with the rush itself. Every day has its own rhythm. A slow trickle that catches up to us. A flash mob that comes from no-where. A million combinations in between. I think of it like a new set of numbers needing to be sorted and solved.

I can easily take ten orders at once and not get one thing wrong. Not a meat or a cheese or a garnish or a condiment. Sometimes it's shitty to remember some things without even wanting to but not remembering other things. These orders will stay with me for days, but I'll have to study for hours to do well on next week's science test. How unfair is that?

Nora stands beside me as the first two customers enter the building. There is a moment of hesitation as their hands first pull on the door. Will we be open today? Most of the customers know that Coop owns The Triple S. Not everyone has heard that he's dead. They see that we're open, and come inside.

Country music blares from speakers in the ceiling. Helen must have put it on. There's a Helen on every show I've ever seen. Dating apps, country music, inflated self-esteem. The music reminds me of characters like Helen who are meant to annoy you, and then the words rhyme and repeat and repeat and repeat and get stuck in my head and I think that maybe I now hate country music as the customers approach the counter.

Janice chooses to be at the grill even though the smell of grease will cover every inch of her. But today, she says, she doesn't think she can do more than weigh meat and turn it with the spatulas. It's the job that requires the least amount of concentration. Janice doesn't want to slow us down out here while her thoughts are on Coop and on her worries that she can't shoo away.

Lettuce tomatoes pickles onions. Lettuce tomatoes pickles onions.

By noon, a long line has formed. I am focused like I've never been focused before, taking orders, calling out to the line for new ones. Nora helps me from the other side of the island. Tracey tries to keep up at the register. Helen slices the bread faster and faster.

By one thirty, the line is almost gone and the dining room is full. Every seat taken. A few stragglers stare at the menu board that hangs above the metal counter, undecided, and we use the time to clean up. The counters and floor are covered with the ends of the bread loaves, a few pickles and onion slices and, of course, shreds of lettuce—all the things that spilled out of the sandwiches as they were cut and wrapped.

Janice takes a break to wash her arms and face in the back room, and, I imagine, to let the worry have its way with her. I can almost feel her thoughts floating out from the prep room, spinning through every possible scenario.

Helen looks at men on her app. She glances at Nora, who shakes her head with feigned disapproval. Helen has tried to convert her, but Nora loved her husband and he was killed in the army and that's that. Still, she likes Helen and humors her when time allows, like now when the only customers left to serve are still deciding, and when it's good to not seem nervous about a man you wanted dead actually being dead.

Nora turns from Helen to look at me. Her arm reaches out, her hand rests on my back, firm and reassuring. She nods her head, and I nod back as if to say *I'm okay*.

But then we see the car pull into the parking lot. We see its red-and-blue lights and white paint and black letters that say *Sawyer Police*.

I look back to Nora in time to watch her back straighten. She gasps in a deep breath. And then her eyes move, from the car pulling into a spot labeled *no parking*, to a place in the dining room. A place way up high where the ceiling meets the wall. I follow her eyes with my eyes until I see what she sees.

A small black ball mounted just above a poster of a large Triple S steak and cheese.

A light flashes inside. A red light, just like the ones inside the small black balls they have in the hallways at school.

In three years, I've never noticed it. I wonder how long it's been there. Then I think it doesn't really matter, because from the look on Nora's face, I know it was there last night.

The night Clay Cooper was murdered, and I was captured on camera, at the scene of the crime.

CHAPTER FOUR

The cop's name is Ian Maguire, and he steals my breath. It's not just because I know why he's here.

Ian steals my breath every day he walks through the door. Next to Keller, he's my best friend. Since third grade, they've let me take classes with the grade above, and so even though Ian is a year older than me and Keller, I knew him from math and science. He graduated last spring and joined the police force. He didn't even try to go to college. He says it's because he needs to help support his mother, who's a widow and works at the grocery store. That's part of the story.

But I've done the math, and if Ian went to college, he could have a higher-paying job that didn't keep his mother up at night worrying. He qualified for financial aid and merit scholarships and didn't have a Dusty in his way with a catch-22. Ian could have made it out of Sawyer.

I've also done another analysis. Ian could have stayed in town and worked a less dangerous job, at a local bank or selling insurance, for example. Everything I know about people, and everything I know about Ian, tells me that he's a cop because no one ever solved the hit-and-run accident that killed his father eight years ago. The driver is out there, walking around, living life, cruising in the orange Buick LeSabre that ran a man over. There's been no justice for Cullen Maguire, so Ian Maguire tries to balance the scale.

Rule Number Eleven: Emotions keep people from making rational decisions.

I have loved Ian all this time. I loved him on the playground when we were in elementary school and raced each other on the monkey bars. I loved him when we were in middle school and had to build the solar system out of Styrofoam balls and pipe cleaners. And I loved him in high school when he grew six feet tall and his eyes turned a deep shade of brown and I felt my insides stir, just like my mom told me they would.

But that's another story.

He steps to the side of the counter where customers collect their orders.

"Hey, Charlie," he says when I walk to where he stands, the counter between us.

"Hey, Ian."

"Listen," he says, and that's when I know he's not here for his usual large steak and cheese with onions. "They have some questions about Clay Cooper. I can give you a ride."

I study him head to toe. The eyes that dart away just as his face struggles to display indifference. The shoulders that are lifted almost to his ears and the feet that shuffle side to side. He's making this seem like it's no big deal, but the things I've just described are signs of deception. I learned that from an excellent show about a lie detection expert who solves crimes.

But even though I see all of this and know he's worried but trying not to show it, I smile and scrunch my eyes together with surprise, basically letting him off the hook. His deception is coming from a place of kindness, and that's a different thing altogether.

"How long will it take? I have to prep for dinner."

Now he shrugs and looks at the floor. "They didn't say."

Nora comes to stand beside me, and I fill her in. She flinches, which is very uncharacteristic, and so it makes me flinch as well.

"We can handle your shift. I'll call your mother," she says. "Don't answer questions until she gets there. They can't make you, do you understand? You never have to speak. Never. And especially if you ask for a lawyer."

Nora knows these things and I nod in agreement.

I tell Ian I'll meet him at his car, then I go to the back room. I take off my apron and place it in the dirty-linen bin. Next, I wash my hands while Janice and Nora stand beside me discussing what this could be about. Going through the scenarios. Mapping out plans to help me.

But a plan has already formed in my head.

When I leave, I imagine there will be an awkward silence, because between the three of us, I was the one who wanted Coop dead the least.

I get my purse and my coat from the hooks and let Janice hug me while Nora finishes talking.

"Remember," Nora says, taking my face in both of her hands, "no answering questions until your mother gets there."

Ian is waiting in his police cruiser. I walk to the passenger side and reach for the door but then catch his eye.

He signals with a remorseful expression that I need to get in the back, so I retreat two steps and reach for the other handle.

We don't talk on the drive because he's convinced Google and Zuck are always listening when his phone is with him. He even proved it to me once by speaking loudly about having back pain with his phone right next to us. Later that same day, he had three spam emails about products guaranteed to cure back pain. We laughed about it then. It happened before we stopped laughing together.

I didn't need him to show me about the phone, or the car. I always believe what Ian tells me. He's the kind of person you can do that with, and he's taught me about some very important things. Like irony and sarcasm and looking people in the eye when you talk to them, but not so much it creeps them out. And never, ever standing too close because then you're a close talker, which is an actual thing that people don't like: *Seinfeld*, Season 5, Episode 18.

The car smells of old leather and gasoline, and the lingering, stale odor of humans. Men. Women. Old. Young. Drunk. Scared. Homeless. Deranged. Mad as hell and pumped up on adrenaline. There are only so many reasons a person gets into the back of a police car. I imagine I'm adding to the aroma today. The smell of lettuce, tomatoes, pickles, and onions.

We take the interstate because that's the fastest way. I have so many things I want to ask him, like did they find out how Clay Cooper died, and what time did they think he died, and did they find anything on him that might be a clue as to who did this, but I keep my mouth closed tight.

When we reach the top of the on-ramp, the billboards appear. We both look up at the same time and look away at the same time because we are both thinking the same thing, having the same memory from one year before when we decided we couldn't be *that way* with each other. It was the worst night of my life.

It happened under the billboard we call The Hand of God. It has a picture of an old man's hand with his scraggly finger pointed down toward us, the humans, and from the very tip is a bolt of lightning but then a soft white cloud. The old man's hand is attached to an arm that's draped in a flowing white robe, but that's all we get to see. The arm. The robe. The hand and finger and cloud of light. The words on the billboard are in bright-pink Gothic Script letters: *Repent and Turn to God.*

All the billboards in the next row have the usual ads—pictures of steak, ads for tobacco, the exit for the waterpark. There is nothing special about The Hand of God except that it is set back from the interstate and in front of it is a row of thick evergreen bushes that are tall enough to cover the top of a pickup truck. If you line up just right, half a dozen cars and trucks can fit beneath The Hand of God and be hidden from the road. It's a popular place for kids to get lost for a while and do the things kids do when they get lost.

Keller and I go there sometimes when she needs to get lost. Caring for her grandmother has become demanding. She quit school after ninth grade and now has two jobs working for Clay Cooper. One at The Triple S and one at the diner.

Ian and I used to go there before we made our decision. It was the place he first kissed me. It was the place I first felt a hand on the small of my back, on my skin, soft and warm like the light coming from God, literally, right above us.

It was the place where I tried to ignore the fear my mother had injected into me over the years.

Ian sighs as we pass the billboards, and I close my eyes as tight as I can to stop what happens to my insides when I feel it—the stirring that my mom warned me about years ago, telling me this was the one thing that would be the same for me. Exactly the same, because of biology, she said. "There will be a stirring and it will make you do dangerous things."

It took many years and many conversations for me to understand that I was the result of a stirring, and a boy from her high school whose family moved away the second they found out about me, and how, basically, I was part of the whole shit storm that ruined her life.

I try to fight it, but I still feel something burning in my gut, an impulse to whisper in his ear. *Just keep driving . . . away from this place. Away from the decision I forced us to make. Just hold me again. Touch me like you did that night, and never, ever, stop . . .*

In the fastest flash that sweeps through me, more like a feeling than a thought, I imagine us together the way I've imagined it before. I've stored away the kisses and the touches and the things Keller has told me—things about how it is when you're with a boy—when Keller and I have sat beneath The Hand of God on the hood of her car and I've begged her to tell me and she's relented.

"Only if you drink a beer with me," she always says. Sometimes, my mind doesn't settle easily when I'm thinking through new information. It spins like a washing machine, faster and faster until something turns it off. Beer turns it off better than tapping my fingers or anything else I've found, and Keller knows this because she's my best friend and that's the sort of thing best friends know about you. I know things about her too.

I always drink the beer and maybe even take a drag of her cigarette until the machine stops spinning. And then she tells me.

About his tongue brushing her ear and his hand on her breast and then sliding down between her legs. And then when they're naked, lying together, before, during, after, the oneness of them. The passion. The love. The desire.

Levi is a strong boy, a man really, with olive skin and dark, earnest eyes, and Keller says he holds her so tight she has no choice but to surrender completely, to let go of everything and give in to him, letting him lead in some wild but beautiful dance.

"You just disappear, Charlie. Into each other. You become one."

Her face fills with wonder when she tells me this, like she's just seen a UFO land in front of her. Like it's a miracle that no one else has ever experienced. And from the way Levi looks at her when they're together, I know they both believe it. They believe in this kind of love, and they don't care if it's just because of Keller's storybook face and curvy body or Levi's chiseled cheekbones and broad shoulders, or if she'll have to have a baby if there's an accident, or if the baby will steal their dreams the way I stole my mom's. Ian taught me about irony, and there is no greater irony in the world than how the best feeling I've ever felt comes from the most dangerous thing I could ever do.

Still, in these moments with Keller, when my mind stops spinning, I forget the great irony and all I want is to believe the way she believes. I want to step inside her body and feel what it feels like to believe that way. When she speaks of it, I want it to be true. I want her to believe in love the way she does as badly as I want to get out of this place.

Because each time I imagine it for myself, with Ian, even after a beer and a cigarette with my best friend, listening to the cars on the interstate just beyond the bushes, their drivers maybe seeing The Hand of God, but not us, because we are hidden and lost for this one moment—even then, and even right now, I hear my mom telling me it will steal my dreams and then the love will die. *That kind of love isn't real.*

As hard as I try, I can't prove her wrong, so I know I will never have what Keller has, and so Keller must have it and hold it for the both of us. And I feel like I would fight to the death to let her keep it.

On that one horrible night, Ian and I decided we couldn't be together like that. We decided because I decided. After he kissed me for a long time and told me he loved me. He said the words.

Charlie, I love you.

And I tried to say them back but they got stuck inside me, trapped in the prison my mother had built. I could feel them rattling the bars, begging to come out.

I wanted to say *Ian, I love you too!* And then have the kissing become more because I felt it in my entire body and I wanted more and more and more. The feeling was not contentment. It was hunger. And as far as hunger goes, I was starving.

But fear won out. I told him I couldn't love him. That we had to stop kissing. Stop everything or I would never go to college. He didn't understand. He said one thing had nothing to do with the other. And as much as I wanted to believe him, the evidence was on my mother's side. Fewer than ten percent of the girls in Sawyer ever left. Numbers don't lie. People do. Even if they're just lying to themselves.

He took me home and I cried into my pillow.

And now all that's left is this. A sigh. The silence. Regret. Me in the back of his police car.

We turn off the interstate two exits later. The moment has passed. The urge has dissipated with the sound of his voice which causes me to open my eyes and remember what is happening. Remember last night. Remember Keller and the beautiful belief she holds in her heart and which is always in need of protecting.

"You ready?" he asks.

And I don't know how or why but I am.

I'm ready.

CHAPTER FIVE

My mom's not happy she's been dragged down to the police station. Today is Saturday, and that's the one day she has help with her boys, because Dusty is home. On Sundays he plays golf. But what really has her in a tiff is that they've messed with her daughter.

I hear her before I see her as I sit in a chair in the hallway.

My mom has a loud and commanding voice after being Mrs. Dusty Madison for seven years.

"You have no right! This is a travesty! My husband is a lawyer, he's on the town council! Someone will pay for this!"

She turns the corner, sees me, and stops. She's in her tennis clothes, which means she got pulled from her game with her friends at their club. We've come a long way from our shitty apartment.

She says nothing but gives me a serious look that says *I'm here now, you see? And I'm taking control, so you just be a good girl, Charlie, and sit there quietly.*

A uniformed officer puts us in a small interview room with a fake wood table and metal chairs. It's not intimidating, like *Law and Order* or any cop show, really. There are no two-way mirrors or cups with bitter coffee or overflowing ashtrays. It's just a room.

She makes one more declaration while she has the chance.

"You have no idea how sorry you're going to be!"

I am her cub and she is my mama bear. It must be primal the way I want to let her fight to protect me, because I can't stop it and the feeling becomes a spoonful of glass making its way down my throat and into my stomach. This is the same woman who put things into my head and took other things out like a brain surgeon performing some creepy lobotomy, and now I can't love the one person who wanted to love me. And now he's not my boyfriend, he's barely even my friend. Now I'm just a girl who had to ride in the back of his police car.

They leave us alone while they wait for the detective to become available. My mom sits beside me pretending to be calm now, like she's done this before and knows what to do, even though we both know that's not true.

"Don't say a word. Not one word, you hear me?"

I open my mouth to say "*Yes, I understand,*" but she shushes me before I get out a single syllable. She is not kidding about not saying one word.

A woman comes in. Her name is Detective Pittfield. She smiles and asks us if we want something to drink and my mom says no for both of us. The detective sits across from us.

"You're Charlie Hudson, correct?" she asks.

But my mom puts an end to things right then and there. "My daughter wants a lawyer," she says.

Detective Pittfield sighs with frustration. My mom has this effect on people.

"Did you bring a lawyer with you?"

My mom shrugs and waves her arms in front of her. "Do you see a lawyer?"

I shift in my seat. The detective senses my discomfort. I think she must wonder if it's because I know something about Coop's death, or because my mom is this woman she now wants to strangle and I've had to live with her for seventeen years.

"Your daughter is not under arrest," she says.

"So we can leave?"

"Technically, you can leave, but we do have some questions, and I think you'll want to know why. Can you wait just another minute?"

She excuses herself politely and leaves the room.

"See?" my mom says to me.

I don't so much as part my lips this time.

When Detective Pittfield returns, she has a man with her and he has a folder. He opens it and slides it across the table so it sits before both of us. Inside is a photo of me at The Triple S.

"What is this?" my mom asks. But I know exactly what it is. My seesaw begins to tilt.

Hot head. Hot Head.

Coop had that camera at the store, and now I'm in a heap of shit.

The man's name is Detective Slater and he's the one who answers my mom.

"It's a still shot of digital surveillance. From the dining area of the sandwich shop last night. It was recovered from Mr. Cooper's home computer."

We both lean in to study the image. It's grainy but unmistakable. It's me, crouched beneath the metal counter where customers stand to place their orders. The same counter I stood behind all morning.

"You were at the store last night, Charlie. Hiding under the counter. You stayed there for one minute and forty-two seconds."

He pauses to observe my mom's silence and shock, which she tries to cover with a haughty expression. I don't know what else to call it when she does this. Leaning back in her chair. Arms folded. Head askew with a toss of her hair as her lips smirk and her entire face relaxes like she's beyond bored. I've seen it a hundred times on *The Real Housewives*. My mother should have her own show she does it so well.

Detective Slater turns the photo to reveal another one beneath it. Again, it's me, and I look scared.

"You can flip through them if you want. Charlie, you were there last night, and it's pretty clear from the footage that you were listening to something unpleasant."

I stare as he turns the pages, slowly. I can't bear to even touch them as I see myself. My face curious, concentrating, listening. My hands covering my ears, trying to block it out. I wince.

My mom's expression cements because she's fighting against her anger, realizing that I didn't tell her about this.

In my defense, I've been really busy today.

Also in my defense, I cannot think about last night. I cannot talk about last night. I have made promises, to myself and to others, and I will not break them. Not for anyone or anything.

"I don't see how any of this is relevant. Wasn't Coop found near his house? On the street by his car? It's been all over the news," my mom says.

Detective Pittfield leans back, crosses her arms just like my mom. I know what's coming next.

"We have reason to believe the body was moved."

My mom holds her face steady except for a slight tremor at the corners of her mouth. Like what happens when you have to smile too long for a school photo.

She doesn't look at me. She doesn't look at the detectives. She reaches up and neatly stacks the photos of her daughter hiding beneath the counter at The Triple S last night, slides them back into the folder, and closes the cover. Then she pushes it back to where it came from. Across the table.

She holds her *Real Housewives* expression but I now see something else there too. Something she told me about years ago, before she had the right to have that kind of expression. Before Dusty saved us. It had to do with a snow globe she had growing up. She'd thrown it against our bedroom wall when we still lived with my grandparents. It shattered into a million pieces and Granny screamed at her through our door for what felt like hours.

She told me that Sawyer was a snow globe like the one she broke. The people were glued to the bottom, and all they knew were the same snowflakes that kept falling on their heads. And they liked it that way. They didn't want different snowflakes. Not like her. And not like me.

She told me she hated Sawyer and all the people glued to the floor and she never planned to stay here. She'd had big dreams.

And she's scared now, because they have something on us. On me. She's scared because no matter what she's done to be a snowflake that belongs here, and to make me one, she never will be. And neither will I. And she doesn't know what they'll do if they have the chance to get rid of us.

The TV show plays on as my mom says her lines.

"My daughter wants a lawyer, and this interview is over."

CHAPTER SIX

My mom calls Dusty the second the detectives leave. She walks to the corner where she thinks I can't hear her whispering to him about how I might have done something terrible and can he come down here right away. He must have said something about the boys and what would he do with them, because she gets frustrated and tells him to "call someone from his office then!"

She hangs up and sits down, and I look at her but don't ask about the lawyer because she told me not to say one word and that's what I'm doing. But I can see she's not happy.

I think then that if Dusty is a lawyer with his own firm and we can't get a lawyer to come and help us right now, then we are not really that far away from our shitty apartment after all.

"Come on," she says to me. "We're going to the bathroom."

"Why?" I ask.

She looks at me like I don't know a single thing about any single thing, and says, "To buy time!"

In the bathroom, my mom checks beneath all the stalls, then takes me by both arms, squeezing them tight.

"You have to tell me everything that happened last night," she says. "Oh! I can't believe this! I can't believe it!"

She releases me, then goes into a stall to pee. She doesn't stop talking. She talks and pees at the same time.

"I mean, a murder, Charlie! A moved body! For Christ's sake!"

She comes out again and washes her hands.

She takes four paper towels from the dispenser, pulling each one hard, like they're going to put up a fight.

"Sometimes I still don't know what to do with you."

The door opens and we both turn to see who's joined us. I think I hear my mom swear under her breath, or maybe she just says *Jesus Christ*, which is one of the worst things you can say in our town. Worse than the "F" word. But my mom says it all the time, and with different configurations of the Lord's name: *Christ. Jesus. Jesus Christ.* And the longest one, *Jesus H. Christ.* No one knows what the *H* stands for, although there are a bunch of theories that I looked up once because she says it so often and it makes Dusty so angry. They're all long and boring.

Coop's wife, Regina, stops and looks at us. Her face is red from crying. Tears drip from her chin.

"Charlie," she says.

Then she takes three steps toward us, and as my mom watches, she pulls me into her arms and sobs right in my ear. It startles me and I stay stiff as a board until it ends.

Lettuce tomatoes pickles onions.

She was always nice to me when she came to The Triple S, which was once a week, even though her version of nice was to speak to me like I was a child, slowly and with simple words. She even raised her voice, like maybe my lopsided seesaw had also impacted my hearing.

Regardless, I never liked Regina Cooper. Her mind always seemed stuck in some kind of groove, like when it snows around my mom's car and no matter how hard you press on the gas, the wheels spin in place. The world was what it was, and she was winning and no one was going to take that away.

Still, she used to say I was like a second daughter to her and Coop, so I think she's expecting me to cry with her.

She didn't know the first thing about her husband. If she did, she wouldn't expect me to cry over his death. And if she ever got unstuck from her groove, not one single tear would drip from her chin either.

My mom finishes drying her hands and stands beside me.

"We're sorry for your loss," she says.

Regina pulls away and says something she's supposed to, like "*Thank you*" or "*Yes, it's been very hard*," but she doesn't look at my mom even as my mom glares at her.

I make a note. My mom hates Regina Cooper. And Regina Cooper seems wary of my mom. I don't know why, and feel angry with myself that I never noticed their dynamic before. I think then that maybe it goes back to high school, because that's the last time they were in the same corner of our snow globe. My mind starts to spin with theories.

Regina wipes her face with the back of her hand.

"The IRS came to the house this morning and wanted to take things before the police could even investigate. When I refused, they said they would come back with a warrant, so I'm here trying to get someone to stop them. And poor Lillian—I had to leave her with my mother who drove up from Pittsburgh. It's just so unbelievable . . ."

Lillian is Regina and Coop's twelve-year-old daughter. She's a brat and no one at The Triple S likes her. But what would you expect? Apples don't fall far from their trees. The best they can do is try to roll away.

Regina starts to cry again.

"Yes," my mom says even as she squints her eyes, "that must be very hard. For both of you."

Regina goes on then about how, in addition to the IRS, the police have been to her home and all the stores.

"They thought it was a robbery at first, but he had his phone and cash in his wallet and they didn't take his truck. It's valuable, with the detailing he had done for hunting."

More sobs. I get her a paper towel while my mom watches. I could be wrong, but no. I'm not wrong. She's enjoying this.

"He was good to his people. At all of his businesses—he was so kind, wasn't he, Charlie? Now they're saying he had a fight with someone yesterday, but they won't say who, and they're asking about his records, and the IRS is involved, and it's as if they're blaming him, like something *he* did might have made someone want to kill him."

As a new wave of crying overtakes her, I think to myself that they won't find anything. Coop didn't want Nora keeping records, not even the Excel spreadsheet to track the sales and inventory that I created. Coop handwrote the register reports every day, on paper, then deleted them from the machine. He always took the papers with him when he left.

Nora said our food costs dropped after we started to use my Excel model. She told me she was going to show Coop. She thought he would be proud of me.

But Nora was wrong. Coop told her to stop using the spreadsheet and to go back to doing what she was doing. That was the day Nora started locking the door to the office and staying late, after Coop was sure not to come back. Over time, she expanded the model to include other things, like how many sandwich sales we make and how much inventory gets delivered. She's done all of this behind Coop's back because he didn't like anything written down.

And at the end of the year when he had to file papers with the government, he made Nora sign things with numbers she knew were wrong. I know it upset her—she always started smoking again if she was in the middle of trying to quit. She was the manager, and so the recordkeeping was her job, and something she could get in trouble for if it wasn't right and the government ever came to check. I know that because they did fight about it, Nora and Coop. Just not yesterday.

Yesterday he fought with Janice.

"Charlie," she says now, "do you know anything about that fight? Do you know anyone at The Triple S who'd want to . . . who'd want to *hurt* my husband?"

She seems so sad about it. Not fake sad, but actually sad. Coop must've been so different with her.

I can feel my mom's thoughts like they're being transported to my brain by telepathy. Regina Cooper doesn't seem to have a clue about the surveillance footage. No idea why I'm even here. Otherwise, she would have asked me a different question.

I'm about to answer Regina Cooper, though I still don't know how or what words to use, when my mom saves me.

"It's probably best if no one talks about the case. I mean, not that anyone has anything to hide, but just because it looks bad, like there's an effort being made to cover things up, you know? Like, maybe, influence is being used to get certain answers to be given, or to be withheld." She lets this sink in, then she finishes with, "I presume you're the new boss, right?"

Regina hasn't considered this. We both see it by the surprise in her eyes.

"Oh," she says, "I suppose you're right. I'm sorry, Charlie. I didn't mean to make you feel uncomfortable."

My mom speaks for me—again. "She's fine. Don't worry about my daughter."

Regina gives us one of those smiles people use before they slink away. And I think this is over, but then she says, "I heard the detectives saying you asked for a lawyer."

My mom puffs up her chest like a male peacock. "Yes, well, my husband is a lawyer, so it shouldn't be a problem."

Regina knows this of course, which is exactly why she's brought it up. Regina is a snowflake that belongs here. "Well, if you need someone sooner, there's a woman in the lobby wearing a suit. I heard her say she was waiting for her client, so she's probably a lawyer. If she's just waiting around, maybe she can help you. Those lawyers are always looking for new clients, right? There's a reason they call them ambulance chasers."

My mom gives her a *Real Housewives* laugh, then takes my hand and leads me back into the hall, where we head toward the lawyer who might be waiting there for an ambulance.

As we walk, she tells me. "Do not ever trust that woman. Tell me you understand?"

I nod and finally say a word. The only one my mom wants to hear. "Okay," I tell her.

CHAPTER SEVEN

Sawyer has a lot of stories that keep getting told: no one ever leaves to take them away, and no one new ever comes to dilute them. Some get bigger, some get smaller, and others just become part of the air we all have to breathe.

There's just one story I know that connects my mom and Regina Cooper, and it goes back to their time in high school.

Regina and Coop were seniors when my mom was a sophomore. That meant they spent two years at the same school. And the last one was a very bad year.

The story about that year never gets smaller because it was the biggest scandal Sawyer has ever seen. Ian heard the story from his mother, and he told me and Keller. Ian's parents were also seniors that year, along with Coop and Regina.

It happened on a field trip up in the mountains. It was an annual event for the senior class after exams were finished and they were getting ready for graduation. It was meant to celebrate the fact that they were moving on, although none of them really were. They just weren't going to school anymore. The students went to the same place every year, but once they arrived, some of the kids went on hikes, some swam in the river, others found places to be alone so they could drink and smoke and have sex, which is what teenagers like to do even when they're about to graduate.

That very bad year, one group of boys went up a steep part of the trail. Coop was there. So was Ian's father, Cullen Maguire. There were a dozen other boys, but they had spread out into clusters, some moving faster, others slower. The cluster with Coop and Cullen Maguire also had a boy named Rudi Benton, who fell off the trail down the side of the mountain. And died.

According to Ian's mother, seeing Rudi fall to his death traumatized all the other boys, and they each found a different way to cope. One boy moved away right after graduation. His parents had the good sense to get him out of here. Mr. Maguire drank alcohol and sat around a lot, getting fired from multiple jobs and disappointing his family. And Coop—well, they say that's how Coop got so mean. It's hard to believe that, because it's hard to imagine him being any other way.

But then again, Coop has given me one of the most important rules about human behavior.

Rule Number Twenty-Four: No one is all good and no one is all evil.

This is what I mean.

The summer I turned fourteen, I rode my bike down Highway 65, which is really just a four-lane road—stopping at every store and restaurant that didn't sell alcohol or tobacco, searching for a job. The owners and managers all looked at me, head to toe, and scrunched their faces and pulled their heads back into their spines until their necks nearly disappeared the second I asked for an application. Like it was so absurd that they couldn't even comprehend the idea. Some let me fill out an application, but I could tell they were going to throw it away.

One lady at a bakery was honest about it. She said things were tough around here and other people needed jobs to support their families, while I had a family to support me. She also told me that I looked like a child still, like a girl, and it made people feel bad to see a child having to work. It made them feel like things were really, really bad, like in China where they force their children to work at barely five years old. People in America did not want to see themselves that way.

I almost rode right past The Triple S because it was the next stop and what that woman said had made me cry. I needed to make money and I had no way to get it. Anger. Frustration. *Hot head. Hot head.*

I had my spreadsheet and I knew exactly how much I needed. My mom had agreed to open up an account for me at the bank. It's called a 529 and you don't have to pay taxes if you put money into it. She had to be on it as well, which annoyed me, because it would be my money from my work, but you have to be eighteen to have your own account. I would be in college by then if I got everything I needed. Federal loans. The town scholarship. Money from a job in my 529.

Dusty already told me he couldn't help, so unless money started falling from the sky, I needed all three of the things in my calculations.

Dusty is another story, and not one that's even worth telling, except to say that I'm not his daughter and there was an unspoken agreement that I could feel between him and my mom that even after they got married, she would never expect him to treat me like one. It was set in stone, just like the rest of their lives together: he had to be a lawyer and make money, and she had to be a housewife and take care of everyone. I think there were other things that were more negotiable, like how much she had to look at him and whether she had to try to hide her repulsion, which she did less and less as he got more and more worthy of it.

I think that people can get easier or harder to look at depending on how they behave over time. Dusty got harder to look at every single day.

As I was riding past The Triple S that afternoon, I saw Nora sitting at a table on the side of the building, smoking a cigarette. She was still wearing an apron from the lunch rush, but she looked dignified. Proud. I must have stared at her for a long time, because she finally looked up at me and when she did, she smiled.

It was the kind of smile you give someone who has just brought you a moment of happiness. Maybe a memory from the past, or a glimpse of hope for the future.

I have wondered if what she saw in me reminded her of herself when she was a girl, or maybe just of girlhood itself. I never asked her.

But it was enough for me to turn my bike into the parking lot and go inside. Clay Cooper was eating a sandwich and talking on the phone at a table in the back. I didn't know who he was at the time, but when I asked if they were hiring, the round, jovial woman behind the counter pointed him out. That was Janice, and she, too, smiled at me the way Nora did. Both of them smiling like that made me feel like I had found my new home. My new temporary home, until I could get out of here. She gave me a short application, which I filled out. Then I walked to where Clay Cooper was sitting in the dining room.

"Sit," he told me, motioning at the bench across the table.

I sat down and handed him my application and told him I was fourteen, legally able to work, and that I wanted a job to pay for college.

All of this amused him and made him snicker at me.

"Is this your full name? Charlie? It's not short for something?"

"No. It's Charlie. Just like I wrote it."

His face grew curious. I was used to that. I'd been asked the same question my entire life. By teachers and doctors, even kids who usually don't care about things like that. My mother was sixteen when she named me, and she was given two choices by her mother. Charlene, after my great grandmother, or Eunice, after her great aunt. Charlene it was, because, as my mom later explained, she knew she could then call me Charlie. When we were finally on our own, my mother legally changed my name to erase everything about the past, which was just fine with me. I had always been Charlie, and from what my mom says, Charlene was not a nice woman.

"Fourteen, huh?" Coop looked at the résumé I'd brought, which had my grades, SAT scores, the list of classes I was taking, and of course, my race times.

"You're a runner?" he asked.

"Not anymore," I answered. That was true. That's another story.

He looked up then. "Why not?"

And I told him the truth. "It's not useful to me."

"Not useful?"

"Right. Not useful."

He put the paper down and stared at me, no longer amused like I was a child, but curious, like I was a piece of information he'd just learned.

"You're a little spitfire, aren't you?"

He wasn't looking for an answer, so I didn't offer one.

He stared a moment longer, long enough that I could smell the to-bacco on the breath he was exhaling from across the table. He had a clean shave, but there was still something dirty about him. A shadow that never left his face. A bald spot on his head that was speckled with brown spots. The dark, thick hairs on his arms, which you could see when he rolled up the sleeves of his button-down shirt—always a button-down, collared shirt; khaki pants; a belt; loafers; and even cologne. Coop did his best to look clean, but he just never did.

"Okay," he said finally. "You're hired. Come on."

I felt my eyes light up as I followed him into the service area and then the prep room in the back and then Nora's office where she was then, seated at her desk sorting through papers. My smile beamed as I took in the smells for the first time, the cleaning solution wafting up from a dirty mop bucket, the scraps of food spilled on the floor from the lunch rush, the peppers and onions and even the slight rot of the bad produce in the garbage that was bagged but hadn't been taken out yet. It entered my brain, making me feel things I couldn't control. But these things felt good, like I said before, like freedom. And for that brief moment, even though Clay Cooper was a dirty man inside and out, he was also my hero.

————

As my mom talks to the lawyer we find in the lobby of the police sta-tion, my thoughts have gone in a straight line from Coop in high school seeing that boy die, becoming mean but still having some good about him, to the question Regina asked me in the bathroom about who would want to kill her husband.

Then, obviously, the list begins to form in my mind.

First: Janice. Coop fired her husband Shane from the tobacco store in town because Shane punched him in the face. Shane punched him in the face because Coop had called their son Ollie "half-pint" again after they'd both asked him not to. Coop said half-pint was a term of endearment and mentioned some show called *Little House on the Prairie*, which is so old it isn't even on Netflix, but to Shane and Janice it was a reminder that Ollie was born sick and so his growth in all directions, up and out, was delayed, maybe forever.

Bottom line—Coop knew any reference to Ollie's size was hurtful, and he made that comment anyway. He did it because he wanted to hurt them. He did it on purpose. It was no more complicated than that.

This is another way I think of Clay Cooper. With one hand, he gave you a job. With another, he stole your dignity, your pride, your something or other. No matter the employee, with that second hand, he always took away the one thing that should be more valuable than money. But it can't be when you need to feed four children, with one like Ollie, or when you need to pay for college, or support your sick grandmother. Or just because it was your life's work and there was nowhere else to go.

Coop gave Shane his paycheck one day, and Shane said thanks a little too little and a little too late for Coop's liking, so Coop said, "How's half-pint doing?"

And Shane punched him right in the nose.

A man has his limits. Shane went home and told Janice, who came into work the next day, both crying and yelling because as much as she loved that her husband had defended their child, he had no right to do it, because what their child really needed were the doctors that job was paying for.

"When do I get to punch someone?" she said that day, to me and Nora and Keller and this new kid who only lasted a month because he couldn't even remember that a Number 9 was a steak pita with American cheese.

"He can lose his job over his manly pride, but what about my pride? What about my heart that breaks every time that son-of-a-bitch calls my baby that name? When do I get to lose my shit!"

Janice then apologized for her "French" because Janice doesn't believe in swearing. She says it offends Jesus. And Janice believes in Jesus. She believes in a way you won't find on any of the billboards along the inter-state that runs through our town. She believes from her nose to her toes.

Nora nodded solemnly but said nothing, because Janice was not wrong so there was no point in trying to analyze the situation or make excuses for anyone—not Coop or Shane. It just was what it was.

Later that day, Janice begged Coop to take Shane back and swore he would never do that again and then told him how hard it was with their son being so sick, and we don't really know what else she said as we watched from the service area while they sat in the dining area, but it was a lot. Coop leaned back with his arms folded, a man in control. A man with the power. And he made her beg and plead a good long time before he finally nodded his head yes.

He got up with a straight back and a nod and a smile and walked to the prep room where he washed his dirty hands.

Coop was good about Ollie for a while. He didn't mention him for almost two months, but then he just couldn't stand it. That was the thing with Coop. When he knew your weakness, he was like a kid holding a lollypop, its wrapper off, its sweet smell reaching up into his nose. He just had to lick it, just a tiny bit. Just to get a taste.

That was the part of him he couldn't control. Just like his greed and his lust (which is another story), he craved power, found it irresistible.

I don't even remember what he said to Janice yesterday. I only know that he used *half-pint* again, and this time, Janice was just so filled up with rage, or maybe so empty of pride, that she couldn't stop herself. And like a breath that rushes in when you've tried to stop breathing, she called him every "French" word she could think of. She did it loud and she did it in front of all of us in the prep room, and then she threw her green apron in the bin and slammed the back door on her way out.

We all stood there, all except for Keller, because she was working her second job at the diner, and we waited to see what would happen next.

And what happened was surprising yesterday, but now makes per-fect sense. Coop did what a person like him always does when you've bared your soul and let your weakness be known to them.

He laughed.

He laughed so hard he buckled over and had to wipe tears from his eyes. Then he sighed and shook his head dismissively and told us the show was over and to get back to work.

Did anyone want Clay Cooper dead?

Well, Janice, for one.

CHAPTER EIGHT

The lawyer in the lobby is a woman named Dana Blakely, and she wears a navy pantsuit and black pumps and has hair pulled into a tight bun at the back of her neck. There is not one single strand out of place and not one root showing, which is a sign that she takes very good care of herself and, by inference, will take very good care of me.

She says she isn't a criminal lawyer but deals with *corporate matters*. Dana Blakely says that she and the client she's waiting for are from the city, but he was held overnight on a DUI and she came here to get him released. She said she didn't mind talking with me until her client got out and she could drive him home.

Then she tells us she charges $350 an hour, and my mom chokes on her own breath. I wonder how we'll pay for it, but I imagine this is what it will cost Dusty for not finding us someone from his firm. A small price to pay to save him from the wrath of his wife.

Dana Blakely and my mom go through the whole thing about the photos and how I was at The Triple S and maybe the body was moved and how I have a lopsided seesaw and so while I might have seen something, I might not be capable of processing what I saw and talking about it without getting myself into trouble.

When Dana Blakely agrees to help, my mom looks at me with satisfaction.

"There," she says. "You see? Now we have a lawyer."

There's no point reminding her that we'd have one for a lot less money if Dusty cared enough to help. My mom is great at conveniently forgetting things that would disrupt her denial of who Dusty really is inside. Like his refusing to co-sign any private student loans for me because it would reduce his credit rating, and what if they need to refinance the house or get a car loan? Or refusing to take me off his tax returns as a dependent so I could maybe qualify for financial aid, because he saves money when he claims me on his taxes, and that money pays for the house and food.

Sometimes I want to scare him by saying I won't go to college after all and will live in his house until some man decides to marry me. Dusty has said before that he worries about that, how no man will ever want to. He doesn't understand that just because I don't look like I'm listening, I still have ears that work perfectly fine.

I almost say that we should thank Regina Cooper for telling us she saw this lawyer in the lobby, but then I decide to keep my mouth shut. I still don't know what the bad blood is between them.

We find the detectives and show them our new attorney. They send me and my mom back to that same room where we wait while they speak with her. Dana Blakely with the navy pantsuit.

When she returns, she has a copy of the security footage, which we view on her laptop in the interview room. My eyes watch the one minute and forty-two seconds of footage, but my mind is wandering back in time, to the night before. With my people, my family, Nora and Janice and Keller and Levi and Ian. And even The Triple S itself.

Lettuce tomatoes pickles onions.

It spins with the decision that is now before me, now that they know I was there but don't know what I saw. Or even if I saw anything at all.

The recording plays. I see myself come into view after leaving the bathroom. I am about to enter the service area, but then I stop. I freeze. I hear something and it causes me to drop to the floor and crawl around to the front of the store on hands and knees and hide beneath the counter.

I watch my mom's face, I see behind her skin to the ferocious instinct to protect her child as she watches me wince and then cover my ears on the screen.

And then I watch the lawyer and see behind her veil of professionalism turn into something voyeuristic, her base curiosity as she observes this skinny teenage girl in jeans and a T-shirt and a long brown ponytail start to crawl back to the entrance of the service area, then carefully lift her head, just enough, to try to see into the back room.

There is no audio on the recording. The tape stops when I crawl into the service area, still on hands and knees. Still trying to see, something.

For these few precious minutes, I consider my entire life. My brain gets hot. My heart races. I tap my fingers. *Together. Together. Left. Right. Right. Left.*

I feel a scream so I hold my breath and push it down, like when I have to get rid of hiccups.

Meanwhile, my mom starts to ramble. She tells Dana Blakely how hard she's worked with me to *improve my communication style,* which was not true—it was TV and Keller and Ian and my family at The Triple S that got me where I am now—but I was told not to say one word and so I don't say one word.

Everything I've learned from my mom has been in spite of her.

She tells Dana Blakely about my math skills and about my taking classes above my grade and my SAT scores. She leaves out how hard I've had to work for these things, because that would be too ordinary, and if I'm going to be seen as extra-ordinary in any way, as worthy of protecting, it will be in this way. A savant like Dustin Hoffman in *Rain Man.* Then she tells Dana Blakely how she *had* to get me out of this mess because I was headed to college. I was getting out of this shithole, not getting trapped like every other person who's ever grown up here, and then she asks Dana Blakely if she grew up here, and she tells her "Someplace like it," and my mom says, "So you know—look at you now. You're a lawyer. No chance that would have happened if you'd stayed in a place like Sawyer."

Dana Blakely is very interested in my lopsided seesaw and my mom's obvious take on our entire situation. She asks her if there are any medical records on file about me.

I know exactly which story my mom will share, and she launches right into it. She tells Dana about the time I was admitted to the psychiatric unit because I wouldn't stop training for marathons and had become dangerously underweight. She tells her how scary it was because social services got involved and Dusty was so embarrassed he brought in a special doctor to treat me. All of that was now in a record with the state and also in my medical file, and I will never be able to get rid of it.

Dana Blakely looks at me because my brain has become so hot I've started to cry, which I only do when I'm mad, and this makes me madder and my brain hotter and so more tears fall and it's all just one big horrible shit show.

Dana Blakely speaks in a very soft, even voice. She asks me if I knew about the camera in the dining area, and if I knew if there were other cameras at The Triple S, inside or outside. She says Clay Cooper was required by law to tell us if we were being watched while we worked. And I tell her that I did not know about any cameras.

"Technically," she says, "the one in the dining room doesn't reach into the workspace, so he didn't have to tell you about that one. I assume if they had any footage from the back room, you wouldn't be here at all, because they would know what did or didn't happen at the store last night."

She pauses now, because this is the obvious time for me to say what did happen, or at least the part that I might know.

But I don't. I made promises.

My mom sighs deeply like she wants to reach inside my mouth and pull out the story, but then she realizes she may not like it, so she stops herself. Me being me might be useful after all.

Instead, she asks, "How do they know the body was moved?"

Dana Blakely says that it could be many things, like the amount of blood they found at the scene or the way the blood had pooled inside his head. Maybe it wasn't consistent with him being struck there on the side of the road, then falling to the ground and bleeding on the street.

She says it could also be from surveillance cameras in town. Maybe someone caught an image of his truck on its way back to his neighborhood.

And after they do the forensics, they may find other things, like dirt or particles that came from somewhere else, not the street or his car.

And I think that she must have learned all of this from TV shows because she said she wasn't a criminal lawyer, and because I knew all of those things from TV shows, and so would my mom if she watched anything besides *The Real Housewives*.

"So he was killed somewhere else, then driven in his truck back to his house?"

Dana Blakely shrugs. "They don't have to tell us anything, so all we can do is guess. They might even be lying about the body being moved. Right now, Charlie is just a possible eyewitness. Not a suspect. Certainly not a defendant in a case. There are no disclosure rules. They don't have to tell us anything and we don't have to tell them anything. That much I know—I represented a corporate officer once who witnessed a robbery."

My mom doesn't look at me, because she's returned to her thinking.

"What about your phone?" Dana Blakely asks.

I pull out my phone and place it on the table.

"Have they asked you for it?"

I shake my head no.

"Good," she says. "They'll have your call and text log soon, if they don't already. They got a warrant based on the camera footage. But the actual content of the texts will take longer. You don't have to unlock it."

I nod.

Now my mom does look at me.

"What will they find, Charlie—on your phone?"

I shake my head. "Nothing unusual" is all I say. And that's the truth. Everyone I called and texted that night would be on my phone any day of the week.

But it still sits there, the question they're both waiting for me to answer. My mom hasn't asked because she doesn't want to know. And the lawyer hasn't asked because she's trying to win my trust or make it seem like it's my choice to answer when I'm ready. But it's coming. It has to be. The moment where I decide who I am.

And then it does.

"Charlie?" my mom says. "Tell us what happened last night. What did you hear in the back room of The Triple S? What did you see?"

I look at them, these two women with wide eyes and hungry curiosity.

I consider what Dana Blakely said, about there not being any disclosure rules. About me not being under arrest, just a possible witness. I've already looked this up myself, and I know that people don't have to say what they see—even a brutal crime.

They can make me sit here like a good girl.

They can do all of that.

But what they can't do is make me speak.

Not a word.

Not one single word.

I did not kill Clay Cooper. And I don't know who did. But I do know that people I love are about to be suspects. And once I open my mouth about one single thing, they will want to pull the rest of it out. Things I've observed and things I know about people who trust me.

If I open my mouth, and if I say one single thing, I will then have an impossible choice to make between lying and breaking that trust.

So I will not say one single word. I am not a liar and I won't betray my friends. Because:

Rule Number Five: Once you betray a friend, you lose them forever.

CHAPTER NINE

Half an hour passes after I refuse to speak. The detectives return. Pittfield and Slater.

Dana Blakely tells my mom that we should finish the interview because maybe that will satisfy them. Otherwise, they could get more warrants and cause all kinds of trouble.

So we let the detectives start asking their questions.

They have the text log and they can see that whatever happened last night, with me at least, had to do with Keller.

"She sent you an SOS, didn't she? That's what all of this was. She needed your help," Slater asks.

I don't answer.

Sighs and frustration follow, just like before when my mom refused to let me answer, only now it feels different. Now the refusal is coming from me and I feel like a lone soldier on a battlefield facing an army.

Pittfield jumps in.

"We know Keller's family. The Joelles. They've been in the system for many years."

My mom groans. She hates Keller. She told me straight out one day, "Keller's headed down a dead-end street—so don't you follow her!"

Dana Blakely leans forward with scrunched eyes and asks what this is about, who are the Joelles and what do they have to do with me?

Slater answers her.

"Keller Joelle was a truant. She left school after ninth grade. She has a boyfriend who's twenty-two. You get the picture."

As much as my mom dislikes Keller, she suddenly rises to defend her.

"You don't know anything about it. That girl dropped out of school to take care of her sick grandmother . . . because her own mother is dead . . . and because she has no father . . . and her half-brother could care less about anyone but himself . . . and because the state won't pay for the right medication . . . so don't you dare put down a girl who does that! Who sacrifices her own future to care for a woman society has thrown away!"

She pauses, looks at the ceiling and then back at them. "Don't you dare!"

For a moment I think she's going to cry, and I don't know if it's for Keller or for every girl from Sawyer who was dealt a shitty hand. But what I do know is that maybe she doesn't hate Keller after all. She just doesn't want me to follow her down that dead-end street.

Pittfield comes to Slater's rescue.

"We didn't mean anything by that, and I apologize if it came out wrong. We're just noting that Keller Joelle has a complicated life and that last night, she needed Charlie's help. Was it about her boyfriend, Levi? You must know him, Charlie. He works across the parking lot from The Triple S, at the gas station. And Keller—she works two jobs for Clay Cooper. One at The Triple S and one at the diner. Maybe there was something . . . that made Levi jealous? Or maybe it was about money?"

My mom is starting to lose her shit as she thinks about me being wrapped up in some mess on that dead-end street with Keller and Levi and her crazy, sick grandmother.

"Charlie," she says, calmer now. "What happened with Keller last night?"

I look at Dana Blakely, who looks back, and I think tries to tell me with her eyes to stay quiet. So I shake my head. *No.*

Dana Blakely speaks next.

"My client declines to comment at this time."

And then we are off to the races.

Pittfield asks, "What about the call to this 526 number? It's not traceable."

Dana Blakely responds firmly, "My client declines to comment at this time."

"And the call at 10 p.m. to Clay Cooper?" Slater asks.

My mom interjects, "Jesus H. Christ! You called Clay Cooper?!"

Dana Blakely repeats, "My client declines to comment at this time."

Now Slater again.

"Charlie, you don't need to be scared. We can see from that footage that someone else was there last night and that what they were doing and saying in the back room was upsetting to you. And all of that leads us to the conclusion that you either didn't see what happened or what you saw involves someone you care about."

He pauses then and gives me his best puppy dog eyes. "It's admirable, Charlie, wanting to protect a friend. But it's not the right thing to do."

I look at Dana Blakely again. She nods then shakes her head at Slater. Suddenly, his eyes aren't so sweet.

"Okay. Well, before we let you go, be aware that this is an ongoing investigation and that we will be looking into these calls and texts, analyzing the footage from The Triple S, conducting forensic examinations . . ."

Dana Blakely says, "With proper warrants of course—if anything is needed from my client."

Slater responds, "Of course. But we will find out who killed Clay Cooper. This town won't rest until we do. He's the head of our council and a church board member and the largest property owner in the county, which means he writes a lot of people's paychecks."

I feel a knot in my stomach when he says all of this because I know it's true but I also think how unfair it is that no one ever says all of the other things about Clay Cooper. I wonder if that's because they figure no one will ever believe them, or because no one would care because men like Clay Cooper also have seesaws, and if they put enough things on one side, the side of good things like church and money, they're allowed to put a lot of things on the other side too. The mean side. The ugly side.

Lust and greed and insatiable need. That's what's on the ugly side.

My mom has an even bigger knot, as it turns out.

"Oh, so it's more important to find out who killed Clay Cooper than someone else in this town?" she asks, but it's not really a question. "What about old Mrs. Watkinson, who died of a heart attack after a break-in scared her, literally, to death? And the clerk at the gas station a few years back—shot in a robbery? That case was never solved. And even Cullen Maguire! Run down on the highway by a stolen car? How many hours has this department logged looking for him this year? Or last year? Or the year before? But for Clay Cooper, you won't rest until there's justice?"

Detective Slater tries to calm her down. "We're just saying that his murder is likely to involve a lot of suspects. Many of whom your daughter is connected to. People won't take kindly to that fact—that she's not saying what she knows."

And then my mom has the last word. "You know something, detectives? I have found that giving a shit about what people take kindly to is a waste of time. Because they're always not taking kindly to something."

Pittfield looks at Slater, then drops a new bomb on all of us. "There is one last thing," she says, and the rest of us take a breath and hold it in all at the exact same time. "We found an incident report in Keller Joelle's file from last June. It was a report made by someone who claimed to be concerned about bruises found on Keller's arms and neck."

Now she pulls some papers out of a manila folder.

"Keller said it was from a fall she had at her house, tripping down the stairs. But the woman who reported it thought it might be from a man. Possibly her boyfriend."

My mom grows quiet like a sleeping volcano. Keller's dead-end street just got shorter and she sees me on it.

"Who made that report?" she asks.

They can't tell her. But I already know. Janice is a mother to all of us and she can never help herself. We all saw the bruises on Keller, and not just once.

The volcano erupts the second the detectives leave the room which is after they give us more warnings and threats.

"I knew it!" my mom says. "I knew that Levi was no good! And now they've dragged you into this mess."

I look at my folded hands and feel surprised that my head has stayed cool as a cucumber.

I could look at my mom, and at Dana Blakely. I could look them both right in the eye because Ian taught me how way back when and because I've gotten very good at it and even like to do it now with Ian and Keller and my family at The Triple S because that's where love is, and not just the kind between Keller and Levi. Every kind. Every. Single. Kind. Right there, in a person's eyes, if you can stand to look long enough. But I don't.

My mom and Dana Blakely start talking like I'm not in the room.

My mom repeats, "I knew it! I knew that Levi was no good! And now they've dragged Charlie into this mess . . . although . . . they could just be working an angle, right? This could be nonsense, smoke and mirrors, to protect the Coopers."

Dana Blakely asks curiously, "What do you mean?"

My mom says, "Well, Regina Cooper just told us that the IRS is investigating her husband. They may even have a warrant by now."

Dana Blakely asks, "The IRS? Did she say what it was about?"

She shakes her head. Then Dana Blakely asks me if I know anything about the books, or the manager acting strange lately, and I tell her no.

"Nothing unusual going on with the business? No strange people meeting with Coop? Changes in the routine, how the register is handled?"

No, no, no . . .

She asks if I'm sure and my mom waves her hand dismissively and tells Dana Blakely straight out that if I say no then that's the truth because I'm a terrible liar.

Dana Blakely says she'll let the detectives know and maybe that will turn attention away from me.

My mom likes this. "Yes!" she says. "That's the thing to do! Let them focus on someone else."

But then she gets a new thought. One she doesn't like as much.

"Ms. Blakely . . ."

"Yes?"

"You don't think Charlie's in any danger, right? I mean, if Coop was doing something illegal. She's just a girl. A kid—right?"

CHAPTER TEN

Dana Blakely goes outside to execute our new plan. This day feels like it won't end. My mom calls Dusty from that same corner, and my thoughts return to the question Regina put in my head while we were all in the bathroom.

Who may have wanted Clay Cooper dead? I continue making the list because it's impossible to stop now. I need to sort things out.

One: Janice.

Two: Nora.

Nora knew things, maybe too much, about what was going on with Coop and his shady recordkeeping. Nothing kept on computers. No papers stored in the office. No spreadsheets, not even to track the pans of food we went through each week so we could get better at the ordering. Well, none that he knew about. And Nora is wise. She didn't go to college and she never left Sawyer, but she was married to a man who died in the army, and this gives her a kind of wisdom that you can't get in school, or even just from being old.

She didn't trust Coop because she learned to see the world through the eyes of a widow.

Coop said his methods were necessary because of agencies like the IRS—the entire government even. He explained it all to me one

afternoon at The Triple S: Coop was convinced that one day the government was going to seize all the banks and all the companies who traded
in the stock markets, and then the stock would be worth zero. And he
said they would take all the money in the banks as well. He said cash
was king and one day we would all come running to him for a loan.

Turns out, there are people who fear the government more than
anything else. They talk about places like Cuba and Venezuela and hide
their money under their mattresses. It didn't take much research to make
my own decision about whether my money was safe in the bank, and
in an account that allowed me to pay fewer taxes.

So Nora taught me how to file my tax returns. She said, "Don't mess
with the IRS." It was like a giant beast with no head. Once it got its
hands on you, it would just squeeze you until you were dead and nothing you could do or say would make it stop. The best thing to do was to
report all of your income and pay all of your taxes on time, to stay out of
trouble. And in my case, putting the money into the 529 plan allowed
me to legally avoid taxes and the headless beast that collected them.

All of this explained why Nora kept those spreadsheets, and other
things as well, about the register receipts, the payroll, the rent, insurance, taxes, and whatever else she could find, all on a thumb drive that
she slipped in and out of the laptop when she knew Coop had left. She
worked a lot of late nights.

And I'm not the only one who knows this, it turns out.

When Dana Blakely returns for the last time, she tells us that the
detectives promised to keep the security footage a secret if they could.
But when she mentioned the IRS and Coop's possible shady books, they
told her that they also knew about Nora signing the documents and
staying late to work on those books, so maybe *she* was the one cooking
them. And maybe she and Coop fought about it last night, and maybe
she killed him.

Then Dana Blakely explains to me what I already know.

"Everyone is eventually going to find out about that recording they
have. And that it proves you heard something and maybe saw something.
And the trouble for you, Charlie, is this: the person you're protecting

might be grateful. But it sounds like there are also people you could be hurting by not talking, and they are not going to be happy. They are going to be angry that you won't exonerate them."

She looks at me with serious eyes as she moves on from Nora to another member of my family at the shop.

"I know about the fight Coop had with Janice yesterday. An employee already told the police about it. And about her husband punching him, getting fired and then rehired . . . there's a history there."

Dana Blakely gives the details, which I already know, though I'm not at all happy that someone told the police about it. And I know who it was. Tracey worked the dinner shift last night. It had to be him. He's weak like that. The snarky kid who talks shit but then collapses into a pile of it the second he's confronted.

"You see what I'm saying? Nora often stayed late to sort the books—books that might soon be under investigation. Janice left in a rage after Coop ridiculed her child. And Keller—she reached out to you for help last night. They have the texts and, well, they're going to find out what happened if they don't know already."

Here we go. My mom perks up because she has this thing about Keller.

"Find out what? What else about Keller?"

Dana Blakely tells us with a heavy, remorseful sigh, "There are rumors, I'm told, about Clay Cooper dating young women that work for him. Was Keller one of them, Charlie? Is that why she was upset last night? Was she dating her boss?"

Now my mom gasps and covers her mouth.

"Oh—Jesus H. Christ—and she had those bruises!"

Dana Blakely goes on to explain how everyone was talking about Clay Cooper today, things she overheard in the lobby and just now from the detectives, and most of it was probably gossip. Rumors. Word of mouth. Shit talk. Coop employed lots of pretty women. Young women. And he flirted with them. Ogled them. Supposedly dated some of them in exchange for better shifts. It could all be nothing. It could be things he talked about with his friends when they were drunk at his club or playing golf or at the old warehouse he owned that he supposedly used for illegal poker games. It could have just been talk.

But my mom is shaken as she processes this information and puts it into her own mental files, very large files, about the inequality between men and women, especially in towns like ours, and I'm sure she thinks about her lost dreams and our shitty apartment and the man she has to tolerate in her bed every night.

And while her mind is doing all of that, Dana Blakely is finishing her own thoughts.

"You can't save them all by saying nothing, Charlie. The best you can do is save the ones who are innocent by telling us what you know. You need to be honest, Charlie. You don't have a choice. If you tell me, I can work with the police to get you a deal."

My mom nods her head in agreement now.

The two of them discuss how to make it work without me getting in any trouble or ruining my college admissions by having all of this come out, and I stop hearing them.

I can't save any of them without saving all of them, because I don't even know which one I'm saving from what thing.

Lettuce tomatoes pickles onion. I need to get back to The Triple S.

CHAPTER ELEVEN

My mom is silent the whole way home, which gives me time to think more about the people who wanted Clay Cooper dead.

First: Janice, because he used his second hand to take away her pride and her dignity and that of her husband and even her child, poor little Ollie.

Second: Nora, because he put her in a position that could expose her to criminal charges for crooked bookkeeping and who knows what else when she's all about personal integrity and honor, and also this job, which has been her whole life since her husband died in the army.

Third: Keller.

Keller has been my best friend since we started elementary school. Ian was my next best friend, and all three of us were inseparable until life started to change. We had nothing in common aside from the fact that we all had *broken* families. And by broken, I don't mean single-parent homes, divorced parents. Common things like that. Ours were broken in ways that become plots in novels and movies, the ones that make people think and cry. The ones that make people think *thank God that isn't my life*. That was the glue that held us together.

I learned that I had a broken family like that in the fourth grade. I remember it was a Tuesday because they always served meatloaf on

Tuesdays. I had asked a girl in my class if she wanted to come over one day after school. I'd asked her the week before, and I figured seven days was enough time to wait for an answer. In the fourth grade, kids still just say whatever they've been told. They don't have filters yet, at least not good ones. So she told me she wasn't allowed to come to my house because *her mother* couldn't be sure that *my mother* ran a home with *the right values*. Even with Dusty and their boys, I was a reminder of my mother's past that made her a different snowflake.

I never told my mom about the playdate thing because she would have shit an enormous brick.

And she would argue that it didn't matter about the past. She put our family back together with Dusty and the boys, but it wasn't the same. It's never the same. Dusty didn't love me and I didn't love him. We were like the pictures the TV shrinks use to diagnose their patients—where there are some things that belong and one that doesn't, and they ask, "Which of these things doesn't belong?" Like a bowl of fruit with one potato, or a rack of boots with a pair of high heels. It was subtle, but still obvious if you bothered to look closely enough. My mom belonged to me, Dusty, and the boys. The boys belonged to my mom and Dusty. Dusty belonged to my mom and the boys. I was the only one who just belonged to my mom, like a cancer that can be cut out without killing the patient.

Ian's father died when Ian was seven, and his mother never remarried, which seemed acceptable, since she had already been married and had a child. She had proved herself to be normal. With Ian's family, there was also a tragedy hanging over them, and that garnered sympathy from the community. Sympathy is better than scorn. Still, they were broken in a way that reminded people of sadness and loss, and nobody likes that.

Ian's family was broken like a heartbreak. But Keller—her family was broken in the worst possible way. It was broken like a TV set that's thrown from a window ten stories high, its pieces littering the street, metal and glass and plastic everywhere, injuring anyone too close when it hits the ground. Broken in an ugly, messy, shithouse way.

Her mother had two children without being married. The first was a boy named Rickie. His father lived in Boston, and now Rickie had his own wife and two kids himself. Rickie moved just far enough away from Sawyer to make it impossible to help with their grandmother, Dot, who has a dozen physical ailments along with her dementia.

She wears adult diapers, a Life Alert necklace, a brace on her leg, and an oxygen tank that she wheels around from room to room, all while leaning on a walker. Keller says she could be a spokeswoman for pretty much every old-age product that's ever been invented, plus Marlboro Reds, which Dot won't give up. One long infomercial. One giant billboard, right next to The Hand of God and The Triple S. Except for the fact that it was so painful to look at her that people might crash their cars. Keller and her mom lived with Dot until Keller's mom died of breast cancer when Keller was thirteen. Social services came to see what to do about Keller, and she lied and said her dad was going to come live with them, because she didn't want to have to live with some *rando* foster parents, and she didn't want Dot to be sent to a state facility. The last time that happened, they gave her the wrong medication and she tried to cut her wrists with a butter knife in the cafeteria.

Things had not ended well between Dot and Keller's mom—she didn't even go to her funeral. Keller's mom and my mom had a lot in common, but Keller's mom didn't have babies until she was nineteen, so there was that difference. But they both got called whores by their own mothers, and I think that should be its own special club where everyone in it gets a million dollars and can live their lives without men like Dusty or shitty apartments or cancer. But I don't make the rules.

Instead, there are people like Dot. She is unforgiving and believes, even now, that her only daughter is burning in the eternal flames of Hell for what she did. Two babies out of wedlock, and one with a married man.

Keller had a plan. After ninth grade, she stopped going to school so she could make the money needed to keep living in her house with Dot. I got her the first job at The Triple S, which wasn't hard because Keller is the kind of girl Clay Cooper liked, and after that he let her work at his diner as well. She was a woman, really, in every way, especially in her spirit and determination. She cared for Dot like my own mother cared for her boys and Janice cared for Ollie and her three other children. Keller learned how to cash Dot's Social Security checks and pay the rent and the utilities and even how to file all of Dot's medical claims with the government.

But she was also a woman in other ways. She moved through the world in her body like she'd had it forever, the breasts and hips and pouty lips. Like she had never been anything but a woman, and the kind of woman who turns heads.

Coop was disgusting around Keller, and all of us hated him for that. His eyes lingered. His mouth gaped. That spot on his balding head got shiny with perspiration. He stood too close to her. Brushed her behind with the back of his hand when he squeezed past her in the service area, which he only lingered in when she was working.

Keller said she was used to it. She said he wasn't the first old geezer to ogle her.

And she was right—Coop wasn't the only man who wanted to touch Keller. This is the part about Levi from the gas station.

It was at the end of that first summer that a tall, beautiful man came in for a sandwich. He was a cross between Dallas and Sodapop from *The Outsiders*, which every teenager has to read—he has a bad-boy exterior with an innocent inside that all made him irresistible. He walked across the parking lot from the gas station, where he'd just gotten a job as a mechanic. He was twenty then, and had moved here from New Jersey. He'd come looking for work, which makes me think New Jersey must be even worse than Sawyer, if that's possible.

I remember seeing him in the line, then seeing him again as my eyes took over my brain. That's how beautiful Levi is. He stood patiently, waiting his turn. And when Keller asked him what he wanted, he stumbled over his words, barely able to look at her, which made her blush and look away and then made him do the same.

Keller stood next to me at the wood counter, where I was making a tuna-salad pita with lettuce and onions, and she said, "I think I just fell in love."

That was over two years ago. And in that time, three things have happened.

First, Levi and Keller became inseparable. They became best friends. They became lovers.

Second, Janice started to notice bruises on Keller's body, and then so did Nora and I because we all started looking for them after Janice told us. Janice eventually told the police as well—about the bruises and about Levi.

All of this confused me. I thought about the times Keller and I lay across the hood of her car under The Hand of God, drinking beer so my mind would stop spinning, and she would tell me about their bodies being one, and I just could not reconcile that image with the story Janice was telling about the bruises. One second, Levi stroking her face and gazing into her eyes, and the next second, grabbing her arms so hard he left them black and blue.

Once I started looking for the bruises, they seemed to be every-where. There was the one on her cheek. The one on her neck. The one on her ankle.

But then I thought, what do I know about any of this? Keller also said there was something powerful when she and Levi were together like that, a feeling of being overpowered by his strength, which she said was exciting, and maybe that's what caused the bruises. Maybe it didn't hurt when it was happening because she was so excited by the rest of it.

I only asked about it once, and she said she fell and not to worry. I did worry, but what can you do in a situation like that?

Coop was not happy about Levi and Keller, even though Keller was too young for him and he was married. His flirtations took on a new flavor. Suddenly, she was something he couldn't have, not because of his own self-control or his priorities like his family and his reputation with the town council and the church, but because of another man. And so whatever fantasies he'd allowed himself inside his head—well, those had been stolen right out from under him.

He cut back her hours. He put her on shifts that made it hard for her to care for Dot and to see Levi. He threatened to fire her every time she was late, which was almost every day because she was always being pulled in different directions. And he touched her wherever and whenever he wanted, tempting her to make a scene so he could have a reason to fire her.

The look on her face when she felt his hand run across her thigh while she was prepping the food or mopping the floor—I don't have the exact word to explain it. Vacant. Dead. Resigned.

Back in the prep room, Janice would sometimes bite her lip until it started to bleed, because, as her husband Shane once said, "We all had to eat whatever pile of shit Coop served up for us."

Levi could kill Coop with his bare hands, but if he did, we would all suffer. So he saw what Coop did to Keller and heard about what Coop did to Keller and couldn't do a thing about it for the same reason Janice couldn't and I couldn't and Keller couldn't.

Coop got whatever he wanted.

The third thing that happened since Keller met Levi has nothing to do with Keller and everything to with me and what I knew about Clay Cooper.

It happened one night after my shift at The Triple S. I had just turned sixteen and finally had my driver's license. My mom was in the kitchen with the boys. She was cooking them dinner, and they were watching TV, which meant Dusty wasn't home. When I walked in, she was mumbling to herself the way she does when she's really, really upset.

I opened the fridge to get a soda.

She grabbed my arm.

"I need to talk to you."

She put two plates of chicken nuggets and apple slices in front of the boys and pulled me into the family room.

"It's happening," she said.

"What's happening?" I asked.

It was Dusty. He was having an affair and getting ready to leave her, only she wasn't going to let that happen, no way, no sir.

"I have a plan, don't you worry!" she said. I was just one year away from getting into college and winning the town scholarship. What happened in this house was so close to not mattering I could feel it in my bones like the shiver of excitement you get on Christmas Eve before you know the truth about Santa.

Still, she carried on, telling me about his late nights and his excuse about some case, but how she checked at the courthouse and the case had already gone to trial, so it was over until the judge made a ruling, which could be months away. He always slowed down after a trial, only not this time. This time, he was using it as cover to have an affair.

She knew it.

"Take the car, Charlie," she said next. "I can't leave the boys, and also, he'd see me and know I was out looking for him. But he wouldn't think anything if he saw you. He'd just think you were meeting friends."

"Take it where?" I asked. I was tired. I wanted to have a shower to get rid of the grease smell from working the grill and the pickle-juice stains on my fingers from stocking the pans for the next day, and then watch some shows and go to sleep.

But, no. That's not how my night would unfold.

My mom told me about the place where they go, the people having affairs. How it was just over the border in the next town. How it was a Marriott Hotel with a restaurant and bar in the lobby, and not a family place, but a place for out-of-town businessmen who wouldn't recognize anyone from here.

"No one local goes there for any other reason. It's overpriced and the food is terrible. Just the businessmen from out of town and the teenagers trying not to get carded. And the cheaters."

"Mom . . ." I tried to complain, to stall, to tell her she was crazy because, after all, she was so beautiful and like she was always saying, Dusty couldn't afford to leave her now because she had two kids with him and had "become accustomed to a certain lifestyle which he would have to keep her in if he left." He couldn't afford to do that and also provide a nice life for another woman. She had been telling me this for years. And years.

But it was no use.

Half an hour later, I was parking the car at the Marriott. She was right about that place. I had no idea it even existed, and there were a lot of license plates from neighboring states.

I walked through the lobby and into the restaurant. I still smelled of grease and pickle juice. I was still wearing my jeans and The Triple S T-shirt.

I didn't find Dusty that night. When I told my mom later, she seemed more disappointed than relieved. I began to wonder if she'd been hoping for a reason to leave him that would put her on the high road and him on the low road. Like maybe she wanted a divorce with alimony on the side and sympathy poured over the whole thing like hot fudge on a sundae.

I didn't find Dusty. But I did find someone I knew.

A couple was sitting in a small booth, way, way in the corner. It was the back of the man's head. The scruffy hair on his neck and the pattern it made as it crept from his hairline until it disappeared beneath the collar of his button-down shirt. The shiny bald spot. Even the shape of his ears, the way they protruded farther from his head at both the bottom and the top, make the letter "C" on the right side and a backward "C" on the left.

It was Coop. And sitting across from him was a girl I knew from the diner. I guess she was a woman, because she was nineteen, and she was dressed like a woman and she was acting like a woman, the way she held her wine glass and laughed like she was actually happy to be there with a man like Clay Cooper. And it was then too that I knew why she got all the dinner shifts where people paid more money in tips, while Keller only got breakfast and lunch, if she was lucky.

And just like the curiosity that had grown inside me from Coop's strange recordkeeping, a new curiosity was born. I could easily imagine Keller sitting at that table with Coop too. And now that she was eighteen and still with Levi, and Coop kept cutting her hours at The Triple S and at the diner, making her desperate for money, well, it seemed like it was only a matter of time before Keller could be the girl at the Marriot.

So, yes, Keller had reasons to want Clay Cooper dead. I guess, by association, so did I.

CHAPTER TWELVE

When we get home from the police station, my mom cooks while I have a shower. Dusty has taken the boys out to the park, and when I hear them come home, I get nervous. Dusty is not going to be happy with me.

I stay in my room until my mom calls me. I come downstairs and take my usual seat, next to her on my right side, with the boys across from me and Dusty at the other end. He calls it the head, although I don't see how there can be a head when there are two ends to the table that are exactly the same. But in Dusty's house, there is a head and Dusty sits there. A king on his throne.

Dinner always starts with a prayer, and we have to hold hands in a circle like we used to do in nursery school. I know it sounds normal. Maybe it even sounds nice. But for me it means touching my mom with my right hand and touching Dusty with my left hand, feeling their skin on my skin on both ends of me, and it makes me feel like losing my shit.

On this night, though, Dusty does not reach for my hand or for DJ's hand on his other side, and everyone seems a little confused. We all just follow his lead and let him say his prayer thanking God for the food while we stare at our hands folded in our laps.

When he finishes, we look up again, and my mom starts to pass around the food: tonight, tuna casserole and peas. She didn't have much time to cook since we were at the station so long.

My mom asks about the park. The boys shrug and say it was fun, and Dusty goes on and on about all the things they did, like throwing balls and playing tag with some kids they knew from school. Dusty says he ran into so-and-so, and my mom says that's nice, and nobody talks at all about Coop being dead and me being recorded and getting hauled down to the station for questioning.

Dusty decides to speak then.

"Did you tell them?" he asks my mom.

She doesn't answer. She gives him a look.

"Because they should know. It might help. Even if we have to take her back to the hospital."

I stop chewing and forget to swallow. I sit with a mouth full of mushy tuna casserole, which is not pleasant. But I can't move my mouth or my tongue or any part of my body. I'm frozen thinking about what Dusty has just said.

Finally, my mom says something. "That won't be necessary."

But Dusty is not satisfied. "How do you know? I mean, this was just the beginning. The first interview. What if they come back with more questions? What if they find more evidence?"

My mom shuts him down. She sees my mouth full of food and my cheeks getting red.

Hot head. Hot head. Hot head!

"Charlie—drink your water."

I do as I'm told, and she's right to tell me because when I drink the water, I have to swallow, and at least that part is over.

"Eileen—I'm serious. If this blows up and the college finds out, they could withdraw her acceptance. And then what? What will she do then?"

Now he cares about me going to college? *Now* he wants to help?

This is horse shit.

"Don't you remember when she started running?"

Rule Number Twelve: People tend to repeat the past.

———

I was eleven when my mom and Dusty's second boy was born. Their first was named Dusty, after his father. We call him DJ because he's technically Dusty Junior. DJ sounds like the name of a jerk—I hope that doesn't happen, because their DJ is a sensitive boy, and I actually don't mind him.

The second one started growing a year after DJ arrived. My mom said she wasn't *messing around*. Two babies in two years made it impossible for her to go back to work, and that made her a stay-at-home mom, and that made her a candidate for alimony, and that made it all worth the effort.

Dusty was with her when DJ was born and he didn't like it one bit. He looked like someone had ripped out his eyeballs and scrubbed them with sandpaper then put them back in his head. So when it came time for the second one to be born, he went on a golf trip with the partners from his firm. He said he couldn't get out if it because it was one of those team-building things where they're all supposed to get to know and trust each other more so they work together better. But there were only five of them, and they were all men, so all they were going to do "was play golf, get drunk, talk about porn, then jerk off in their hotel rooms." My mom told that to one her friends, a woman named Leah, who liked to come over with her baby and pass the time by putting the babies in one room together, drinking coffee, and talking about their husbands and the other women at the club. Leah laughed when my mom said this.

It turned out Dusty planned the trip and decided the timing on purpose, and when my mom found out, she made him sleep in the guest room for a whole week—which I don't think he minded. My mom is not fun to be around after she has a baby.

This baby, named Everett after Dusty's dead father, came at night the way babies like to do. My mom woke me up. She told me she was having the baby and I had to go with her to the hospital. She said we were dropping DJ off at Leah's house but I had to be with her in case she needed me. It was already decided, and I could tell it had been decided the second Dusty told her about his "mandatory" golf trip.

The hospital was not crowded, and they took my mom into a room right away. I sat in a chair in the corner and stared at the muted tele-vision that hung from giant metal hinges on the wall across from my mom's bed. There was a commercial playing, only it never ended. It had an old woman with blond hair and perfect teeth speaking with plead-ing eyes and a serious mouth, and I could tell she used to be someone important, like an actress, because why else would she be on the com-mercial for so long when she wasn't very attractive?

Behind her were emaciated children walking around in the dirt, their eyes hollow like they were already dead. The camera zoomed in on one, and I could see flies buzzing around the baby's head. I couldn't tell if it was a boy or a girl, or even the age.

Nurses came and went. They put wires and tubes into my mom's arms, and she was NOT happy when they told her it was too late for some medicine that she wanted. She yelled at them and even swore at them to "give her the medicine because no way in hell was she doing this without it!"

They left to get the doctor and she started to cry. Her eyes found me, and she summoned me to come to the side of the bed and take her hand, which I did. But my eyes couldn't leave the flies eating that baby's head and so her eyes followed mine until she also saw it. Then she said, "Look at that, Charlie! Those poor women forced to have babies they can't even feed! Don't ever forget it, because even though you don't live in that place, you'll turn this place into that place for yourself if you don't listen to the things I tell you." Then she asked me if I understood, and I lied and said yes when really I couldn't put one single thought together.

The pain came again, and she let go of my hand to grab the railing on her bed, and she screamed so loud I had to look at her. I wondered how this kind of pain wasn't killing her. How much pain did it take to kill someone? It didn't seem like there was much more pain someone could ever feel, even when they were dying.

Alarms went off. People rushed in. Nurses and a doctor. A man. He told my mom the baby was coming, and they pushed me aside. Then they strapped her feet in the metal stirrups and pulled off all the sheets and gathered between her legs.

You know the rest—except for this part.

While it was all happening and she was screaming and yelling at them for not giving her the medicine, the pain subsided for a moment, and they told her to rest and catch her breath. It was then that she looked around and found me—and she told me to watch what was happening to her. To remember what was being done to her body, how it was being tortured and ripped open, and how this was the most pain she would ever feel in her life. "Never ever forget this, Charlie. Never, ever. This is all God's trick." And then the pain returned.

I couldn't think about anything while I was watching this thing happen to my mom, with the flies eating the baby going on in the background. There was nowhere to escape to in that room.

When the baby ripped out of her and they cleaned it up, wrapped it in a soft, cuddly blanket, and placed it on her chest, she cried again, only this time with joy—I had learned the difference by then—and she kissed it and stroked its face and said it was a *miracle*. She called me over and said, "Meet your new brother, Charlie. Isn't he beautiful!"

But I would never forget. I would never forget how much pain she endured, how much strength it took to push that thing out of her, and how angry it made her that she had to endure all of that, even though she could, even though she'd now done it three times. I would never forget how she cried when she kissed his face and how I knew she would love him forever, as fiercely as she loved me, whether she wanted to or not. And I would never forget the images of the flies eating that baby's head because the mother couldn't find enough food or enough strength to keep the flies away.

All of that became a new rule.

Rule Number Fourteen: God's Trick, whatever it was, is a very, very good trick.

———

It was all of this remembering that led to the running that Dusty had brought up again after so many years.

Because not long after, when we were all back home and Dusty was made to sleep in the guest room, my mom and I cuddled on her bed while she fed Everett. She had been tending to both her babies day and night. Everett screaming in the night for a feeding. DJ screaming in the day because he wanted more cookies or TV or for no reason whatsoever. My mom tried to hold them both, together or one at a time, all through the day. She was ragged, but she still kissed their faces because she couldn't help herself.

I didn't know what to make of this except to see that she was under the spell of God's trick, which was bigger than even she knew. And I watched this carefully too, like a spy gathering intelligence. *Watch and file. Watch and file. You'll need this one day.*

I sat beside her on the bed, and she showed me her swollen breasts and told me how the milk was stored there and how it came down and squirted out when she heard the baby cry and wasn't that crazy how biology works?

She stared at me then and told me to come closer, on the other side of her. She reached out her hand and touched the front of my nightgown where my own breasts would have been if I'd had them. I flinched but then steadied myself because it's not okay to flinch when your own mother touches you.

I felt her hand brush over my nipple, though I didn't call them that, even in my mind. I didn't call them anything, because they were irrelevant to me. She brushed over one of them and then paused, pressing her fingers into my skin like she was feeling around for loose change under the couch.

She sighed with relief.

"Nothing yet," she told me. "But it's coming." The first sign, she said, would be little bumps on my chest—there, where my nipple was.

This was when she decided to tell me about puberty—the part they left out in health class. It was all a big joke to us back then. But what my mom told me wasn't funny—it had to do with what would happen to me if I didn't listen and remember. The conversation was nothing like *Are You There God? It's Me, Margaret.*—my only reference point for "the talk."

"They will come, the boys, like animals at the farm. So you have to be ready to resist them, because they will make your insides stir and then things happen and babies can come from it. And the next thing you know, you have to duct-tape your floorboards to keep the roaches out."

I hadn't remembered the duct tape, but suddenly I could see the old apartment in my mind. How one night, my mom got up to pee and turned on the light and saw cockroaches everywhere. She let out this horrible cry and started beating them with a shoe from her closet, squashing them until their guts exploded.

The next day she bought a whole bag full of duct tape and went around the entire apartment taping up the cracks where the walls met the floor, and all around the pipes under the sinks and around the heaters. We almost never saw a roach again. Just the silver tape reminding us that they were just on the other side, waiting for their chance to get back in.

"Where do you think you end up, Charlie? With a baby at sixteen and no education?"

My mom was still so young and so beautiful. It was hard to believe her dreams were all dead. But she said they were, and that it was because of puberty and boys being animals at a farm and making your insides stir. And I believed her because back then, I still believed everything she told me, making new rules at every turn.

I knew how to look things up on the computer. Puberty was sometimes delayed in girls who are overly active. Girls who do gymnastics, for example. They didn't have enough fat for the hormones to work the right way, and they used too much energy doing their exercise.

When I was eleven and my mom told me about what was coming any day now, and after I'd seen her give birth while the flies ate that baby's head on TV, it confused and terrified me, and I knew I had to stop it. It was too late for me to get into gymnastics. I read all about how the best gymnasts get started young, taking lessons at four or five years old. But I could run. And for the next three years, that's what I did.

I ran every day. I ran one mile, then two miles, then five miles. I found a training schedule for people running long races—not just one, but several throughout the year. I ran in the morning before school.

I ran for hours after school. And when it was too cold to run or when the roads were covered with snow, I ran in place, in my room.

They took me to a therapist because Dusty couldn't stand the pounding on the floors and my mom couldn't stand how strange this made me.

One night when Dusty had had enough of the pounding, they both came to my room, Dusty leading the way and my mom racing behind him as best she could with a baby in her arms. He saw me there, knees popping into my chest one after the other as fast and as high as I could make them go, panting for breath, and he told me to stop. I shook my head, *no*, and he told me again, and then he walked to me and picked me up off the floor, my legs flailing in the air.

"Why, Charlie?" My mom was crying. "Why are you doing this?"

I stopped air-running so he would put me back down, a look of satisfaction on his face, and when they both left, I put on all the clothes that would fit on my body and went out to run in the snow.

When I came back, the police were waiting at the house, and the doctors were waiting at the hospital, and they kept me there for three terrifying days. It wasn't easy to concentrate. But by the second morning, I had observed two things. First, no one showing emotion was allowed to leave. Tears. Screaming. Yelling. Moping around, avoiding activities and people. Emotions did nothing but ensure they'd keep you another night. So I managed to smile. I watched TV in the common area. I made conversation with another kid who actually did seem kind of crazy. I did as I was told.

The second was something I should have known before stepping foot in the place. I needed to apologize. Just like the teachers at school and Dusty at his house—anyone with power over me would bend if I said I was sorry. So when my mom came to see me and we sat with the doctor, I said I was sorry for running and hurting myself and making everyone worry. I said I didn't know why I had to do it, so the doctor fed me the answer. I was punishing them for having another baby. Classic sibling rivalry. "I think that might be it!" I told them. "I'm sorry. Thank you. I'm sorry. Thank you." Over and over and over.

On the third day, a new doctor came to see me. She didn't ask me about the running or my new brother. It was a complete shift from every-thing I'd been asked to do in the last few days. She started off by asking me if I had any questions for her, and I said *yes*. I asked her if it was true that exercise could keep my body from making babies. They let me out later that day, after a lot of tests, and on the way home, a word was passed back and forth between my mom and Dusty like a tennis ball on the court at their country club. It sounded like a question when Dusty said it. *Autism?* And like a revelation when my mother said it. *Autism!* No one said it to me. Not then. And not ever. I don't even know if they ever said it to anyone else, because nothing changed in my life. Not a single thing.

But as far as tricking biology goes, it couldn't last forever. When I turned fourteen, it happened. Right during the lunch rush at The Triple S.

Janice gave me something from her purse and tried to console me in the bathroom.

"You can't stop your body from growing up, Charlie. And look at you—what a beautiful young woman you're becoming!"

When she said that word, *woman*, I burst into tears. Not just tears, but inconsolable sobs that made her scared for me. She brought me to the back room and got Nora from her office, and the two of them watched me cry until I was all cried out.

I couldn't explain it to them. I wanted to. But I didn't have the words. I never said *hot head* out loud, and they wouldn't have under-stood it anyway.

It had not been easy to trick biology. But I thought I had done it. I really thought I had won, and it had made me feel like I had skipped over the part of my life where my dreams could die.

I told myself that it wasn't over. That I still had the power to con-trol my destiny. I had the job at The Triple S, and my grades were so good that I was probably going to be first in line for the town's college scholarship, which pays for almost one semester of school and is only given to one student.

If I could keep the animals from coming around, and if I keep my insides from stirring like my mom's did when my father circled around her, then I stood a chance of getting out of here—this place where I could wind up like that sad woman watching the flies eat her baby's head. Where I was an unwanted snowflake. Where I might become the last turkey and have to look at a man like Dusty for the rest of my life. All of those shitty things.

I don't know why I thought this could only happen in Sawyer, but I did. And I became as obsessed with dodging God's trick and leaving this place as I had been with running.

———

I hear Dusty and my mom still talking about me as if I couldn't hear their words or have any feelings about them. I am at the end of everything. My patience. My rope. The heat in my head.

My mom reaches out and grabs my hands to stop my fingers from tapping, and I yank them away so quickly I nearly pull her to the ground.

"Don't touch me!" I yell, because I can't keep it inside for one more second. I am a volcano. A hot hot hot volcano, and they have made me erupt. All of them. Dusty. My mom. Detectives Pittfield and Slater and even Dana Blakely. And most of all, Clay Cooper, who had to be such a bad man that in the end, someone had to kill him, and now I had to find a way out of the mess I was in or I would never get to college. *No one will want me. No one will want me. No one will want me.*

Because I'm a girl *like that.*

Because of my lopsided seesaw and hot head and tapping fingers.

"Charlie!" Dusty tries to be scornful, but I don't care about him and his stupid words.

I am saving my family at The Triple S and I am going to college and no one can stop me.

Nora will have her truth. Janice will have her pride. Keller will have her love. And I will break the glass on this snow globe and fly away.

CHAPTER THIRTEEN

The day after I was brought into the police station, my mom let me take her car because it was raining and she didn't want to drive me. It was Sunday, and on Sundays Dusty usually played golf after church, but because of the rain, he stayed home, which meant she could go back to her bed and not have to feed the boys until dinner time. Dusty was making them pancakes for lunch and then taking them to the toy store.

I first see the stranger right outside Dusty's house. I see him but think nothing of it. He's just a man in a car drinking coffee. I only notice him because the house is on a dead end, so people come here to see us or a neighbor, or to fix something or sell something, but not to park and drink coffee. I've never seen him or his car, a black SUV, before, so it enters my brain as a small thing. I don't even look a second time as I drive past.

I see him again at the end of the lunch shift. But a lot of things happen before then.

Nora comes in at ten thirty and she sees me when she pulls into the parking lot. I wave. She waves. I let her get to the door first because she needs time to open the lock and turn off the alarm. When I see the door swing open, I make a run for it, because I don't have an umbrella and the rain is coming down hard.

She hangs up her coat. I hang up my coat. I put on an apron. She goes to her office, puts her purse on the floor.

"They went through the place yesterday," she tells me. "Top to bottom."

A rush of adrenaline comes and goes.

It goes because of the tone of her voice and the intonation and inflection and all of those subtle things that I watch for when someone says something important like that.

That's how I knew what she was about to say next before the words left her mouth.

"They didn't find a thing."

She comes back out and we both lean against the sparkling metal tables. The place smells especially clean today.

I'm waiting now, waiting for her to tell me what she thinks about the fact that I was here the night Coop was killed.

"That was the only camera," she says. "I feel bad that I didn't tell all of you, but Coop insisted. He wasn't trying to spy on the employees—you can hardly see in the service area from where the camera is positioned. But he didn't want you guys telling other people who might then know how to sneak around the camera. I don't know what he was afraid of. Maybe someone coming in and opening the register, taking the cash. He said he liked seeing everyone who came into his places."

Coop did like his cash. He offered lower prices for customers who used cash, and he didn't accept any credit cards except Mastercard and Visa. Nora tried to tell him that no one used cash anymore. The kids didn't even have wallets. But Coop wouldn't budge. He came every day and emptied the register and went to Nora's office and counted it and then either took it with him or put it in the safe. Every day, and for all of his businesses.

"I'm sorry if the camera got you into trouble."

Nora places her hand on my shoulder, and I can see that she's sincere. She feels bad for me. But I feel bad for her.

"Are you in trouble with the police?" I ask her. And she knows what I mean. My hiding under that counter and looking scared had turned The Triple S into a possible crime scene, made all of them would-be suspects.

"Not any problems that weren't already there. I had my differences with Coop. Janice had the fight with him yesterday. The police spoke to us, and Tracey and Helen. I imagine they paid a visit to Keller and Levi too. But that was all. Just questions."

I nod my head.

She says then, "I was at a meeting that night—a support group for people who lost loved ones in the military. They have them once a month, and this was our annual potluck dinner meeting, so it was on Friday—more of a festive evening. I brought a pie. Stayed until about ten. Janice, well, she was home with her kids and Shane, of course. I don't know about Keller. I'm hoping she'll be in today, but I haven't seen or heard from her."

Nora rattles off the facts that will give them alibis for the night of Coop's murder. They haven't told us the time of his death, if they even know it exactly, or why they think he was moved.

I consider their alibis and think that they aren't really that good. Nora didn't know if anyone at that meeting would remember when she left. And Janice only had Shane and her kids to back up her story, and who's to say that they wouldn't lie for her? No one was in the clear.

"Charlie," she says next, looking at me right in my eyes. "Do you know what you're doing?"

I don't answer because I'm not sure what she's asking.

"Coop was the kind of man who attracts bad people. And bad people do bad things. And sometimes good people defend themselves against bad people. I don't know what happened that night. But I do know these things about Coop."

The door opens then, and Janice rushes through it, soaking wet from the rain. I have only a second before she will see me and come to me and hug me, and this moment with Nora will be over. So I look back at her and tell her with as much conviction as I can muster: "I'm good."

That's what people my age say now, even though I agree with my mom that it's annoying and stupid because it doesn't really answer any question. But it's very useful today.

Before Nora can reply, there's Janice, right on cue.

When she's done with the hugging, she rattles off a few things Nora hadn't told me.

Like, "Oh, it was so crazy after you left, Charlie!" And "They closed us down, brought in about six people in those white suits with their shoes covered and hands covered, you know . . ."

"Forensics people?" I ask.

"Yes!" she says. "And they went through everything, dusting for fingerprints, then taking all of our fingerprints, even poor Tracey, so they know which ones don't belong back here, but we told them, didn't we, Nora? About all the vendors who are in and out every week, delivering food and the aprons and the paper goods and my gosh, the bread! Every day the bread delivery and always a different guy, well not always, but you know—there have to be a dozen drivers the bakery uses."

I remind myself that nothing was found. *Nothing was found. Nothing was found.*

"And the best part," Janice continues, "was when they did that thing where they look for blood with that special light—and do you know that they didn't find one drop—not one! And think of all the blood from the steak that drips on the floor from the slicing and stocking and all of that. That's how well we clean this place! I know it's all terrible, what's happening, but I felt very proud that our cleaning is the reason we're open today and all of us can work our hours."

Yes, I think. A lot of blood is spilled here. And the reason there wasn't a trace, even with the Luminol, is because of the special kind of bleach we use that removes even the invisible proteins of blood, which is what the Luminol detects. A lot of people think regular bleach will do the job, but all it does it get rid of the stain. It leaves behind hemoglobin, which can still be detected by the police. Janice asked Nora to order bleach with active oxygen because she used it at home for Ollie when he was sick and swore that it got rid of more germs. It also gets rid of the hemoglobin in blood.

Anyone who's ever watched any season of any *CSI* series knows that. And I've seen them all.

Nora adds, "We also need to thank Regina. She could have closed us down, but she agreed to let me run the place until she figures things out."

"That's nice of her," I say, although she had no reason to close it down and lose money on selling sandwiches. Especially with the IRS investigating.

"We all need the work," Nora says, reading my mind.

Janice sighs with relief. "Amen."

Lunch rolls around. Keller is a no-show. She calls in to tell Nora, and Nora tells us. I told her not to show her face anywhere until her bruises healed, so I'm relieved when she calls in sick again.

There is a small line around eleven thirty. Maybe five people waiting. It's then that I see the man for the second time. He sits in the same black SUV from the morning. The SUV is parked in our lot and pulled in backward so the man can watch us working inside the store through the windows. I swear I can feel his eyes on me as I take the orders.

Still, I'm too busy for this thought or the image of him to worm through my brain and find the matching image from the car on my street that same morning. I'm pretty tired, and I have a lot of orders to take and sandwiches to make. So I dismiss it as a coincidence and file it away.

I haven't slept much since Coop was murdered. When the lunch rush picks up, I fear that exhaustion will prevent me from concentrating. That I won't be able to clear the line, and it will weave out the door, and everyone will be upset and then not come back again, and the store will close, and Nora and Janice and Keller and me—we'll all lose our jobs and the money we so desperately need.

But it's the opposite. I'm on fire today, just like I was the morning after Coop was killed. Three more customers enter. I yell to them, "What will you have?" And they look at one another, confused because there are customers before them in the line and I'm already making their sandwiches, loading things on the French bread and inside the pitas.

I yell it again—"What's your order?" And this time they answer.

"Chicken salad."

"Steak and cheese."

"Italian sub."

Back and forth we continue.

"What size?"

"Medium."

"Large."

"Pita."

"What's on it?"

"What have you got?"

"Lettuce, tomatoes, pickles, onions, ketchup, mustard, mayo, oil and vinegar, salt and pepper . . ." I know this list like I know my own name.

Within twenty minutes, the line is cleared. It's then that I remember about the man and the black SUV parked backward in the lot. I look outside and it's gone. He's gone. And I even wonder if it was ever there to begin with. I saw it before the mess was cleaned up, and no one sees things clearly with a mess to clean up.

While I'm looking for this disappeared SUV, I see another car, a different car, pull in from the main road. It's not a police cruiser this time. It's a pickup truck. Ian's pickup truck. And there it is, right on cue—the stirring. I hear his voice telling me that I'm wrong when I break up with him. I hear him saying before I got out of his truck that "love is everything."

Love is everything.

Love is everything.

Ian is off duty today, and he wears jeans and a soft flannel shirt, which I want to press my face into and disappear. Maybe forever. The feeling sweeps me away as I place two carefully sliced tomatoes on a medium ham and cheese for the woman before him in line.

Janice sees Ian, then she sees me, and she takes the sandwich from my hands.

"I'll finish this," she tells me.

She rings the order and shoos me to the dining room.

Ian and I walk to the very back of the store. I lead him to where the camera can't see.

"Hey," he says first.

"Hey," I say back, because that's another thing young people do now.

I haven't heard from Ian since he drove me to the police station. He left me in a row of chairs waiting for the detectives because, he said at the time, "It won't look good if we're together in here."

I wonder now if the detectives kept their promise to Dana Blakely. I wonder if she was able to scare them enough not to tell anyone who didn't need to know about the security camera and what they saw on it. I wonder if her hair pulled into that tight bun and her navy suit and her black pumps and fancy corporate client with the DUI worked for or against her in the intimidation business. On the one hand, she looked important. That would be a plus. On the other hand, she was a woman, and that was always a minus. Sorry to say, but this is true. Women are always discounted.

I make myself look into his eyes so I can find the answer, and I'm relieved when I do.

"How are you?" he asks. "It sucks they had to question you at the station. Was it because of Keller?"

I try to answer him, but it's too much now. It's all just too much. I cover my face with my hands, and Ian lets me fall against his chest and hold him with both arms, and I feel the soft flannel against my cheek as the tears fall.

"It's okay," he says. Because that's the only thing you can say to someone who is suffering from a swell and crying into your shirt.

He closes his arms around me, and I feel myself calm because of the neurological response that's happening in my cerebellum, which is only ten percent of my brain's mass, but holds over fifty percent of its neurons. I remind myself of this. It's not Ian. It's just his touch. Anyone's touch could do this. *It's not love. It's science.*

I move away and he releases his arms and nothing is said about it.

"Do they know anything else?" I ask him, wiping my eyes and getting my stupid shit together like a person whose seesaw is just right. Perfectly even.

He shakes his head but also shrugs his shoulders. "I don't know. They're keeping it in a tight circle. The detective squad and two senior units."

Ian is as rookie as rookies get, so he's not going to be put on this case. And I'm grateful for that.

"Do you know anything?" he asks me. I wonder if I should be worried now.

"Like what?"

"The others—Nora, Janice. Keller and Levi . . ."

"They say they have alibis. And there was no . . ." I am about to tell him about the bleach and how the police didn't find anything here, but then I stop myself, because why would I need to tell him that unless I was worried? "They're fine for now." I finish my thought with something else, and he doesn't notice.

"Will you tell me? If anything changes?"

I promise him I will, and then I ask him to do the same. "Only if it won't get you in trouble."

He says he wants to stay as far away from the case as he can, and I tell him I understand. Because that's the thing about people you care about.

Rule Number Eight: If something hurts someone you love, it hurts you too.

This is a heavily weighted rule. It cannot be changed. It's in our nature.

There are people here who wanted Clay Cooper dead. Nora. Janice. Keller. Levi. I care about all of them, and Ian cares about me. When he leaves, I think about this circle, because that's another thing people do. They don't tend to look outside of their snow globe. They see their world and forget it's not a world at all. It's a speck of dust so small God would need a microscope to see it. This is why I don't think about the black SUV or the man inside and the fact that I'd seen him twice in one day, and in two different places.

———

I take a long break before my second shift, but I don't use it to rest or eat or clean up. Instead, I check the inventory. I write it on paper because that's all we've been allowed to do, and I check every pan in the refrigeration units and then the cans and jugs and buckets of things stacked on the shelves that line the walls. I give the paper to Nora and expect her to do what she always does, which is to take her thumb drive from her bag and plug it in and put the numbers into the spreadsheets. But she doesn't do that today. She takes the paper and folds it into her bag.

Of course, I think. That thumb drive is in a place where no one will find it. The real numbers for inventory, but also for sales and payments to vendors. All the things that she and Coop used to argue about. The arguments that put her on the list of suspects.

I work the dinner shift. I clean the grill, the service area, the prep room. I sweep and mop and then collect all the trash from the bins and take it out to the dumpster.

This is the third time I see the man. He sits now in the same black SUV that was parked on my street and outside the shop window. I watch him and he watches me, and I walk a little faster back to the door, which I close and lock behind me, even though I am almost ready to leave for the night.

I am alone closing the store because Keller didn't show and no one could come in to work her shift. It's always slow on Sunday nights, and I was happy to have the place to myself.

I wait inside for another half an hour. I wait with all the lights out until, finally, I see the car, the black SUV, drive out of the parking lot.

I grab my coat and phone and my mom's car keys. I turn on the alarm code and check one last time to make sure everything is off. I don't have store keys, so once I close that back door, the main lock will lock and there's no getting back in.

I don't see the car as it drives back into the lot.

And my mom's car is parked on the other side of the dumpster, so I don't see the car parked sideways behind it.

I click open the doors. I open the driver's side, get in. Put the keys in the ignition.

What I don't do is lock the doors.

And so the man also opens a door and also gets into my mom's car, right behind me where I can't see his face, except in the rearview mirror.

Then he says, simply, "Don't turn around."

CHAPTER FOURTEEN

Don't turn around.

I do as I'm told and stare into the rearview mirror where I can see just the right side of his face. Other than my eyes, I am frozen with fear.

Lettuce, tomatoes, pickles, onions . . .

He speaks then.

"I'm going to give you something."

His hand reaches through the space between the seats in the front and places a small wallet on the console.

I look at it but then quickly go back to watching him in the rearview mirror. Having a man behind you and not knowing what he might do next, like strangle you or shoot you, is a bad feeling.

"Go on," he says now, like he's surprised at how stupid I am for not looking at what's inside. He's obviously never been in this situation, and his tone makes me almost as angry as I am scared.

I reach down and pick it up.

"Open it."

I flip it open. It's some sort of ID but I can't read it because it's too dark so I take my phone from my jacket and hit the flashlight, but then he gets a sudden thought and snatches my phone from my hands. He knows I could just as easily hit 911.

I go from scared to less scared to more scared again.

He holds the phone up so it shines on the ID. And when he does this, his body is closer to me and I can smell the Old Spice soap and bad coffee breath and old man odor, which is a real thing. Dusty has it and Coop has it and so does this man in my mom's car.

The ID has a badge on one side and then an official-looking card on the other. It has a lot of writing but what I first see are the large black letters. FBI.

I look below that to his name. Max Zellman. There's a number, a title, and a photo that matches the man I saw three times today, and now the side of his face which I can see in the rearview mirror.

"I'm with the FBI. I'm looking into Clay Cooper. You don't need to be afraid."

My brain thinks that he is telling the truth but my body is still reacting. Heart pounding. Breath shallow. A frozen animal awaiting her fate.

He reaches for the ID and puts it back in his jacket pocket.

"I've been working a case in Pittsburgh," he says in a serious voice. "Following some bad men. One bad man, in particular. I followed them up here. I followed them to Clay Cooper and the businesses he runs. Including The Triple S."

I have a million questions but I tell my brain to stay silent. It's always better to listen because sometimes you get answers to questions you don't even know you should ask.

"Do you know what money laundering is?" he asks me.

"Of course. In season five of *Breaking Bad*, Walter White launders money through the A1A car wash," I tell him.

He laughs but this does not help the situation. I think it even makes it worse.

"That's right, Charlie. I love that show. Walt mixed the illegal money from the drug business with the legal money from the A1A car wash so no one could tell the difference, and it all looked like car wash money, right? Now, this operation in Pittsburgh is run by a man. I can't tell you his name, so I'll refer to him as Barry, but the name's not important anyway— what's important is that Barry is very dangerous. Do you understand?"

No. I don't understand any of this.

"Why are you calling him Barry?" I ask.

Agent Zellman sighs like he's frustrated. "You don't need to know his real name, okay?"

"Okay," I agree, because what else can I do? He followed me all day, probably making sure no one else was. Then he snuck into my mother's car. And now he wants to tell me about Barry and money laundering at The Triple S.

"First," he continues, "we believe that Barry has been laundering money through Clay Cooper's businesses here in Sawyer. He has The Triple S, the diner, the tobacco store, and some apartment buildings. Second, we believe he does this at The Triple S by creating false reports that inflate both his sales and his inventory costs. That way he can account for the money Barry gives him, but also deduct the money when he gives it back so he avoids paying taxes. The money going out isn't really going to vendors for inventory. It's just going into Barry's pocket, in cash. Coop then gets to keep some of that cash as a fee for his services. Now, imagine he's doing this at all of his businesses. He can clean a lot of Barry's money without raising any red flags with the IRS. Do you understand?"

My mind goes to the spreadsheets and the register and the discount on the cash sales and all of Coop's strange behavior when it came to recordkeeping.

"Have you seen anything like that?" he asks me, and I don't answer.

He tells me I'm a good girl and I don't need to be afraid to tell him the truth. He says they've been investigating everyone at The Triple S.

"I know a lot of things about you, and your family," he says. "For example, I know that you have the highest GPA in your class. It's a 4.4 because you get extra points for all of your AP classes, isn't that right? And I know that you got a very high score on your SAT, and that you have been accepted to MIT, but you have to find a way to pay for it because your stepfather, Dustin Madison, claims you on his taxes. You've saved some money, but you also need that town scholarship to make it through your first year. See—that's a lot of information I have that comes from investigating."

I tell him that everyone knows those things. They're not secrets and they don't prove that he's got some inside source or something. He's trying to make me doubt the people I love. That's what this is!

But then he says, "Well, how about this. I know that the town has voted on the scholarship recipient and they plan to announce it next week. I also know who they voted for."

My heart jumps into my throat and I start to turn around.

"Stop! Don't turn around, Charlie," he yells at me.

"Then just say it! What do you know about the scholarship?"

But he won't. Instead he asks me what I know about the cash transactions at The Triple S, and I tell him I just make sandwiches, and yes, Coop liked things paid in cash but so what? A lot of people are like that. Then he asks me about Nora.

"We know you help the manager, Nora Olman, keep the records. We know she puts them on some kind of thumb drive and takes them home at night. And we know that some of the vendors Clay Cooper pays for the *fake* inventory have addresses that don't match any real locations for any real companies. Now . . . Let's talk about Friday night. You see, even though Clay Cooper's body was found on the street outside his house, we know that you were here that night. And that you heard something, and maybe saw something that you shouldn't have. We also know that the safe in the office was empty when the police broke it open, and that Clay Cooper's cell phone was not found on his body. Very strange, don't you think?"

I shake my head. "I wouldn't know what's strange or not strange about a crime scene."

"Really?" he asks me in the most annoying way. "Even after watching five seasons of *Breaking Bad*? I bet you watch a lot of shows. That's what kids do these days, right? Binge Netflix and all that?"

Now I want to turn around and punch him in the nose and I think the fear is giving way to something else.

"Okay," Agent Zellman says. "Let's go back. When a person deals in cash like that, cash they're trying to hide, it either goes through secret bank accounts or it's physically transferred from one person to the other person. Now, I'm betting Clay Cooper isn't a big fan of banks, right? But see, that means there was probably cash in that safe, and information on that cell phone about upcoming drops of larger amounts of cash. Cash that Barry wants, and will do some pretty scary things to get. Because it's his money, really."

Now I have an idea. "How do you know he didn't kill Coop and take it himself? If you know everything?"

"Well, that is certainly a possibility," he says, but I can tell he doesn't believe it. "And if that did happen, if he does have his money because he, or one of his men, was there that night and killed Mr. Cooper, what other reason would he have to be in town? Come on, Charlie. You know the answer. We know Barry is here in Sawyer. So he either wants his money because someone killed Clay Cooper and took it, or—what?"

Suddenly, I understand. I think it but don't say it out loud. *He thinks I can identify him as the killer.*

Agent Zellman senses that I know. "He'll be watching you very closely, won't he? And if he thinks you know something that could hurt him, or if he thinks you have the cash and Clay Cooper's cell phone—either way—you're in great danger."

He doesn't stop there. "And your friends, Charlie—think about them. If Barry didn't kill Clay Cooper, and if he thinks you know who did but aren't telling the police, then he's going to assume it's someone you care about, don't you think? And that if you don't have the money and the cell phone, then maybe one of them does. The one who killed Clay Cooper. The one you're protecting."

This is the shittiest thing I've heard. Maybe ever. I can't believe this is happening.

"We can protect you, Charlie. If you help us catch him and make an arrest, he'll go to jail and you'll be safe. You can go to college, just like you planned, leave Sawyer and never look back."

I can't breathe. My fingers are tapping and I can't breathe and my head is hot, hot, hot . . .

"I'm going to place my card on the console now. And your phone. Think it over and call me, anytime. Day or night. That's a direct line."

I don't move. I close my eyes and tell myself to just pull in the air. Just pull it in slowly.

He keeps coming at me with his words.

"There may also be some reward money for you, which you are going to need. Because the vote by the town council? Well, it didn't go your way, Charlie. You're not getting that money."

Now the air rushes in and then out with a scream. "That's a lie! You're a liar!"

"I'm afraid it's true. It went to a kid named Doug who plays football and got into Alabama."

"Liar!" I scream again. Doug barely has a three point average. Doug has never even made honor roll.

"Why don't you ask your stepfather? He's on the council, right? And the vote was unanimous."

This isn't true! Dusty wouldn't do that to me! Not that, of all things.

Zellman is done with me.

"Goodbye for now, Charlie. We'll do our best to keep you safe. And please—be smart about this. Don't tell anyone we spoke. Don't tell anyone we're investigating Clay Cooper's murder. Our best chance of getting Barry off the street is to catch him unaware. And that's also your best chance of keeping yourself and your friends safe."

Agent Zellman reaches through the seats one last time and squeezes my shoulder. I flinch and pull away because only three people are allowed to touch me and he isn't one of them. I flinch the way I do every night at dinner when Dusty takes one hand and my mom takes the other.

He gets out of my mom's car and disappears into the night.

CHAPTER FIFTEEN

My hands shake as I drive. They shake so hard I can barely hold the wheel. I think through what Agent Zellman told me. Some criminal named Barry either wants me dead because I saw his men kill Coop, or he thinks I stole his money and he wants it back.

Maybe he's right. Maybe Nora's right. Maybe there is more danger here than I thought, where men like Coop own everything in sight and worse men like Barry from Pittsburgh own men like Coop. I have been fighting so hard to get out of this place that I wasn't paying attention to what was actually here, all around me.

Coop taking money from Barry, cleaning it with crooked books, forcing Nora to turn a blind eye even though her signature is on everything.

Barry making that dirty money in dirty ways.

Suddenly the things I know feel too big to wrap my head around. Suddenly they feel too heavy to carry alone.

My hands turn the wheel to the right, the way that leads to Dusty's house. That is my instinct, even though I know there's no one there who can help me.

I take my hands from the wheel. I close my eyes. I don't know what I should do. But I know what I have to do. I've put people in danger. People I love.

Taking the wheel again, I turn to the left. The way that leads into town and then to the other side where we used to live in our shitty apartment, where Janice and Shane live and where Keller lives.

It's quiet on the street. Nothing is open on Sunday night. I drive past the grocery and the gas station on the left, then a small strip of shops on the right. Among them is Coop's tobacco store and then his diner. I think about how those places also dealt with cash and how Coop made his rounds every day. Picking up the register receipts. Picking up the cash. Bringing it somewhere.

I step on the gas, leaving the town in my rearview mirror.

I drive past a small condo two miles out. It's in a cluster of condos that sit close together. They are cared for, but overcrowded. Old cars in their driveways. Garages doubling for patios, some of them with artificial turf and lawn chairs. Kids' bikes piled up on the lawns.

The third one on the left is where Janice and Shane live, and I drive past it slowly now, looking for lights in rooms and people moving around. Looking for strange men in black SUVs watching from the street. Looking for any sign of anything not right.

It's quiet. A man sits on his front step smoking a cigar, and he waves at me, and I wave back. I slow to a stop long enough to see a body move across a room through the draperies, and then a second body. They move at a normal pace. A light turns off in the room. A light turns on upstairs. Janice and Shane heading up to bed. The kids probably all asleep by now.

What did I think I would find? What has this man put inside my head?

The night of Coop's murder, something entered my body, my blood. A chemical. A drug. I've been too wired to sleep. My head hot then cold, hot then cold. It's been two days, and there's been a shift. Maybe from the exhaustion. Maybe from Agent Zellman and the fear he's injected into me. Maybe from the shock and then anger when he told me about Dusty voting against me.

I have no idea what's happening inside myself.

I make the turns and drive until I get to Keller's street. Now I'm even more careful, because Keller is my best friend, and if Barry wants to hurt me, and if he's been taking these two days to find things out about me, then he will know this.

I turn off the headlights. I pull to the curb where I can see down the street to Keller's house. One light is on upstairs, in the back. It's either the bathroom or Dot's bedroom. It seems quiet. The doors are all closed. The car is in the driveway.

I take my phone and send two messages. First to Nora. She lives ten miles from town in an apartment so I won't be able to see anything just by driving by. I text her with something simple. "We need to order lettuce. Thanks. See you tomorrow."

I send a second text, this one to my mom. I say that I'm at Keller's house and I will have the car back before she wakes up tomorrow.

I wait for the replies, which come quickly.

"Thanks for letting me know, Charlie." That was Nora, and I think she must be okay.

And, "You'd better be." That was my mom, acting annoyed, which means she's okay.

Janice, Nora, my mom. And now to Keller.

I leave the car and walk down the street. I lace the keys between my fingers and close my palm around them. I am paranoid. Made delusional. Or maybe not. Maybe I'm focused. Maybe I'm clever. Every scary movie I've ever seen emerges, memories of scenes with a terrified woman on a dark street, people after her, danger lurking. Bad guys everywhere all around. Jason and Freddie and Ted Bundy. These stupid keys won't stop them with their chain saws and knives, and they won't stop Barry, who would surely bring a gun.

I walk behind her neighbor's house then cut across the lawn to Keller's yard and back door. I take the spare key from the top of a small lantern that hangs on a shingle and I let myself in.

I hear them the moment I step inside. One voice yelling. One voice pleading. I walk through the kitchen to the foot of the stairs and listen again.

They're in the bathroom. I hear water splashing. Their voices are strained. I bound the steps two at a time until I reach the top, then run down the hall.

The door is open but neither of them sees me.

Dot is in the water. Naked. Struggling. Keller is trying to keep her from climbing out. It's not difficult because Dot is frail and weak, but she won't stop fighting.

I step inside.

"Let me help you," I say. And if Keller is surprised at the sight of me, she's too upset to show it.

Dot sees me as well and hisses.

"Another whore, just like you. You're all a bunch of whores!"

She pushes Keller's hands away.

"Don't touch me, you filthy whore!"

Keller lets go and Dot tries to pull herself out of the water using the sides of the tub, but she's too feeble to even lift her body.

She lays back down and begins to cry. The cry becomes a sob and then a wail. A woman into a small child.

Keller kneels at her side. Her hair is drawn into a ponytail, and I can see the bruise on the back of her neck. She wears old sweatpants and a T-shirt, and I think to myself that these are the same clothes I helped her change into Friday night.

She draws a breath, takes a washcloth that floats on top of the soapy water.

"Dottie," she says in a quiet voice. "It's me. It's Keller. And this is Charlie. Remember? I'm your granddaughter and this is my friend."

She gently washes the tears from Dot's face and leans in close until the woman can lock eyes with her. Dot is beginning to calm down. The child soothed.

"Keller? Is that you, sweetheart?"

Now comes the heavy sigh that always follows one of these episodes.

"Yes, Dottie. It's Keller, and Charlie is here. See?"

Dot looks at me, and her face grows soft and loving. "Oh, Charlie! You came to see me?"

I nod. "Yes, Dottie. I came to see you."

Keller turns her head around to look at me. She places her hand on my wrist and gives it a squeeze. Her face shocks me. The bruises have grown darker. Black mascara is smeared around her eyes, worn down from crying and rubbing. She hasn't showered. She hasn't changed her clothes. She hasn't even washed her face.

I don't say anything about any of it because I fear she might fall apart more than she already has. She's let Coop touch her and threaten her and belittle her every single day for years. She's let her grandmother call her a whore while she changes her diapers and washes her sagging skin clean.

Keller is on a tightrope. She has to keep her eyes where they are, only a few inches ahead of her feet, so her balance will remain perfectly calibrated. I am not going to be the one to make her look away and fall.

I get a towel ready, and together Keller and I help Dot out of the water. Her body is worse than I've ever seen it, skin hanging from bone like it's on a hanger in a closet. Blue veins protrude and run from her feet to her chest, up her legs and across her arms. She is wasting away.

I wrap the towel around her, and we walk her to her bedroom. Keller finds a night gown, and we get her dressed.

"Oh, you lovely girls. Good girls. That's what you are. Good girls, good girls, good girls . . ."

She says this over and over as though trying to stick it in her mind so she won't forget.

We put her into her bed, on her back and propped up on pillows. Keller tucks the blankets tightly under the mattress so she can't get out easily, if at all. She lifts the metal rails that flank the sides so she won't roll off.

Then she kisses her on the cheek.

"Good girls, good girls . . ."

The words echo as we turn out the light and close the door. Keller locks it from the outside.

Then she falls into my arms and cries.

When she's done, we sit on her roof outside her bedroom window. It's slanted but not too steep and faces the side where we can see over some of the rooftops of her neighbors.

The sky is dark and there's a chill in the air. We huddle under one blanket and lean back against the side of the house.

"It's bad, right?" Keller asks me. "She's not eating anymore. I thought it was enough, but you saw her, right? She needs to be in a facility, and not the state one where she tried to kill herself because those idiots gave her the wrong pills. She needs people who know what they're doing."

She stops herself long enough to light a cigarette. She takes a drag then hands it to me. The nicotine is like magic on my nerves. A rush washes through me, and I close my eyes and give in to it. Intoxication is every bit as intoxicating as they warned us in health class.

We don't speak. We just smoke. We smoke until the cigarette is down to the butt. Keller smashes it out on the roof then flicks it onto the ground.

"He's gone for good," she says then.

"Who?" I ask.

"Levi. He says he doesn't want to be with me. Not after the fight we had Friday. After I lied to him. And now Coop is dead."

She shakes her head, then hangs it in the palms of her hands.

I don't know what to say. My heart breaks right beside hers. I find words but they sound hollow. I think about rule number five: *Once you betray a friend, you lose them forever.*

"He'll be back. I know he will. He loves you! And he has to understand. Doesn't he see what's going on here?"

In all the time I watched Keller put up with Coop, I never said one word to her. I never said things like *how can you let him look at you that* way or *how can you let him say those things to you.* I can easily calculate the money she must need to pay for this house and the car and Dot's medicine. I've never had to do anything but save money for college because I'm lucky. I'm the lucky one who has a chance of getting out of here.

I was not going to judge Keller. But I'm not Levi. I'm not her jealous boyfriend.

She shakes her head.

"I don't think so, Charlie. You don't know him. He has this pride that is just so big. There's no room in it for this. For me being anything but his girl."

"But you are his girl. You've never been anyone else's. I've known you almost all of our lives."

And then she makes me look her in the eye, which I do, because it's Keller and she needs me to see inside her so I'll know she's telling me the truth.

"I never let Coop touch me. Not like he thinks. Never. I swear, Charlie. I swear!"

I tell her "Okay," and then I look away because what is behind her eyes is bright and loud but also dark and fading and the contradiction confuses me. I can't let myself get confused now, not about anything.

I picture Levi opening a door for her. Putting his arm around her and giving her a soft kiss on the top of her head. Stroking her cheek. Running his hands through her hair. They have been inseparable since the day they met.

Now I picture him Friday night. Thinking the wrong things about his girl. His woman.

Keller waits for more words from me, but I don't have them. The truth is, Agent Zellman is in my head. My mom is in my head. And my childish delusions about Keller and Levi and their true love defying gravity, all of it is up for reevaluation. My very foundation is crumbling.

She looks at me as she lights another cigarette.

"Charlie?"

"Yeah?"

"About Friday night . . ."

"Don't," I stop her. We swore not to ever talk about Friday night, and we have to stick to it. "I haven't said a word about anything to anyone, and I don't want anything else in my head that could come out if they make me."

I've done what I've done to protect her. I've come here tonight to protect her. But also Janice and Nora and Levi. All of them.

She says then, "Can you just tell me if he's safe? If Levi will be okay?"

I take the cigarette even though it's started to make me sick. I'm grasping at anything to stop feeling what I feel. To shut down my brain.

I open my mouth to give her an answer, but something catches my eye. Out on the street.

I toss the cigarette and pull her back against the house, tighter, so we're less visible.

"What's wrong?" she asks.

A car is creeping slowly, then stops far enough away from the front of her house that I can't tell what kind it is. There is one person inside, a faceless shadow, and it doesn't get out.

"Go inside," I tell her.

And we do. We climb inside the window and I close it and lock it behind me.

Then I tell her to go downstairs and lock every door. I do the same up here, with the windows.

When we're done, I make her take a shower and wash her face and change her clothes. I give her one of Dot's sleeping pills, and it clouds over the worry, the despair, the sorrow, and the fear, and she goes to sleep.

And me—I get a knife from the kitchen, and I sit in a chair in the living room where I can see out a crack in the draperies. I sit and watch until the car backs up, all the way down the street, and the headlights disappear.

CHAPTER SIXTEEN

That night, I sleep in fits and starts. I sleep long enough to dream about things that I don't want to see. Not ever again.

I see everyone I love in pain. I see Nora smoking outside, her face swollen with worry. Powerless to stop what's happened on her watch and in her good name. I see Janice exploding in tears and rage and Coop stifling laughter right in front of her as she stands before him protecting her child's honor. His dignity. I see Keller with bruises and Levi opening doors and Coop touching her and Dot in the bathroom, skin hanging from bones. I see my mom back in our shitty apartment, crawling on hands and knees as she duct-tapes the floor boards.

I see the things Ian and I did last summer when we were alone with the stirring that had finally caught up to us. How it makes me think about Ian day and night, night and day, his hands on my body, my hands on his body, under our clothes, inside our clothes, deep, wet kisses, and a longing that still feels like a runaway train, pulling me off the tracks that I have so carefully laid down to get me out of here.

I see Coop's face, always dirty, that spot on his head shining with sweat.

I see metal pans with shredded lettuce, plastic wrap. A tomato slicer. Rage and money and blood and bleach.

One giant thud in my chest hurls me into consciousness as thoughts of Agent Zellman and Dot and a car backing down the street chase away the remnants of the dream. Adrenaline surges, then recedes, leaving me more exhausted than when I felt my eyes start to close.

The knife is on the floor beside the chair, fallen from my hand.

I check my phone. It's just after six a.m. I look outside through the crack in the draperies and see nothing but a boy walking a dog and a woman bringing a garbage bin to the street. The sky is still dim.

I shuffle to the stairs, groggy, head spinning, stomach sick from the cigarettes and no food and churning fear. The house is quiet, and cold, and dark. The heat is off to save money, but I find the thermostat and turn it on so they can wake up with some comfort. I start the coffee pot in the kitchen the way I do for my mom on Saturday mornings when she likes to sleep late. I want to stay and be here when Keller wakes up and has to handle Dot, get her up and dressed and fed and then settled in front of the TV so she can watch her shows. It's Monday, so they will all be on. That will make her happy and give Keller some peace. Maybe she'll come to work today. She needs to get out of this house.

But I have to go. I leave cash in the coffee can on the top shelf of a cabinet, where I always do, every week. One-third of my paycheck, which I have allowed for on my spreadsheet and which Keller has been saving to pay for a room in a private facility for Dot. When she has enough for one full year, she'll use the time to work more and save more for the next year, and she'll keep doing this for as many years as are left for Dot. She just needs that one leg up. That first year to get out from under. It's such a small thing, but the can is not nearly full enough.

I leave through the back door, locking it then replacing the spare key to the lantern. I find my mom's car on the street and drive.

Ian lives two miles away on Rosebury Lane. I've never been there— he moved after we broke up over a year ago, after he graduated from high school and got the job as a cop. I've never been there because of the things my mom told me and that I know to be true, even if I hate both of us for it.

I drive to Rosebury Lane and I look for his police car. It's easy to find.

I park on the street a few houses down from the car.

I don't see any lights on, so I wait. I know it won't be long before he's up and getting ready for work. I settle in, wrapping my jacket tightly around me. I pull my knees to my chest. Lean my head back. And my mind goes to him in that house as I study every inch of it—the windows and the shades and the curtains and the front porch and the flowers that line the walkway that I'm sure his mother planted.

I wonder where he sleeps, where he eats, where he cooks and makes his coffee. I wonder if he sits on that porch and drinks a beer and thinks about anything beyond the day before him, or looks for the orange Buick that ran over his dead father. I wonder if he cares about his future. About me. Or someone else.

I wonder what it would be like to be in that house with him, away from my mom and Dusty and their boys. Free like Nora to do what I want. In love like Keller, lying in bed, under the covers, bodies wrapped together, hands, mouths, skin, everything moving together to become one.

Ian is the only boy I have ever loved. The only boy who has ever made me feel the stirring. The only boy who has ever made me want to run as fast as I can away from childhood and into his arms, into my body and out of my head.

I remember the very first time I felt it. When I knew what my mom had warned me about. When my eyes lit up and my heart nearly exploded with joy.

Ian knew me. He knew the things that caused my body to shake and my fingers to tap and my head to get hot. It happened one day outside the school. I'd missed a question on a ninth-grade science test, of all the stupid things. It was about the respiratory system, which I knew better than anything, better than algebra and sandwiches and the smell of my mom beside me when I was younger. It was just a brain hiccup. I'd been moving too fast. My eyes danced over the last part of a multiple-choice answer, one of those dog-shit tricks teachers like to play on us because they think they're clever, and I answered wrong. I knew it the second we left the class. My mind was still on the test, seeing each question and each answer and checking my work as I walked to my locker with Keller and listened to her talk about some party we should go to, and I just saw it suddenly. The tricky end to the question appeared before my eyes.

I ran from the building. Keller chased after me. Ian was outside already, in the line for his bus, and he left the line to come to us. I couldn't breathe. I was hyperventilating, tapping my fingers furiously. My head was on fire. Keller was frantic, calling out my name because I wasn't responding. But Ian was calm.

"Charlie . . ." he said. "Follow my breath." And then he inhaled and exhaled and inhaled and exhaled. Slowly and with a loud sound, and it was impossible not to do the same, like the way someone's yawn makes you yawn too. I felt a wave of something hypnotic. A drug, a potion. My heart steadied and I caught a huge gulp of air that reached deep in my lungs.

"You're all right now," he told me. And I was. I was all right.

I looked at his face. My eyes met his eyes. And that was it. The moment I felt the stirring for the very first time.

The night I decided we had to stop never leaves me. It sits in the back of my brain like a faucet, and from that faucet is a constant drip of remorse. Lying together in the back of his truck, under The Hand of God. Feeling his body close to mine. Feeling his hands on my back, touching my skin.

"Does it feel good?" he asked me. But he knew it did, because my shoulders were dancing against his chest, and that was one of the many things he knew about me. And loved about me.

We might as well have been cast in a cautionary video they showed at school, about abstinence and consent and safe sex. "It's hard to stop," the commentator warned. When you get to that point where hormones have taken over. Where biology has been let out of its cage, let off its leash, let loose to trample your will, your better judgment, your self-control.

Ian said we could stop. And there were ways to be safe. And yet, there was always a chance of a mistake. That's what I said to myself. It was about the risks and the fear of being on the bad side of the statistics. A failure for the system that tries to get us past this stage without a mishap. That tried to trick God's trick.

But that wasn't it.

No one talks about what happens to girls in towns like this. No one but my mom. It makes me hate her. It makes me love her. Because she's right but I don't want her to be.

"The stirring goes away the second it's ruined your life." Her words have stuck in my mind, and I don't even remember when she said them because she talks so much and all the time.

The question lingered that night.

"Can I kiss you?"

The answer was yes. And I wanted him to. But I wanted other things more. And I was the only one who could save me.

I didn't cry that night. What I felt was too big for tears. Too big for tapping fingers or rocking back and forth. It was so big I turned into a zombie.

Ian drove me home, angry, frustrated, but also sad because I told him it had to be over. I could never be this strong again. He let me out in front of Dusty's house and he drove off. And that was that. A lifetime of friendship. And now love finally expressed. And I had blown it to shreds.

His mother begged him to leave. When he didn't, she begged him to live at home while he saved money. She begged him to take the scholarship at the school he got into up north in Maine.

I remember when he was accepted to that college. I remember his face when he showed me the letter. I will never see that face again.

Because what his father put inside him is something worse than what my mom put inside me. Cullen Maguire was a good man. That's how the story goes. He was a good man who had been a good kid until he saw something that he couldn't stop seeing. The boy from his class dying on that mountain, falling from the narrow trail and tumbling down, bouncing off of rocks that lined the ledge, which bashed in his head and scraped off his skin until he landed on the ground below. People like a gruesome tale, and this one had been embellished over time. How could it not? Only three people saw it happen, and one of them was tortured, one of them was gone, and the other was Clay Cooper, who never let a chance to shock and awe pass him by.

Coop liked to tell people about the thud the body made when it hit the ground, far, far below.

But Cullen Maguire never spoke of it again. Not after he told the police what happened. How the boy, whose name was Rudi Benton, was there one second and then falling the next. But none of that matters. What matters is that Cullen Maguire never got over it, and he made himself feel better by drinking, and this made it hard for him to hold down a job. It's why his wife only had one child—Ian. And why she worked two jobs the whole time he was growing up.

His father was even drunk on the night he died. The police came to believe he got out of his car on his way home from a bar to take a piss, and some passerby hit him in the dark, then drove away, thinking maybe he was a deer. The police knew the make and model of the car from the tire marks and the paint scrapes left on Cullen Maguire's car, and even some on his body. They found an old woman in Sawyer who owned a car like that, but she had reported the car stolen two weeks before. The officers say they looked as hard as they could for as long as they could, but the car never turned up, and the case went cold.

Ian was only ten when all of this happened. But when he got older, when he was old enough to think about it and draw his own conclusions, he came to believe something different. He thought that the stolen car and the back road, which wasn't on the way home from the bar his father liked to frequent, and the fact that there was paint on his car didn't add up to the story the police had fed his mother. Who would think they'd hit a deer if their car scraped another car enough to leave paint marks? As Ian said when he first told me about it, "Why would a deer be standing next to a parked car on the side of a road?"

Ian believed someone hit his father and drove off. A hit and run. And he didn't care that it was probably an accident, maybe even his father's fault for being so drunk he was pissing in the middle of the road. He wanted that someone to pay. So he started looking for that 1996 orange Buick LeSabre—and he was still looking to this day. The VIN for the car was never registered again. He told me once, and I wrote it down in case he forgot to: XPG749TYW8643PL97. Everyone tried to tell him it was probably sold for parts or junked after the accident. But it was his only lead.

Ian Maguire, the boy I love, the only boy I have ever loved, would never leave Sawyer or go to college or stop looking for that car or stop being a cop, where at least he could make other people pay for other crimes. He would never get over his father's death, who never got over his friend's death, and that's one of the saddest things I've ever seen, even next to Keller and her sick grandmother.

I knock just once, then wait. Ian answers. He's taken aback when he sees me.

I can't imagine what I look like after the night I've had.

"Hey," he says. We stand there, awkwardly, even though I just saw him the day before and cried on his flannel shirt.

"Do you want to come in?" he asks. He opens the door, and I see inside, and God help me, I want to walk in. But I can't. I just can't do it or I may never, ever leave.

"I'm good," I say, like an idiot, and he pulls the door closed behind him and stands with me on his porch.

He's dressed in his uniform, and it hugs his body, and my body responds, defying the orders I have just laid out.

I get to the point. I tell him about Agent Zellman and I show him the business card. I wrote down his badge ID number on the back as soon as he got out of the car because I knew this could be one of the times my memory failed me. I'd been terrified, and terror is not good for remembering—or for anything, really, except maybe saving your life. I tell him about the car in the back of The Triple S. How Agent Zellman followed me all day and knew things about me and snuck into my mom's car.

I have no reason to doubt Agent Zellman. But there is a rule about trusting strangers.

Rule Number Thirty-One: Trust but verify, because everybody lies sometimes.

"I don't get it, Charlie. Why does he think you know something?" Ian looks worried, and I remember that he has no idea about the camera at the store, about the video the police saw.

I stall for time because I have never lied to Ian. But now I think, I have to, somehow. I have to protect him. I have to protect everyone.

My head is getting hot as I make my list of them, and then I think that I have to get out of here. I shouldn't have come, because what if Barry is watching me and now he knows that Ian is one of my people. And the car that was at Keller's—he knows about her too. I am making things worse and worse and worse!

"Charlie . . ." Ian reaches out because my fingers are tapping, and he thinks he can just work his magic and calm me down, but he can't. Not this time.

"I have to go," I say, and I think I really do. I have to leave this place—the worst place in the world. It's the place where dreams die and girls go down dead-end streets and men like Coop and Dusty take everything that's good and keep it for themselves. And now Barry is here, watching me and wanting to hurt the people I love.

Ian backs off. He looks at me with more concern than I've ever seen before. *Ever.*

"I'll check out this agent for you, as soon as I get to the office. Okay?"

I nod. Breathe. Force my fingers into a fist so they remain still. And then I run, like a scared little mouse. I run down the steps of his porch on Rosebury Lane and across the street and into my mom's car. And then I drive away.

CHAPTER SEVENTEEN

When I get back to Dusty's house, I find him and my mom waiting for me in the kitchen. It's Monday morning, and I've been out all night. Plus I should be at school. Plus the boys had to take the bus because I had my mom's car. Plus Dusty should be at work but now he has to go in late because of me and the worry I've caused.

"Where have you been?" Dusty speaks first, in his most serious voice.

I try to get away without sitting down at the island as I ramble about Keller needing me to help with Dot and falling asleep at her house.

"Can you please sit down?" he asks, now in his nicer voice. There's not much difference between the two.

Dusty is a successful lawyer, even if, as Regina Cooper said in the bathroom, they were all just ambulance chasers. Dusty doesn't chase ambulances exactly, but he does have his picture on a billboard out on the interstate. I think if you have a billboard, you may not be chasing ambulances, but you are still telling them where to drop off the sick patients.

Dusty says that in towns like this one, that have been wrecked by problems with the economy and then never "bounced back," there's no more money that ever comes in. What's here is here, and that money, he says, flows like water, finding its way through any crack and crevice a person can chisel. People with more try to build dams. People with less chip away at those dams with whatever tools they can find. Charity programs. Welfare programs. And suing.

Dusty says it's ironic that some of their tools actually just move money from those with more to others with more, like him, because he gets one-third of everything they're awarded when they slip and fall. He always makes air quotes with his fingers when he says those words. "Slip and fall."

The point is, Dusty is clever. Maybe not as clever as Clay Cooper was, but clever enough not to risk his good reputation by protecting me. He's worried now. I can see it on his face. But not like my mom is worried.

I sit down on the stool at the end of the island, and the two of them turn so they can see me.

Now my mom speaks.

"We think you should quit that job, Charlie. Those people at The Triple S—I didn't realize the sort of people they were, and now they've gotten you into this mess."

I try to make sense of her words. I know what she's saying of course. I just don't see how Coop's murder makes them all a *sort* of anything. Nora is different from Janice, and they are both different from Keller, and Levi doesn't even work there. Tracey and Helen are, as far as I can tell, irrelevant to the conversation.

Then I think about Agent Zellman and the things Coop was involved in. I think that maybe I should just blurt it all out and let them sit there with their mouths gaping open in disbelief. But I don't know what would happen next. If they would tell the detectives or my new lawyer with the navy pantsuit, or if Dusty would use his power to track down Agent Zellman's boss and demand some answers. If I was in danger, then being in his house meant that his boys were in danger, and Dusty may not love me, but he does love his boys, who are named after him and his father.

I don't want to act out of a desire for momentary pleasure at the expense of my long-term best interests.

Rule Number Ten: Impulsive behavior happens when the emotional brain hijacks the thinking brain.

I'm tired and freaking out, the perfect cocktail for an emotional hijacking. My brain is in fight-or-flight mode, and that's never a good time to make any decision, unless you really do need to fight or take flight. I have to stop the words that want to explode out of my mouth.

"Charlie?" Dusty says when I don't answer. "Did you hear your mother?"

I can feel Dusty's disdain from across the marble countertop, and my fingers start tapping. *Together together. Right then left. Left then right. Together together. Right then left. Left then right.*

I can smell his old-man smell. The big-shot lawyer. The town-council member. The man who wouldn't be anything two hundred miles from here, north or south. The slightly-above-ambulance-chaser helping people chisel holes in the dam so he can take a third.

And then I get a burst of something cool and clear. I come up with an alternative that will make their mouths gape, but also serve my interests, and I'm so proud I want to give myself a medal.

I look up and find his eyes, and my fingers stop tapping, and I say, "I can't quit my job. I need the money more than ever now that the council voted to give the scholarship to a football player."

My mom shrieks. "What are you talking about?!"

Dusty is flustered. His face gets red, and I think about his head getting hot just like mine because we all get that sometimes. We're all human, and when you get busted for doing a shitty thing, it's hard to control your emotions. So there.

"How do you know about that?" Dusty asks.

I shrug. This makes him even more angry.

My mom doesn't care how I know—I knew she wouldn't. All she cares about is what she's sacrificed so I could get out of here and how this man she tolerates has just slipped the rug out from under both of us.

"Is it true? Did you vote to give the money to some jock over Charlie?"

Dusty sighs and looks at his hands, which are sweating like Coop's bald spot.

"He got into Alabama. Almost a full ride."

Now my mom—"So what? Charlie got into MIT! Do you even know what that is? What that means?"

Now Dusty gets defensive. "And then what? What happens after that, Eileen? This kid will have to support a family one day. He'll have a wife and a mortgage and kids. And Charlie will do what? Study math for the rest of her life? Who's going to hire her to do anything except make sandwiches?"

I see flames come from my mom's ears like in the cartoons I watched when I was a kid.

They were both mad at me, and now my mom is mad at Dusty and Dusty has to defend himself, and suddenly me working at The Triple S and making our family look bad by being involved with that *sort* of people is the last thing on either of their minds.

It's like a dog in a yard full of squirrels. They can chase one squirrel all day, but the second they spot a new squirrel, they start chasing that one.

Rule Number Six: People are easily distracted.

I leave them with this new squirrel and head for the stairs. I tell them I need to get ready for school, and I don't know if they hear me, but I do know that it's not long before I hear doors slam and cars start, and then my world is quiet and still. In my bedroom, I close the door and turn a full circle. Everything is exactly where I left it not twenty-four hours before, except for me. I am turned upside down and inside out, and I don't know where to begin.

I sit on the floor, which is covered in a shaggy beige carpet. I take off my sneakers and my socks and let my feet sink into the polyester, which I have hated since the day we moved here but which now tickles my feet and gives me enough physical distraction to slow my heart and steady my breath.

I pull my knees to my chest and rest my forehead on them. I don't close my eyes, because then I will see either darkness or images from the last two days, and that will not help.

Instead, I stare at the button on my jeans.

I thought I would go to school and then to work and wait for Ian to tell me about Agent Zellman. I thought I would just carry on, because

I was full of adrenaline, which numbs pain, and that has been useful, but now it's gone. Now, I feel all kinds of pain. The kind that comes from worrying.

I can't deny what Agent Zellman told me. I can't deny what it means. I have to face it. I have to *see* it now.

When my legs start to cramp, I know I have to get up off the floor. I have to think about this new information the way I think about the inventory at The Triple S or a problem on a test, and I can't make a mistake like the one on that test when I lost my shit and Ian calmed me with his magic.

No mistakes. There is a solution to everything. An outcome that can be created or evaded or manipulated.

If Barry is watching me to see what I know or what I might have, then I need to watch him right back.

A plan forms as I stand and let the blood flow through my shaky legs. When they stop shaking, I begin to execute it by making a list and doing the things on the list. One at a time. In order, so I don't miss a step. *No mistakes. No mistakes.*

First—the box of lotion in my mom's vanity drawer. The box that has no lotion inside but wads of money in large bills she's been taking from Dusty, here and there, from his wallet, from his car, from the ladies when they go out for lunch and my mom pays the entire bill on his card then takes their cash. Still there. *Check.*

Second. My closet, and the shelf at the top, and the teddy bear that sits there along with other remnants from my childhood that I no longer cling to. I open the Velcro on the back that hides a very large battery pack, because the bear talks and moves his arms when there are batteries installed. But the battery pack has been removed, leaving just the hole.

I slip my fingers inside and pull out the small flip phone I took from the floor of the prep room, where it fell from Clay Cooper's pocket the night he died. I turned it off before bringing it into this house because I didn't know what kind of phone it was and I didn't want it to send a signal and be tracked here.

What I do know is that his other phone, his fancy new smartphone, was found on his body. So when Agent Zellman said his phone was missing from the crime scene, he must have known that Coop had two phones. Which means he knows even more than he was telling me. Maybe from the police. Maybe from other people he's also trying to turn to for information against Barry. Or maybe from his surveillance.

I wonder how long he's been watching Coop and Barry and whoever else. I wonder if he has photos of them talking and handing off money and Coop using different phones, including the one I hold in my hands, which is now part of a federal investigation.

This phone that I hold in my hands is evidence. The kind of evidence that could cause a lot of trouble for someone. And I don't know what to do with it. My plan isn't finished, because I don't have the tools to finish it. I have math and remembering and everything I know about people, but now I have done things I can't undo, bad things, like taking this phone. Things that have put me in this bad situation. It doesn't matter why I did them. It doesn't matter that I was trying to protect the people I care about, even if I don't know which one I'm protecting.

Who wanted Coop dead? *All of them. All of them.*

I can't remember one second in my life when I haven't been afraid of disappointing someone. Even if they said nothing, I would feel it ooze from their silence. Their hushed words. Their condescending comments. I would know, in my gut and my bones and under my skin. Their disappointment in me would come through loud and clear.

Faces of friends I'd lost pass before my eyes. Countless faces who won't even remember me. That freak from first grade. That weirdo from gym class. I was nothing to them, and each time I had to let them go, I worked harder to be more like them. Enough like them that they would stop noticing how I wasn't. And now, what has it gotten me?

A small circle of people I can trust—Ian, Keller, Janice, Nora. Sometimes, my mom.

It's so little. It's too little. But it's all I have. And I can't lose it. I can't lose them.

CHAPTER EIGHTEEN

Dusty has a gun. His father gave it to him when he "became a man." It was some kind of family tradition. Every Madison gave it to his firstborn son, and that son gave it to his firstborn son, and so on. If no son had a son, then it was given to the next-born male heir. Because apparently women have no use for guns.

The gun is very old, and my mom makes him keep it in the attic. He takes it out a few times a year to clean it and fire at empty cans in the woods with his boys. Seems like it's all a big waste of time, but the boys like it more than anything, maybe even more than video games.

Rule Number Four: All feelings are the result of chemical reactions in the brain.

When Dusty takes his boys to shoot cans, he pats their backs and hugs them and kisses them and tells them how much he loves them, and this releases dopamine in their brains, which is the chemical that makes us feel good. So now just talking about that stupid gun and shooting cans in the woods makes them happy.

I know the gun is kept in a box with Dusty's old trophies from sports when he was little. Dusty wasn't very athletic, so when I go up there to look for it, I start with the smaller boxes in the back.

My mom has labeled the boxes so it's easier to find decorations for all of our holidays. And there are a lot of them. Christmas. Easter. Memorial Day. Fourth of July. Halloween. Thanksgiving. And, of course, birthdays. They are the same every year because, she says, that's how you create family traditions. By hanging the same flags and ornaments and using the same dishes and tablecloths. Every year on every event, I evaluate my dopamine. I wait for a surge to come when I see the things from these boxes. The advent calendar. The fake spiders and ghosts. The little white lights that get strung around the tree we get at the fake farm three exits past The Hand of God on the interstate. I remember when it used to happen. Before, when we lived in our shitty apartment. Somewhere along the way it stopped. Now I only get that rush from things outside the walls of this house. My people at The Triple S. Ian. Thoughts of college. I don't have time to feel sad about it, though it's right there, knocking on the door. I have too much to do.

I go through box after box, until one of them makes me stop. I haven't seen this box since I was ten, a box that used to live in the closet at our shitty apartment, that is sealed with the silver duct tape my mom used to keep the roaches from squeezing through the floorboards.

It was one of the boxes that my grandparents put out for the collectors the day after we ran for our lives when I was five. My mom had a friend who lived down the street, and she called my mom to tell her there was *all this stuff* on the curb, and she could see my mom's old field-hockey stick laid right on top.

My mom waited until the middle of the night, and then she drove us to that curb and loaded all the boxes and bags of our things into her car. Well, not everything, because the car was small. She had to leave my bassinet where I slept after I was born and my baby clothes and toys, and she said it was okay because I wasn't a baby anymore, but still she smoked two cigarettes after we drove away and left them behind. I think she knew she was the one who would miss them.

The boxes and bags stayed there, shoved into every crevice of that car for three weeks when we lived in a shelter with other moms and their kids, and my mom learned how to dress and act grown-up so she could get a job in an office. And when she got a job and saved two weeks of paychecks, we moved into our shitty apartment and took all the boxes and bags out of the car and unpacked them wherever they would fit. She unpacked everything, even that old field-hockey stick, which she kept next to her side of the bed in case someone broke in.

The only box she never unpacked was this one. She opened and then closed it right back up the second she saw what was inside. I never asked what it held because it didn't concern me. But now I can't resist. I pull off the duct tape, open the flaps, and find books. I recognize them right away because I have the same ones in my bedroom. Yearbooks.

I pull them out, one by one, checking the dates. She has three of them, and when I look inside, I find her picture in the ninth grade, then tenth grade, then eleventh grade—the year she had me. She never finished that grade, but her picture was still in the yearbook. I was born in November, after the school pictures were taken.

My heart gets jumpy now as I realize that somewhere in these books is also my father. She said he played football. She said he left before junior year, that his family moved away before I was born so he wouldn't have to deal with being a teen dad and wouldn't have to pay child support. I realize they also wouldn't have to feel guilty watching my mom being called a whore by her own mother and being forced to leave school. They left so their son could live his dreams after he'd stolen my mom's.

I go back through and match all the ninth-grade names to all the eleventh-grade names, and not one boy is missing.

I start from the first page of the first yearbook and look for the things people wrote like *Love you! Have a great summer! Stay sexy!* Yuk. In the tenth-grade yearbook, I do the same, and there are even more comments. And then one that catches my eye. It's on the faculty page. A teacher named Mr. Nelson. He's young and cute, and there's a heart drawn around his face in a red marker.

I know before I open the next yearbook, the one for junior year, what I will find. Or, more importantly, what I won't find.

Mr. Nelson.

I go back to the tenth-grade yearbook and read every single note. And there it is. It's so small I can barely see it. It's from the friend who lived up the street from us, who told us about our things being left on the curb for the garbage collector. Her name is Peg and she wrote, *Loved being in bio with you, Mrs. N.* And then a smiley face shaped like a heart. *Mrs. N.* An inside joke about Mr. Nelson and my mom.

Mr. Nelson. Mr. piece-of-shit Nelson. My father.

Lies lies lies. How did I miss this? How did I not predict it from everything I know? Everything I've learned?

I close the yearbooks and put them away. I shut the box, leaving the silver duct tape to hang from the sides. It droops like a beaten-down warrior, old from eleven years in storage and weary from keeping this secret locked away. And I think that my mom still looks young and beautiful, and so I make a new rule.

Rule Number Thirty-Six: A justified lie is easily told.

Then I continue my search for Dusty's stupid gun.

CHAPTER NINETEEN

I can't get this new rule out of my thoughts. It makes me angry, along with so many other things fueling fire in my head. My mom's lie and what it might mean, my shithead father, Dusty thinking I'm not worthy of financial help for college. But there's no time for being angry. I need a plan and I don't have one. But I will. There's no choice.

I skip school. I call my advisor and say that I'm too upset about everything that's happened, and she believes me and says she'll mark me down as sick. I haven't missed a day of school in over a year.

I text Keller, and she says she's fine. There are no strange cars on the street. I text Ian on his private phone, ask if he's found anything about Agent Zellman, but he doesn't respond.

I call The Triple S, and Janice answers, and for a second, just hearing her voice makes my throat close up and my words leave me, but I don't have time to indulge this feeling, so I close my eyes and think about my plan and say what I need to about the inventory and the stock of pans and how I will rotate everything when I come in because I'm coming in early.

And then, when the rest of my world is in order, I ride my bike to the library.

The building is old and looks like something from *Harry Potter*. A weathered brownstone with creeping ivy, mildewed plaster, thick gray glass, and tarnished brass doorknobs. There are old ladies at the front desk and old ladies at the information desk and old ladies stacking books. It's worn from overuse and disrepair, because no one in Sawyer pays for books.

I go to the old lady at the front desk and hand her three dollars, asking for quarters. Then I go to the lobby, where there's a payphone, and lay the quarters out on the dirty metal shelf just below it. Finally, I take Clay Cooper's cell phone from my jacket pocket and turn it on for the first time since Friday night.

It comes to life. I move through the screens. It has very few. *Messages*—none. *Memos*—one. No words—just a series of numbers. I open the contacts last. There are seven. Then I open the voice memo app on my phone. I start to make the calls, putting in quarters, pushing the worn metal keys.

The first number has been disconnected. The quarters release. I record a note.

The second number has been disconnected. The quarters release. I record a note.

On the third, the phone rings, and I feel my body freeze as the ringing stops but no one says *hello*. My plan was to stay silent and let them speak, because that's what people do. My plan was to let them say what people say when no one replies, like *Are you there? What's going on?* Maybe they would say more. Maybe I would recognize the voice.

Rule Number Sixteen: People do not like silence. If you are silent, people will fill that space with words, and might share information that you can use to your advantage.

But now this rule is being used against me. Several seconds pass, and I feel the discomfort building. I'm supposed to initiate the conversation, but I hold fast. *Do not speak . . . do not speak!* The tables begin to turn. I hear breathing, a sigh of frustration. But then the phone clicks and the quarters drop, this time not into the return slot but into the well where they make a clanking sound. Metal on metal, because no one ever empties it.

I will myself to keep calling. Dropping quarters, dialing. There are no more active numbers. Only that one. Only the one with the breathing and the sigh.

I begin to sweep the quarters from the shelf into my hand when the phone rings, and I leap away from it. I stop, stare at the receiver that hangs on the side. My hand moves, about to go to it, but then I think, *don't be stupid.*

I slide the quarters into my back pocket and use the sleeve of my coat to wipe down everything I've touched. I think about the quarters in the well and wish now that I had not touched them with my bare hands because now my fingerprints are inside this box, on those quarters. And who uses a payphone when they don't need to? The woman at the desk will remember I asked for change because who does that either? So many mistakes already, when I thought I was being so careful and clever.

I have no business doing what I'm doing.

I turn toward the doors and think that I'll head straight to work and forget that I ever made these calls that let someone know I have the phone. Because that's what I have done. I have let him know.

I hear a ping. A text message. I start to reach in my right jacket pocket for my cell phone, but I stop and wait. It pings again. It's not my phone. It's Coop's phone. Coop's phone is pinging. I take it out of my left jacket pocket and flip it open. The number I called from the library first called me back on the pay phone, and now sent me a text.

I can't open it. I can't bear to find out. Do they know it's me? It could be anyone. It could be the police. It could be Regina Cooper.

I started this. I chose this path. I take a deep breath because I don't want to look. I don't want to know what I've done. I want to go back to being a girl who works at The Triple S, keeping her head down so she can get out of this place once and for all.

I feel the air rush from my body, my head is light. I have to do this.

I flip open the phone and read the words. I read them again. I read them a third time before I understand what's happening.

I run outside and get on my bike. I ride as fast as I can, letting the energy out of my body until my mind can make sense of things. The text can only mean one thing.

It reads:

Well hello Charlie!

Someone knows I have the phone.

I think through the possibilities and decide that this is most likely Barry sending me a message. And if I'm right, he knows I have what he wants and he wants me to know he knows so I'll be scared. Not just for myself, but for my people. The people I love.

As my legs move, pushing the pedals, taking me away from the library and the breathing at the other end of the phone and the words on the text, my mind finds space to think.

Barry wants the phone, but really, he wants what's on the phone. The number from the memo app. It must lead to his money. There's nothing else here, no other reason to want this phone. The money he gave Coop to clean, that he's now owed but that Coop can't deliver. Because Coop is dead.

So he needs this phone. And I have it in my jacket pocket.

I stop pedaling on Highway 65, right in front of a small strip mall with a liquor store and a laundromat. I take out the phone, open the memo app, and memorize the number from the one entry. I want to write it down, but that's not the smart thing to do. If it's only in my head, I'll have more power. This is the one time I need my memory to be extraordinary. I slow my breathing and close my eyes and see the numbers in my mind. 345-6292879-21704. I repeat them over and over and then also notice how they relate to one another, the sequence. These are all good tricks for remembering things, and they'd better work. *Please, God, let them work.*

I'm pretty sure this number matches the number I found on a piece of paper in Coop's safe at The Triple S. It's not a phone number. I don't know what it is, but I will. I delete everything on the phone except the text message from the library. I open it and send a reply.

You'll never find it.

It's not the most clever thing in the world, but it will do. Now I have to get rid of this thing.

CHAPTER TWENTY

I ride my bike to The Triple S and see Dana Blakely's white Mercedes in the parking lot. She gets out of the driver's side when I come to a stop.

"Hey, Charlie. How have you been?" she asks.

I don't know what I think about her being here, about this surprise attack. I'm still shaking inside from what's just happened with Coop's cell phone.

"What are you doing here?" I ask her.

She tries to make small talk, about school and work and has it been hard and has anything else come up about the murder or the IRS investigation or any of that. I shrug because that's not exactly a lie or an admission. It's just, well, it's nothing really.

"Your mother told me you were working today."

She asks if I want to sit in her car and I think this is better than everyone seeing me out here with a lawyer. I walk around to the passenger side and get inside.

"There is something that's come up," Dana Blakely says.

"Okay." I act like I don't care.

She folds her hands in her lap. Looks out the window. She tries to turn to face me better but she's wearing a very tight skirt and those black pumps and there's not much room to maneuver in this little sports car.

She tells me that Detective Pittfield called her. That they claim to have a new witness. Someone who came forward after seeing Coop's picture on the news.

"This witness was at the Marriott Hotel. It's about fifteen miles down the interstate," she says.

I tell her I know where it is.

"Well," she says, "the witness said he saw Mr. Cooper at the hotel the night he was killed. Friday night, around nine o'clock. Do you know anything about that?"

"Why would I?" I ask. Sometimes it's good to answer a question with a question.

"Because this witness also saw your friend Keller Joelle. I don't suppose you know anything about that either."

Now I'm silent. I've stopped not caring. Now I care very much.

"I can tell you're nervous," she says, and this makes me more nervous. "You know, your mother told me you get nervous when you keep things from her, or maybe tell her something that isn't completely true. She said you do things like what you're doing now, tapping your fingers together. Charlie—can you look at me?"

"When did you talk to my mom?" I ask.

"We spoke on the phone earlier." Dana Blakely rambles on about how concerned my mom is and how she told her that this hotel is the place people from Sawyer go to have dates with people who aren't their wives or husbands.

"Or maybe with an employee?" she asks. And then, after a pause, "Look, Charlie, I'm your attorney. And that means that anything you tell me is confidential. I can't share it with anyone, not even your mother or the police. Not even if you did something really bad. Not even then, Charlie. Do you understand? Do you want to tell me something? Anything at all? Because maybe I can help you if you tell me about Friday night."

"I'm good," I say. She's already spoken to my mom behind my back.

But she doesn't give up that easily. "Okay. How about this. We haven't really had a chance to get to know each other, right? What if you ask me a few things first. Go ahead—ask me anything you want. Did you know I used to live near here? Over in Bradford. Our high school played football against yours. I used to go to all the games. Okay, I'll admit it. I dated the quarterback, so it was kind of a big deal. Is it still like that?"

I shrug. This isn't helping me trust her.

"I imagine it is. And I actually remember the name Clay Cooper. It felt familiar right away. I remember his father owned the tobacco store. That was it back then. Just the one store. Looks like Clay built a small empire here. It must have been difficult sometimes, working for a man with that much power."

This time I answer with "I guess," which is the same as a shrug.

On and on, she keeps talking. "What else . . . hmmm . . . oh, I re-member hearing about your mother. About you. It was a big scandal back then. I didn't tell her I knew, so don't worry. I'm sure she doesn't want to be reminded of those years, even though now—I mean, look how wonderful you turned out, heading to college, so smart, and she's married to Dusty Madison and has two sons . . . everything worked out just fine. I'm sure there are a lot of people who are jealous."

This I can't imagine. Who would be jealous of my mom?

And then she gives me a long speech which is more like a mono-logue in some boring play. It goes like this:

"I know you don't trust anyone, Charlie. I also know what it must be like for you here. So close to getting out.

"I was just like you, you know. Bradford and Sawyer are very sim-ilar. Too far from the city to have much to offer. People just getting by. And all you want is to keep your head down and get the hell out of here. Go to college and start a new life and see what the world holds for you.

"I remember that feeling, Charlie! I remember when I went to college even though I couldn't afford it, and then working two jobs all summer to make ends meet when the other kids were getting internships that paid nothing but looked great on their résumés. And then law school, and more debt, and more work.

"But I didn't stop. I did what you've been doing. I looked straight ahead and never back, or to either side, because I knew how fragile it was, this path I was on. I knew that one wrong move, and my future would come crumbling down like a house of cards. And that's where you are right now, Charlie.

"Trying to move forward, but this town, this murder, is about to pull you off that road and you're afraid you might never make it back. And so am I, Charlie. Why do you think I stayed on your case? And drove all the way up from the city to see you?"

Now I think that she is desperate for me to trust her so I play one of my own cards.

"Did you know Mr. Nelson? The English teacher?"

"Who?"

"The English teacher at Sawyer High School."

"No," she says. "Should I?"

"You said you heard about my mom. And you said I could ask you anything, so I'm asking."

She says she didn't remember his name but that she knew my father was a teacher. I tell her that my mother lied to me.

"She told me it was a kid from her class. A football player. Like your boyfriend."

"Well, I would have believed that too. Football is everything around here. It's the ticket out for a lot of guys. And a lot of girls want to tag along. I am so, so sorry that your mother lied to you. That must be very hard."

It's not hard anymore because now it's just a new rule. *Rule Number Thirty-Six: A justified lie is easily told.*

But I don't tell her that.

After a moment, she breaks the silence. "Okay. So, now it's your turn. Tell me how I can help you, or Keller, or any of your friends. Let me help, Charlie. Let me help you get out of here."

She doesn't wait for an answer. She just keeps talking—this time about how she would lose her license to practice law if she betrayed my confidence, even though I'm only seventeen. She can't tell anyone what I tell her. Then she says that I probably already know this, which I do, because it's not very hard to find out about things like that.

I decide to take the leap. It's like jumping off a cliff. I must be really desperate.

"The FBI was watching Coop," I begin. "They say he was in business with a criminal, from Pittsburgh. They want me to call him Barry so they don't have to tell me his real name. They say now this criminal is watching me because he thinks I have the things that were missing from the safe and Coop's second cell phone, which had numbers on it, and the numbers lead to something he wants. That's all I can tell you."

She looks shocked. Maybe even a little scared and then tries to hide it.

"Wow. Okay. That's a lot. That's alarming. Okay . . . so, this is more serious than I thought. This is . . . this is a little over my head, Charlie, if I'm being honest with you. I don't handle criminal cases. A few speeding tickets and DUIs, but this . . . the FBI? What kind of criminal activity was Coop involved in?"

I don't hesitate. I want to see how scared she really is. "Money laundering."

"Money laundering? What for? I mean, Charlie—that's serious! Do they know where the money comes from? Is it drugs, gambling?"

I tell her I don't really know that part but it sounds like drugs and some other stuff.

"So can you help me or not?" I ask her.

She thinks about it carefully, then says, "I can try. I know someone at the DA's office. A friend from law school. I can reach out to him. I think we need to find out if the FBI has jurisdiction over the local police and if we can . . . I don't know . . . I'm thinking out loud here . . . but maybe we use this. Get the local police to drop their investigation. We'd have to make a deal with the feds. Maybe offer up anything you know in exchange for immunity. Do you know anything we can trade? Anything at all? You said they thought you might have this cell phone and some things from the safe? Do you, Charlie? Did you take things from the store that night after you heard what you heard and moved away from under the counter? Can you tell me that much?"

This is a lot to take in. So I don't answer.

"Okay . . . okay. Charlie. Wow. This is serious. If you have something that would help them put this Barry person away, and you got immunity, then I suppose you would be safe. Maybe they could protect you until then. I have to think about this, but in the meantime, don't trust anyone. Especially not the police. Not in this town."

I think about Ian and tell her, "But I have a friend who's a cop."

She says I'd be surprised how quickly friends will turn on you and she says it like she has personal experience with this. "Don't trust anyone— not until I know what to do. I'll call you soon. And if you decide you're ready to tell me more, you call me, okay?"

"Okay," I agree.

"Do you have my number?"

"Yes."

She tells me I should get inside before I'm late and people wonder what's going on. We say goodbye.

"Take care of yourself until we speak again."

She says it like she's not sure I can.

CHAPTER TWENTY-ONE

I don't feel right in my head. I don't feel right in my body. It's lunch hour on Monday, and I should be in AP Physics. Then English. Then Math. Then History. And then, only then, would I make my way to The Triple S.

Then, I would open the heavy back door and take in the smell that smells like freedom, hang up my jacket, grab a green apron. Find Janice slicing or cleaning or taking a break to call her kids and make sure they all made it home on the bus, her legs swinging from the metal table, which she's cleaned and then hoisted herself onto because we don't have any chairs in the prep room. Coop used to say that chairs make people lazy.

Then, and only then, would I find Nora in her office, smelling of a fresh cigarette, or of perfume if she's trying to quit again, and she would turn her head and smile and say hello and how was your day, and I would smile and say great, because my days used to be great. They used to be as great as walking down a straight road in flip-flops with the sun shining on your face and nothing but blue skies and white puffy clouds overhead.

Sometimes, then, Keller would be here too, usually on a break in the dining area with Levi, or maybe just talking to him from across the service counter. He would smell of gasoline, his hands stained black, but Keller would still look at him with dreamy eyes. Even if she had a bruise somewhere. Even if she'd hidden it with concealer that would rub off on her Triple S T-shirt, the sleeve or collar.

And soon, I would graduate from high school and be finished with my spreadsheet with the money I'd saved and the federal loans and the scholarship I was supposed to get.

But everything has changed. I've stopped walking down my road, just like Dana Blakely said. I'm standing still. Frozen by decisions that I don't feel equipped to make.

Rule Number Twenty-One: Knowledge is power, so lack of knowledge is weakness.

I open the heavy back door and walk inside. The smell hits me hard, reminding me of what has been lost. Today smells mostly of vinegar, and I see the salad-dressing containers open on the counter.

Helen's shift ended and she's left. Tracey won't be in until later. Keller was a no-show, as expected. Which leaves Janice and Nora.

And, surprisingly, Regina Cooper.

They are jammed in the office. It's only big enough for one small desk, the safe underneath it, and a chair for Nora.

They don't hear me as I enter the building. I go to the table and find the tops to the salad-dressing containers and twist them back on and then put them in the refrigeration unit behind the prep table so they won't spoil. I check the pans, make sure no one's touched them, because that's my job and I said I would do it.

When I come back out, Janice has left the office. She sees me and hugs me, and today it doesn't feel like anything. I have grown numb, I realize. Numb and frozen.

"She's got a bee in her bonnet," Janice tells me, and I ask her who and why and she says, "Regina Cooper. The IRS came back with a warrant. It sounds like trouble."

I leave Janice and go to the office, which smells of Regina's expensive perfume. She wears a tailored suit and stockings and leather boots and gold jewelry that clanks on her wrists as she moves her arms about, wildly, talking and talking about papers and invoices.

The scene overwhelms me, and I wonder if she knows what I know about Coop and Barry and the dirty money. If she does, she's doing a good job of hiding it, playing the dumb housewife who wears knock-off designer clothing to a sandwich shop.

They see me now. Regina's face lights up like help just arrived. Nora seems worried.

"Charlie!" Regina grabs my arm and pulls me inside. I stand with my back against a wall and try not to tap or say the words that run in a loop inside my head about *dirty money* and *lettuce tomatoes pickles onions.* Nora sits at her desk. Regina stands behind her chair, looking over her shoulder. Papers are strewn about, statements from the Sawyer Bank and Trust.

"These were all in a box. In the garage. Bank statements going back three years. He only used the bank for the business—the credit card sales and payments to vendors, and the payroll. We have a personal account for our bills, and the money goes right from one account to the other. That's it. Very simple," Regina tells me. "But we need to see if there's anything wrong. His bookkeeping or whatever. You did some of that, didn't you, Charlie? Coop told me you made some spreadsheets. He always liked you, Charlie." She starts to cry now, but I'm not sure why. "He always said how smart you were. How you were going to come back one day and take over this whole town."

Liar, I think. Coop would never say that about a girl.

I choke on my own breath, then start to cough. A violent, dry cough that forces me to step outside and get water from the utility sink. I run the faucet and put my lips to the stream, and then I realize that my eyes face the prep table where Coop lay bleeding from his head. I take one sip of the water and close them right up.

They say when something terrible happens, like a natural disaster or a violent crime or a horrible accident or even financial collapse, you first go into shock. You do what's needed to survive, literally survive, in the moment until it's over. That's when the heroes come out, rescuing others, giving away their money, opening their homes to strangers, and everybody feels a little better and then moves on. But for those who survive, after a short time, after the shock wears off, this is exactly what happens. The memories. The emotions. The morality. The humanity. It all comes rushing back in, trying to find a new place to live within a mind that has been decimated by the horrific event. That's what's happening to me. My horror. It happened right here, and now I'll have to find a place for all of those things. They want back in. They want to make sense of the world that's left.

Only it's not over, this horror. It's waiting for me in Nora's office.

Back inside, Nora explains to Regina that Coop wouldn't let us use those models and spreadsheets. Regina is quick with a reply.

"Well, this is why, isn't it? The IRS. The government. If there's no paper trail, they can never prove anything, right? Listen to me carefully," Regina says, her voice turning sour. "The papers from the IRS were all addressed to the company that owns the businesses." She picks up a bank statement, and I read the name on the top. *CC Enterprises, LLC.* "That's probably good, right? They're not investigating us, just the businesses?" she asks me and Nora, and I think about how absurd this is. I think that I am just a seventeen-year-old girl trying to get to college, and what do I know about these kinds of papers? I make sandwiches.

I also think about what my mom would say, and that makes me angry because she never gets out of my head. I think that Regina Cooper was a fool to leave her entire financial future in the hands of a man like Coop, and the future of her precious daughter who still needs to get through middle school, high school, and college, and who wouldn't know who or what she was if she couldn't walk through town like she owns the world, because to everyone here this is the world and the Coopers do own it.

Nora says she doesn't know how Coop structured things, so she can't say what will happen if the IRS investigates. She explains that there are no computer records that show the sales and the invoices from the store. But this is a lie—we have the records on our spreadsheets, even if we don't have the papers to back them up. Coop always took those and, apparently, destroyed them.

Regina chews on her right thumbnail, and I think that she's going to ruin her expensive manicure.

"What if they don't stop until they have everything? Except the house, which they can't take because Coop put it in my name and we own it free and clear."

Nora looks at a few of the bank statements. She seems perplexed. "Doesn't he have any holdings? Investment accounts? Trusts for Lillian? Life insurance? He must have left something somewhere, because these bank accounts don't have any meaningful balances."

Regina gets that same look my mom got in the police station. Haughty. She folds her arms and huffs a little.

"Coop and I felt safer staying away from all of that. The banks are all connected to the government through the FDIC. And the insurance companies—what if they get taken over by the government with everything else? We didn't go near anything the government could ever touch. People can think what they want—but look at Cuba. Look at Venezuela."

Nora makes the unmistakable sound of irritation—the loud throat clear. They write this into scripts to indicate annoyance. That's how effective it is, and it works now, only not on Regina. Nora's husband died defending our government, so she's allowed to be annoyed.

"How can we help?" Nora asks her, because we both know if she wiggles her way out of this mess with the IRS and inherits these businesses, she will be our new boss, and I feel the wave of realization drown us all, like a little tsunami.

Regina says it would be helpful if we could go through this box, to start, and see if things match up with the bank accounts and if there's anything the IRS might flag. And then she says something else, almost as an aside, but it's not an aside. It's the real reason she came here and we both know it, me and Nora.

"Oh, and there's this other matter—Coop told me he had some things in storage and that he wrote it down and put it in the safe and also in some code on his business cell phone. And both of those things were stolen the night he was . . . well, you know."

Now she cries again, and this time I can see that she is either very upset about losing her husband or about losing access to what he'd left for her in storage. Maybe both.

"If you find anything that might be useful, please let me know."

We agree, and Regina takes her fancy handbag and leaves us with the box and a million *thank yous*, which are meaningless because this will take a lot of work with no extra pay.

But we're all one big happy family here at The Triple S.

Janice checks the front for customers, then returns to the office.

We stand in a circle and look at the floor, thinking. Knowing. All of us different things. Different pieces to this puzzle. Nora knows that the income on the bank statements won't match what's on the spreadsheets on her thumb drive, and that those spreadsheets are the truth about what we actually buy and sell. I know, or think I know, that Coop has been working for Barry to launder his money through the businesses, and now I also know that the number that was on that phone in the memo app, which is the same number I found in the safe that night, could be the only clue about where Coop's money is hiding.

But Janice knows something as well.

"This stays between us, okay?" she says, and we both nod and stare at her and hold our breath.

She steadies herself squarely on both feet, puts her hands on her hips. Inhales, then opens her eyes wide and lets it all out.

"Shane told me that Coop doesn't keep records at the tobacco store either. That he does as many sales in cash as he can, pays vendors in cash when he can so they get to avoid sales taxes, and then he takes the cash from the safe there once a week in a small duffel bag."

Nora and I exchange a look because we've both seen that same thing happen here.

"And," she says, then pauses and takes another deep breath that seems heavy with fear, "Shane heard from some of Coop's maintenance guys that he collects rent in cash at his apartment buildings—gives the tenants a small discount. Even pays the maintenance guys in cash, under the table. Tells them they're independent contractors, so he's not filing any paperwork for them."

We all take a moment to think about this and what it means.

"Thank you, Janice," Nora says. "I appreciate you telling us that. We won't say a word."

Janice nods. "I just wanted you to know, because me and Shane are both pretty shook up about this. Don't get me wrong—Clay Cooper was a nasty man and God have mercy on him now, but if he's been cooking his books and the government takes the stores away, what will happen to all of us? He employs a lot of people here. This town is hanging by a thread, and this could be the thing that finally does us in. And then what? People like us don't just get up and move. Not with four kids and a condo that's under water and no credit . . ."

Janice starts to tear up, so Nora stands from her chair and pulls her into a hug, the roles suddenly reversed, the boundaries crossed, maybe even erased for good, and she tells Janice, "That's not going to happen. I promise."

We hear a customer call out from the service counter. Janice pulls herself together. "I'll get it. I'm fine. I'll be fine . . ."

It's been hard here with Keller not showing up and me and Tracey only working after school and Helen only working lunch. So we let Janice go and make the sandwich for the straggler, and then we both stand there, silent. Thinking. Finally, Nora speaks.

"Where does he take all that cash?" she asks. Then she looks at me, because the safe was closed and locked the morning after Coop was found dead.

But when the police opened it, it was empty.

I change the subject.

"Why wouldn't he leave the information Regina is looking for with a lawyer, or in his home safe?" I ask. "My mom said Dusty has a will and that she doesn't know what it says because he keeps it with a lawyer. She won't know until he dies and the lawyer shows it to her. But it's somewhere safe."

Nora scoffs. "Coop didn't trust her, that's why. And he certainly doesn't trust lawyers if he hates the IRS and the banks and the government so much." Then she shakes her head. "How can someone so clever be so dumb at the same time? After college, Charlie, you should go out and make millions of dollars in the stock market like those men on all the news shows, only you'll be a woman, and won't that be something."

I smile and nod, and then I say, "That night . . ." I'm about to tell her some of what happened, because I feel like I have to now, I have to get it off my chest, and maybe I can tell only some of it and leave out the hard parts, but she stops me.

"No," she says. "I don't want to know, and you shouldn't tell anyone except the police when you're ready."

I don't ask why. I trust Nora, so I take her advice.

Nora steps outside to have a cigarette.

And while she's gone, I look at the papers in the box. The bank statements and the letters from the IRS. I take pictures with my phone of a few of the statements and an address I see on some of the envelopes, an address for CC Enterprises. An address in Delaware. And the name of the agent who accepts delivery there.

I don't say another word about anything when Nora returns.

"God damned cigarettes," she says. "Don't ever start smoking, Charlie. It never leaves you." I almost tell her it's just the dopamine. The brain chemicals. But that's a longer conversation, and in the end it doesn't matter because no one has a cure for dopamine.

I tell her I need to get home.

I start to leave, but she grabs my arm. "Wait," she says. I look at her and know that she's just now decided something. About me. About this situation.

"Charlie," she says. "There's something else." She looks down and lets out a sigh. "I'm the one who told the IRS about this. But . . . it was over a year ago. The thing is, they never replied to me. They never mentioned an investigation, or sent any inquiries. Those letters Regina has, they all went to Coop's business address. And now, they've gone to see her, not me. Do you understand what I'm saying?"

I do. I understand. They're wondering if Nora's a part of this and if she was trying to cover herself by coming forward.

"But why wouldn't they want you to help them if you do all the bookkeeping? Even if they thought you were doing something wrong, they would use you to turn on Coop, wouldn't they?"

Nora shakes her head and smiles. "You've been watching too much TV. This is the IRS, not the CIA, Charlie. I told you, it's a bureaucracy. A headless beast. They won't be smart like that. They'll muscle their way in and take what they can get and cause trouble for anyone involved." She sighs again, and this one sounds like regret. "I should have known better. But don't you worry. I'll be just fine."

I manage an innocent smile because I don't know what else to do. I add this to my list of things to fix, if I can. I tell her I need to go take care of something and that I'll be back by five. It's already one. She says fine and returns a smile, and then I leave.

I get on my bike. I have gone back into shock, into survival mode. My mind pushes away the things that want to return, to find a new place to live. Instead, it finds new energy to focus, and I pedal as fast as I can, thinking and thinking and thinking.

CHAPTER TWENTY-TWO

There's no way around the conclusion all this thinking brings me to. I need help. I need it more than my pride, whatever that even means. I need it more than protecting myself from what might happen. I hate that I need it. But that probably means that I'm right.

Ian agrees to meet me at his house. He doesn't ask questions on the phone, because even on the one the department doesn't know about—that's not owned by Apple and that doesn't have apps that allow Zuck or the Chinese government to listen in—he still worries. I need to use his computer, and I don't feel safe anywhere else. Not even at the library. Not anymore.

I hide my bike around the side behind his garbage cans, then wait for him on his front porch. I can't say why I hide my bike but not myself. But by the time I think about this, Ian pulls up in his police cruiser, and it's too late.

"Hey," he says.

"Hey."

"Wanna come in?"

And I think, *no. I don't want to come inside and see where you live. Where you hang your jacket, kick off your shoes, watch TV, eat breakfast, take off your clothes, and go to bed. No no no.*

But I say, "Sure."

He opens the door and there we are. I follow him quickly to the kitchen in the back. I don't want to remember anything about this house. I pray that my exhaustion is causing a deficit in the chemicals needed to store memories. I don't want to remember anything, and I never want to leave as long as he lives in it.

"Want something?"

Ian grabs a Coke from the fridge.

"Sure. Same," I tell him. Sugar and caffeine sound pretty good right now.

We sit at a small table pushed up against a wall across from the sink and take sips of our Cokes like we did that night in the back of his truck under The Hand of God. Exactly the same, but also totally different, and I think that should be a rule, but I don't know how to begin putting it into words let alone something I could ever use in any other situation. There is just one Ian and just one love I feel for him, and this Coke reminds me of it. And it is just shitty shitty shitballs.

"So," he says cautiously. "What's going on?"

I don't cry very much. I know I've been crying a lot in the past three days, but usually I only cry when I'm really mad. Today, I'm not mad. I'm not sad either. Today, I'm scared.

The tears start and turn into sobs. He sits with me, and I tell him everything. Almost.

I tell him about the IRS and Nora and the thumb drive and the shady books. I tell him that I think Coop might have been double-crossing this man named Barry, who might have found out and now thinks I know things, maybe even about his money that Coop might owe him and how he can get it back. And how I have a cell phone and a paper from his safe that might tell where he's hidden something that Regina needs. Only I don't tell him that the thing Regina is looking for is all the cash Coop siphoned from his stores and apartments to avoid taxes and banks and stocks and anything that he didn't trust.

That's what I decided while I was thinking on the ride over here.

Regina knows about the money. Maybe the same money Coop owed Barry, or maybe money he was hiding from the government, probably both mixed up together. Regina wants the money, and somehow that money is linked to the number on the phone that was also inside the safe.

"This is a lot to take in, Charlie. Coop being involved with some criminal. The FBI sneaking into your mother's car, asking for your help . . . hidden money."

I start to rattle off all of the things I need to find out.

"Coop ran his businesses under a company called CC Enterprises, and it's based in Delaware, and there's a law firm that serves as the agent there, which I think means they collect official documents and stuff, but I don't know. I need to look all this up, and I need a computer because I can't have it on my phone in case my mom or Dusty check, which they do sometimes, and I can't go to the library because . . . well, I just can't."

I take a long gulp of the Coke. My heart is erratic, fast then slow, skipping beats.

"So you need to use my computer?"

"Yeah."

"Okay. You know I'll always help you. We are still friends, Charlie."

I study his face to see what's there. Hasn't he been tortured the way I have? Hasn't this year felt like a lifetime? Hasn't it been impossible to think of me as a friend after we felt what we felt and then had it stolen away by reason? Cold, cold, black-hearted reason?

These thoughts have made a jailbreak, and now they spin and spin, holding a gun to my head. Scaring me and making me cry, and now I can't tell what I see on Ian's face, which means everything I've thought about us could be wrong. A fantasy I've created to explain what happened that night when I told him we couldn't be together, not ever, because it would ruin my life, as if something like that held that much power. Maybe all of my rules just add up to a giant pile of shit.

"He is real," Ian says.

I look up now with a question mark on my wet, sobbing face.

"Agent Max Zellman. You asked me to check, and I did. He is an agent. With the Bureau."

That's something. And now he has to know I'm not making all of this up. Maybe I'm not crazy.

"When do you need to get back?" he asks me.

I tell him five o'clock. In time for the dinner prep at The Triple S.

"Give me what you want me to research. I'll see what I can find out."

He hands me a notepad and a pen from the kitchen counter, and I write down the name of the company and the law firm in Delaware.

"Can you take a deep breath now?" he asks. Anyone else would not be this calm. This patient. My mom would be calling doctors. Keller would be handing me a beer and a cigarette. Janice would hug me until I was snapped in two like a little twig. Nora—well, maybe Nora. But then what would she think afterward? Would she still trust me with the inventory and the spreadsheets? Would she still let me work there?

Somehow Ian knows I'll be okay, even though he's never seen me quite like this.

"Come on," he says.

I don't ask questions. I get up when he reaches for my hand, and I follow him into his bedroom.

"It's not what you think, if you were thinking anything. You just need to sleep. Even for an hour."

He pulls back the comforter and waits for me to get beneath it. Then he tucks it around me and under the mattress so it's tight. There's a heavy blanket in his closet, which he also gets and wraps around me, and I think about my mom and how she used to do this with her babies, swaddling, she called it. And I think that's how I feel right now. Like a baby that needs to be swaddled, and it's humiliating but also something else. Human, maybe. I feel human.

"Sleep."

He leaves me with this command as he walks out, closing the door.

Suddenly, everything stops. Sound. Motion. Heart.

I close my eyes and breathe in the smells of him on his pillow. I hate that I remember what he smells like, up close like this, but only for a second, because there's no room for that now. His bed warms quickly as my body sinks into the folds. And before I can have another thought, I forget that I can't love him anymore and that maybe he doesn't love me anymore, and I drift into the darkness of my unconscious mind.

CHAPTER TWENTY-THREE

Rule Number Two: Once you love someone, it's hard to stop.

This is why, according to the scientists on Google, and once again, it's just brain chemicals wreaking havoc:

High levels of dopamine are released during attraction. These chemicals make us giddy, energetic, and euphoric. Dopamine is the primary drug responsible for addiction.

Love. Cigarettes. Shooting guns at tin cans. Boxes in the attic. It's just the stupid brain with its stupid chemicals! It's Rule Number Four again! *All feelings are the result of chemical reactions in the brain.*

I think about this as I walk from Ian's bedroom to his kitchen, the smell of him still lingering on my body after sleeping in his bed. It's been over a year, as he reminded me nearly two hours ago, and the triggers that link Ian with happiness are still there. Nothing has replaced them. I can feel the chemicals surging, and they tell my brain I have to have him.

They're still there, and I think they always will be. What has made life tolerable are the new pathways I've built around them. New things that make me happy, like a beer with Keller and making sandwiches and counting my money and even dreaming of college. But they are like specks of dust that blow away now as I remember his hands on my skin and his mouth on my mouth and his whisper in my ear, saying those words: "I love you."

My mom has said a lot of things about love.

But I know other things about love. Things I've learned from other people.

Like Janice, who says that the time she spent with Shane before they had kids, the time when they were really in love, is like cement that then dried slowly over time, and now they are bound together by that cement, which is like one giant block of love that you get to lean on forever.

And Nora, who never got to be out of love. She never got to the baby part and the cement part, but she still has the memory part, and that makes her happy.

And Keller—she's in the heart of the love part right now. The red-hot heart that would make someone want to kill for you. And would make you want to kill for them.

My mom lives without love or even the hope of finding love, because she's married to Dusty, and I think that's worse than having a shitty duct-taped life.

Sometimes I wonder how she gets up in the morning.

But then again, I don't know how I'll get up tomorrow after having these specks of dust blown away, the pathways unearthed, the smell of this man, the feel of his bed, the images of his house and his face fresh in my memories.

The sleep has helped. I know because my mind has made room for these feelings and the thoughts that follow, the ordering of the people in my life into their right places. I needed this.

It also has room for the things that Ian found while I slept in his bed. He found out about Coop's company, CC Enterprises, and the address in Delaware, which is where the company was formed because it has better tax laws. It was formed by a law firm in Wilmington named Huff & Adler, and his lawyer's name is on the website. Daryl Romansky.

"What does that mean?" I ask him, hovering over his shoulder as he sits at the table with his laptop.

"I don't know," he says. "Probably nothing. Coop didn't trust banks.

That's pretty common around here, you know. My mom keeps her savings in a safety deposit box—which is at the bank, but she says it's different because it's real, something she can go and see with her eyes and touch with her hands, and not just some numbers on a piece of paper."

"And what about you?" I ask, worried again about my savings for college.

Ian shrugs. "I get my paycheck. I put it into my bank account. I file my tax return like everyone else. I don't really have time to try to hide things."

"Not everyone else. Not Coop. He didn't pay all his taxes because the IRS is after him, and now so is this man Barry, who gave him money to clean. And I guess he didn't give it back the way he was supposed to."

"Charlie," Ian says now. "I have to be honest. This story—things like this don't happen around here."

"Lots of things happen around here," I tell him. "You'd be surprised."

CHAPTER TWENTY-FOUR

Things are strange when I get back to Dusty's house.

It's dead quiet, and there is no smell of dinner, not even chicken nuggets. I already know Dusty isn't home, because my mom's car is the only one in the garage.

I rack my bike where I'm supposed to, because I don't need any more trouble today. I skipped school and told my lawyer more than I wanted to or meant to, but she got to me with her story about growing up around here and knowing men like Coop. I copied information from Regina Cooper's box of documents, told Ian about it, slept in his bed and felt things I didn't want to feel, made forty-one sandwiches, restocked the pans for the morning, and now here I am. Back home where there is no sign of Dusty or the boys.

"Where is everyone?" I ask my mom. She's in the kitchen, sitting at the counter drinking wine. She's been drinking and thinking, and that's not a good combination for her.

"Gone," she says without looking up. "Dusty took the boys to The Kids' Cabin for two days."

The Kids' Cabin is a giant hotel complex for families. Everyone goes there during the long winter months. It has an indoor water park and a magic game that has kids roaming the halls on every floor with wands and guidebooks searching for clues. If you ask me, it's like a playground for pedophiles. Unsupervised children right outside hotel rooms, in their pajamas sometimes, with their wands, desperate to find magic pixies and elves.

"What about school?" I ask. It's still Monday, which seems impossible. This day has gone on forever.

She takes a long drink from her glass, and I watch as her face softens. "He's punishing me," she says.

"What for?" I am genuinely confused. My mom hasn't done anything. I'm the one who's caused the trouble.

Then she ties it all together, and I feel stupid for not doing it myself, because it's so obvious.

"For you, Charlie. He's punishing me for you. I know you have your reasons, but it's embarrassing that you won't talk to the police. I'm not saying you should. But that's why Dusty's upset."

I have no reason to be stunned. My mom has hurled things like this at me before. Right at my heart. Like when I started running to keep by body from changing and when I wore Ace bandages around my breasts so she wouldn't try to feel them again and a million other times. It seems impossible, and yet I feel wounded, as though I don't know this about my mom. That she loves me but also resents me for the trouble I cause her. It seems to be a lesson I have to keep learning, over and over and over.

She waits for an answer, but I don't have one.

But then, suddenly, I do.

"Well. I didn't ask to be born, did I?"

I stand across from her and tap my fingers and feel my heart pound. I've never confronted my mom before.

I can feel her eyes on me but I can't meet them.

"That's ridiculous."

"No it's not."

And I have other things to say now, but I've already put myself in such a state of agitation that my fingers begin to move and I can't stop them.

Three taps each, *left hand, right hand, both hands. Left hand. Right hand. Both hands.* I force my mouth open.

"Mr. Nelson" is all I say. I don't use more words because those words say everything, and why make this harder than it already is?

"What did you say?" I hear something in her voice I haven't ever heard before. Shock? Surprise? She normally doesn't let these emotions slip past the gate.

"English. Tenth grade," I say.

She pulls herself together now. "I know who he is. Why are you saying his name to me?"

I stop tapping because I need my hands to brace myself against the counter. I feel dizzy, like if I drank one of Keller's beers too fast and then smoked her cigarette right at the same time. A major head rush, which doesn't feel good.

I sit and drop my head into my palms, elbows resting on the marble.

"Take a deep breath," my mom says. "Just breathe, Charlie."

I breathe, and suddenly I'm nine years old watching my shows in our shitty apartment with the duct tape.

She relaxes when my breathing slows. She drinks more wine. And more. And more. Each time setting the glass down with a loud clanking sound.

"Does it matter?" she asks me. "Student, teacher, whatever. It was a man. I let him get to me. All the things I've told you—they're all true. You know they are. I'm not stupid, Charlie. I know about the billboard off the interstate and I know about Ian."

"But Mr. Nelson was old. He could have taken care of us," I say. Because now I think it doesn't matter if she gave in to the stirring and had a baby, because Mr. Nelson wasn't a kid whose parents could move him away.

She laughs, but not because she finds this funny. It's a sarcastic laugh.

"He could have. But he didn't want to." More laughter comes, and it's louder until it turns to a few tears and then stops. Dead.

"In fact," she says, "He didn't want to so badly that he left town the second we were found out. I was sixteen and he was twenty-six and that makes what he did illegal. But you see, that's the difference. He got to choose and I didn't. My choice was made when I gave in to it. When I let him get to me."

I have so many questions now. Like why didn't we just stay in our shitty apartment until I got older and she could be free again? And why, even now, doesn't she do the things she tells me to do while the boys are at school? She could take classes at the community college. She could take them online. She could get herself ready for when the boys are grown and she will still have time. I want to know why she gave up, but I don't ask.

When I can feel her eyes leave me, I look at her, quickly, then away. And I don't know what to make of her, what I see on her face and what I feel radiate off her skin. It provokes the memory from that night we ran from her parents' house when I was just five, and I wonder if all of her dreams died for good when her mother called her a whore and then put our things out on the curb for the garbage collector, even my baby clothes and the bed I first slept in. Like we were both dead to her.

Maybe that's what put the final bullet in her dreams.

"Where is he now?" I ask. I'm suddenly curious if he suffered as well, having to quit his job and move away.

She shrugs. "I don't know. I don't want to know. He never tried to come back for us."

There's a strange pause that feels like a page being turned over, from front to back. And her tone changes from resignation to curiosity.

"Do you want to know? Is that what this is about?" she asks me.

And now I have to turn the page as well. I have never had this thought. Not before, when I thought my father was a selfish jock, and not today, when I found that picture of Mr. Nelson in the yearbook.

"No," I tell her, because that is the truth. "He's not a good man."

She doesn't answer. And words leave my mouth before I can stop them, which means they've been there, waiting, for a long time.

"Is Dusty a good man?" I ask her.

She draws a deep inhale. Gets up, goes to the refrigerator. Finds another bottle of wine. Then she goes to her purse, which is on another counter across the room, and looks for something, which she finds, and then she returns to her stool at the island and her wine, and me.

"Here," she says. And she hands me a small slip of paper.

I look at it. It's a deposit slip from the bank where I have my college fund. There's a deposit listed that I didn't make, and it's big.

"It's not as much as the scholarship Dusty helped steal from you, but I can get more. A little at a time."

I stare at the number and realize it's the exact amount I counted in her lotion box when I checked on all the important things in this house. It's the money she's taken from Dusty when he wasn't looking, and now I think that she knew she might need it one day, and that her handing me this deposit slip is the answer to my question about whether Dusty is a good man.

"There is no good or bad. It's all relative. It all depends on the moment. A good man can become bad in the blink of an eye."

I already know this. It's Rule Number Twenty-Four: *No one is all good and no one is all evil.*

I sit down beside her and wait for more. I know it's coming.

"Mr. Nelson, Jay was his first name, was not a bad man. He was a very good man when I was with him, and he struggled with our relationship. People can say what they want about it, but I pursued him. I wanted him. He was smart, and all the boys my age were so dumb. He made me think about things, you know? And dream about things. About college and a career and yes, about marriage and kids too. He made it seem like I could do all of that. But then things happened. I got pregnant with you. But he did *not* leave because of that. In fact, we decided to keep it a secret, and then, after the school year, we were going to tell my parents and move away together where no one would know us."

This is shocking to me. This is a different story than the one I've been telling myself, a better story. This was the kind of story that would have changed everything for me. Every single thing.

"But then he went on that trip with the seniors, up in the mountains. He was one of the chaperones. He was supposed to be with the group when they went hiking. He was supposed to be up there with Coop and Ian's dad, Cullen, and the boy who died, Rudi Benton, and the others.

"The thing is, Charlie, Jay left the trip to meet me at the edge of the park. I drove there so we could be together for an afternoon. It was sweet, actually. He'd planned a picnic, and we went on our own walk by the lake. I was starting to show under my clothing by then, and he put his hand on my belly, on you."

She stopped then and stared into her wine glass. She was waiting for me to make some kind of connection, but I was lost in this image of her with my father that was rewriting my entire life.

Now I don't understand anything. "So what happened? Why did he leave us?"

My mom sighs long and hard. "Well, as you can imagine, all of the boys' parents, and the whole community, really, wanted to know where Jay was when he was supposed to be on that steep trail with the boys. In fact, no one was supposed to be on that trail, and Jay could have stopped them from going up at all. He should have stopped them. But he wasn't there. He was with me. They asked where he went, and he said he went off on his own to go for a swim—which was bad enough—but not enough to get him fired.

"No—it was a student, Charlie. Another senior who saw us together. There was a group of girls who were spending the day at the lake instead of the trails. One of them spotted my car, and then waited for me to come back. She hid behind a tree like a little spy, and when I did return, Jay was with me. He kissed me goodbye and then kissed my belly and she saw all of it. And then she told the principal."

"And then he got fired?" I interject. "Because he was with you instead of watching the boys and then one of the boys died."

My mom nods her head.

"Who was it?" I ask her. "Who was that girl."

When she says the name, a million pieces fall into place.

"Regina Cooper."

CHAPTER TWENTY-FIVE

It's past two a.m. when I check the street one last time. For the mystery car that parks far away, for the black SUV. The danger feels surreal, like a story I've made up in my head. What is real to me now is what I've done to my mom by making her relive her terrible story. And what she's done to me by telling me a lie for my entire life.

It wasn't love that ruined everything. It was a nosy teenage girl who ruined everything for both of us. My mom could have had a husband, a real one. The kind she could bear to look at. And I could have had a father, a real one. The kind who would love me.

I walk past her room. The door is closed. The light is off, and there is no sound coming from the TV, or from her crying. I go to my room and crawl into my bed and under the covers, and my mind finally goes quiet.

I dream of my mom first. I'm nine years old, and I smell her, the perfume and makeup. I am on our bed in our shitty apartment, and I feel her eyelashes brush my cheek and her hand stroke my face. Then she leaves me, and I hear the door open and close and the key turn the deadbolt from the outside, and the fear creeps in.

I dream of Ian next. We're under The Hand of God. I tell him I love him, and I don't care what happens because I feel good. So good. And I want to feel good. Just once. I want to feel like we are one, me and Ian. One body. One person. I want to feel like we're not alone.

But someone is beside the truck. I can hear the rustling as he moves through the grass and brushes against the side. But then it sounds like my mom and her keys in the lock, metal on metal. And I want to go back to Ian and his body on mine and never have to leave. Never be alone again.

And then I am alone, alone at The Triple S. Alone with Coop, and he comes closer to me in Nora's office. The safe is open, money spilling out of it, and he holds a pile of it up to my face and tells me to smell it. To smell the money. Dirty, greasy money, and the spot on his head begins to shine with sweat.

I wake from this dream and burst into consciousness. The room is empty, but my door is open.

I always close my door.

I sit up and turn on the light beside my bed. It's then I see the mess they've made. Clothes taken from the drawers, pulled from the closet. Everything on my shelf is now on the floor in a giant heap. Books, towels, bags, and hats. And my teddy bear with the missing batteries.

They were here.

They were here!

The space between my bed and the door is only a few feet, but it looks like miles. I can't move. Not one muscle. I am frozen with fear.

Why would they come at night? While I was here? While I was sleeping and could have woken to see them?

Did they really think I would leave anything here for them to find? How stupid do they think I am? I am terrified. I am angry. I am losing my shit.

"Mom!" I call out. I don't know where this comes from—this instinct to call for her. But I quickly regret it when I hear her door open and her feet running—yes, running—down the hall toward my room.

"Charlie?" she calls out. Then she's there, in the open doorway.

"What's happened?"

I open my mouth to tell her, but then I stop. They just did this to scare me. They knew they wouldn't find anything. But they wanted me to know they were here. That they can get to me anywhere, even inside my house. With my mom just down the hall.

She comes to my bed and sits with me. She takes my hands, which are too shaky to tap or do anything else with.

"Did you have a bad dream?" she asks.

Now is the time. If I'm going to tell her about what's been happening these past few days, I have to do it now.

I calculate her reaction. She will call the police. She will call Dusty. She will make sure everyone knows that her daughter and her home were invaded, and she will want heads to roll. Only they can't even see the heads they'd need to chop off. Not the police. Not Dusty. Not my mom. Not even me.

But I know who can.

"Yeah," I tell her. "It was just a bad dream."

She sighs as she climbs into my bed and cuddles up behind me like she used to do in our shitty apartment.

As I start to close my eyes, she says, "Tomorrow you have to clean up. Everything is such a mess."

And I think she's right. Everything is a total mess.

CHAPTER TWENTY-SIX

I wait at the mall, where people begin to gather. Employees, mostly, at this hour. I rode my bike because my mother went out after breakfast to grocery shop. She told me to stay home from school again and rest because of the nightmare and says that everything will go back to normal now because they've done all they can do to me, and it turned out to be nothing. She even said she doesn't care what happened to Clay Cooper and that I just need to finish school and then get the hell out of this place, which is what she's always said.

It feels good to hear her say it again, even if she has no idea how far away that seems right now.

Agent Zellman pulls up in his black SUV. I am standing in front of the entrance to a Sears which closed two years ago and now serves as a giant beige monument to the economic decline of Sawyer. Half the mall is empty inside as well. For every open store, there's a metal wall where another store used to be.

Agent Zellman rolls down the window on the passenger side and tells me to get in. The car smells of stale cigarette smoke and pine and I see an air freshener swinging from the rearview mirror. Agent Zellman chews gum and wears the same thing he wore last time I saw him, black jeans and a black jacket.

"What's going on?"

I didn't tell him much when I asked him to meet me here.

"I'm not good," I say. "Not good at all! They were in my room last night, while I was sleeping."

"Who was in your room?"

"Barry. Or someone who works for him. They went through all my stuff looking for the cell phone and the contents of the safe."

I realize my mistake the second the words leave my mouth.

"How do you know what they were looking for?"

"Because you told me! You said they wanted those things! You said that!"

"Okay, calm down, you're right—I'm just trying to help."

He asks me some dumb questions like could it have been a bad dream or maybe my brothers did it as a prank. When he runs out of possibilities that don't involve Barry and his people, he says he's very concerned.

"This means Barry *is* looking for something you have, or trying to scare you. He's putting more pressure on. Did you call the police?"

"You said I couldn't trust the local police! And so did my lawyer. She said not to trust anyone."

He's surprised now. "Your lawyer? I didn't know you had a lawyer."

Shitty shitballs! Another mistake! I can't keep track of who knows what. I decide it doesn't matter. He's going to find out sooner or later.

"Well I do and she's smart and drives a Mercedes and wears fancy suits. She's helping me because she wants to—even though she has rich clients who aren't criminals."

"Did you tell her that you have the cell phone and the things from the safe?"

"I never said I had them."

He rolls his eyes and lets out a heavy sigh. He reminds me that I called him. I reached out for his help. Why would I do that if I didn't have a reason to be scared?

"I am scared," I tell him. "But not the way they want me to be. I mean, how can they hurt me if they think I have the things they want?"

Agent Zellman tells me I shouldn't be so confident. What if they decide they don't care about the cell phone and the things from the safe? What if they decide they don't need those things after all?

"Because there are numbers they need. Regina Cooper told me Coop hides things in storage somewhere, and I think the numbers lead to the hiding place."

"So you do have them!"

Of course I have them. Wasn't that obvious?

"And no one will ever find them if I don't want them found. My lawyer said I can use them to make a deal with you. That I can make you protect me and my friends if I hand them over."

He leans back and looks at me like I'm a petulant child. He recounts the things I've said about her, like how she said not to trust the police.

"And does she know what's in this hiding place that Regina Cooper told you about? Do you know?"

I tell him I assumed it was money—the money he said Coop was cleaning for Barry and maybe owed him.

He starts to laugh at me and I don't like it.

"You're starting to sound like an undercover agent yourself, Charlie."

"Don't make fun of me!"

"I'm sorry," he says. "You're probably right. It's probably money. But I can't tell how much danger you're in unless you tell me how you got your hands on the cell phone and the things from the safe. I can't help you unless I know what you saw or heard that night while you were in the store. Because if Barry did kill Clay Cooper, then once you hand over the things he wants, he'll want you dead."

I think about what Dana Blakely told me—about the FBI offering me protection. And I ask him if that's true. But he's not interested in making a deal. He's interested now in my lawyer.

"This lawyer you have, what's her name?" He pulls out his cell phone.

"Dana Blakely."

"And what does she look like, besides the fancy suit and expensive car?"

I tell him about her tight bun and that she's tall and thin and how I thought most people would say she's pretty.

He tells me to hold on, then searches for something on his phone.

"Here," he says. "Take the phone and tell me if this is your lawyer."

The picture is her, Dana Blakely. My lawyer.

"Now, look at the name under the picture," he says.

No! This can't be right.

"What does it say?" He wants me to read the name but my mind has already exploded.

It's not Dana Blakely. The woman in the picture is named Daryl Romansky.

"We've been tracking her movements for a while now. She works for Clay Cooper and Barry. She helps them set up corporations so they can create the fake ones that supply the fake inventory that doesn't exist."

This can't be right! I tell him how she knew things about Sawyer and the high school and my mom. Things no one else would know.

Then he puts a new ending on my sentence. "Unless they knew someone like Clay Cooper, who told them."

I think about how sincere she sounded. How easily I was fooled by her.

Agent Zellman tries to make me feel better. "You know what a sociopath is, right? But there are many kinds of sociopaths. We have an entire training program that teaches us about them. What they're capable of. Because sociopaths are motivated by different things than people who commit crimes for money or revenge or power. And they all have one thing in common—

"They're exceptional liars. They don't react the way other people do when they lie. They don't get nervous or sweat or look away. In fact, they can even fool lie detector tests."

I think about whether this is better or worse. My lawyer is a sociopath so I shouldn't feel bad that she fooled me. But—my lawyer is a sociopath!

Then I get a thought.

"How did she know I would be at the station that day? That I would need a lawyer?"

Agent Zellman asks how it unfolded that day and I explain that she was in the lobby waiting for a client who'd been arrested for a DUI and then Regina Cooper happened to see her on her way in, then ran into us in the bathroom, and then I realize how ridiculous this all sounds.

Agent Zellman tells me those are a lot of coincidences.

"And I don't believe in coincidences," he says.

I can't believe this is happening. Agent Zellman reads my mind because again, he tries to make me feel better.

"This is the thing about places like Sawyer," he explains. "Times are tough here, and when times are tough, alliances break down. Loyalty breaks down. There are no sides. No tribes. No laws. Just people pushing other people off lifeboats and looting and corruption that reaches high and low and everywhere in between. Dog-cat-dog. Think about that expression, Charlie. What it means. When members of the same species break from their pack and fight to the death because there's not enough food to go around. Every dog for himself. And now, here, in Sawyer, it's every man for himself—and every woman."

I thought I had it all figured out. I had my rules and my plan.

Agent Zellman reads my mind a second time.

"Charlie, listen to me. I have a plan."

CHAPTER TWENTY-SEVEN

I throw my bike in the back of the SUV and let Agent Zellman drive me to school. It's 9:30, and I've only missed first period, which is math, and I've already taken this class online and even taken the AP exam last spring, so I only go because all the seniors have to.

Yes, this is where my mind is after it's been exploded by Agent Zellman's bomb. But I need to do something normal. I need to be in my normal life. Even though my mom told me to stay home and rest. Even though Agent Zellman pleads as we drive.

"You're not safe, Charlie. They're coming out of the woodwork now, the people who want the money. And now that you've put all these pieces together—you know too much. But that 'lawyer' will lead right to them, right to Barry and his associates."

He thinks and nods and drives while I picture myself in history class sitting next to ordinary kids with ordinary lives.

He doesn't say the rest, which is that the only way to make me *not* know something is to kill me. And I think—Clay Cooper was killed, wasn't he? And I bet he never thought it would happen. Not in a million years, the way he acted like such a big man. Like nothing could ever touch him.

What he does say, Agent Zellman, is that he has a plan, and his face lights up when he explains.

"Charlie," he says, glancing over at me, "let us get her. Let us take down Daryl Romansky. She'll give up what she has on Clay Cooper and Barry—she's a low-level lawyer who's already proven she's willing to do what it takes to get what she wants, posing as Dana whatever. Trying to fool you. That's how we get her. That's how we get Barry. And that's how you get out of this mess."

He tells me he'll call her, Dana Blakely who's really Daryl Romansky, and set up a meeting with her and the FBI, just like she suggested. He says he'll find out what she wants before she'll let me talk to them and hand over the information from the phone and the safe.

He says that she'll probably want to meet me first and see what I have, to hear my whole story. "That's when you'll know—when she suggests bringing her the cell phone first. She'll say it's because she needs to know what to ask us for, in the immunity agreement. She'll probably tell you to leave the phone with her and she'll keep it safe until we all meet and it's time to hand it over, only she won't show up at that meeting, will she? She'll be out of town the second she has what she needs to get the money."

I think about this. I think about giving her the cell phone with the number and with it, all of my power.

"Why wouldn't she kill me, right then and there?" I ask him, and it all sounds so stupid leaving my mouth, like I've made everything up.

"Because we'll be right there with you. We'll have eyes on both of you wherever she asks to meet, and we'll move in the second we sense danger."

He tells me she won't try to do anything out in the open, even if she is using a fake name here. People have seen her around town. No— if she wants to kill me, she'll have someone else do it, or wait until I'm alone somewhere, like in the parking lot of The Triple S or riding my bike home from work. A car might take me out. Something like that.

And this is supposed to offer me comfort.

———

I sit in history class next to a girl named Ginny and a boy named Kyle, and I do not fall asleep today, which is shocking. We're learning about the electoral college system, and it's boring as anything. Next the teacher will probably show us a video, and everyone will fall asleep.

I sit there and think about the number on the cell phone. 345-6292879-21704. It's the same number that was written on a piece of paper in the safe with a small pile of dirty, greasy cash. I've been thinking about this number and how it's separated by dashes, which means each piece is a different element. I think about places money can be hidden. Places that require numbers. It's not an absolute location using longitude and latitude. The number doesn't make sense for that. Where would Coop feel safe leaving all that money?

People hide money between their mattresses. They hide money beneath wooden floorboards and in air ducts and wrapped in tinfoil in their refrigerators. They hide money inside appliances they've taken apart and put back together. There must be a million other places.

But this has to be a place Coop controlled, where he could come and go every week. I have to think about the numbers, but also about Coop. I've done my best to learn and to analyze, but my seesaw will always be lopsided, because that's how it's built and that's what I will have to live with for my whole life. And never have I been more aware of that than I am right now, needing to understand a man like Clay Cooper as much as I understand the numbers hidden in his phone.

I thought I'd been so clever with my rules and all of the information I'd gathered over so many years, but I will never do better than making it through a high school gym class. None of this will get me through real life, because there's just too much to know. Things I can't get from books and TV shows. Intangible things that require intuition and an internal compass, the things I don't have, the side of my seesaw that's too light. I could not see through Dana Blakely. I trusted her.

Frustration takes hold just as the bell rings and class ends, and I put all of that aside because now I have to do something else.

I step into the hallway and pull out my phone.

First, I call Dana Blakely, and ask if she's heard from Agent Zellman. She tells me that he contacted her and that we should meet first to prepare. She says how relieved she is and gives me an address for some shared office space her firm uses. She asks me if I'm okay, and I picture the caring smile I know she would give me if we were face-to-face, and I want to claw it off of her. Just as Zellman predicted, she tells me to bring the cell phone so she can see what I have first and then be able to make a better deal for me.

She's lied to me. And I never saw it coming, because she was supposed to be like me. A woman who'd changed her destiny by escaping where she'd come from. She was supposed to be on my side. I even Googled her firm, which had what looked like a real website with clients and other lawyers, but now I think: how hard can it be to make a fake website with fake pictures? That's on me.

That's the world we're in, even though we have steak sandwiches and tobacco and The Hand of God offering salvation. It's just not enough. Everyone is trying to get what they can, and the liars are having a field day with us.

The second thing I do is text Agent Zellman and tell him I've done it, and that we have a date, tomorrow after school. That should give him time to set up his surveillance to make sure Dana Blakely doesn't kill me. He confirms right away and tells me he will protect me and I shouldn't worry. But I am worried because what kind of shit for brains uses a seventeen-year-old girl who's standing outside her history class to catch what seems to be a pretty mediocre, low-level crime lord named Barry who's dumb enough not to have a plan to get his money back, and who goes into business with Clay Cooper in the first place?

Clay Cooper, who ogles teenage girls and takes them on dates at the Marriot Hotel the second they turn eighteen and who sweats just thinking about it. A man who won't even use a bank or have insurance, who keeps important information on a cell phone that could fall out of his pocket at any moment?

How dumb is it to leave that much money in a place where it might get lost forever? He couldn't be that dumb. He was a shit bag, but he managed to hide all this money in the first place, so he must know how to do some things.

I think then that Coop *wouldn't* do this. He wouldn't leave a string of numbers that his wife would have to decode if he died, unless she knew how to decode it. Unless she knew what the dashes were separating. Yes! That has to be it. Regina Cooper knows what the numbers correlate to. She has to know the code, but there's no way she can get to the money without the number. She needs both. And what all of this means is that she's been lying to me, too.

People are shitty.

I think about Mr. Nelson. And my grandmother screaming those hateful words and leaving our things outside for the garbage collector. I think about two-chinned Dusty sitting at the head of the table, who voted away my scholarship because I'm a girl who can't do anything but study and make sandwiches. I think about Coop and Regina and Barry and Dana Blakely and even Agent Zellman.

And now I am disgusted by everyone and everything in the whole entire world.

I'll never rely on Rule Number Thirty-One again: *Trust but verify.* There's a new rule now.

Rule Number Zero. The Golden Rule: Trust No One!

I hear the bell. Science is next.

I will swallow my anger and pretend to learn facts about physics that I already know.

Then I will ride my bike to The Triple S and make sandwiches all night. I'll restock the pans and rotate them and make the list for the morning, and then I'll clean the grill and mop the floors and accept a hug from Janice and a nod of encouragement from Nora.

As I walk down the hallway to the science room, I miss Keller more than I can even believe. I want to find her, sneak a cigarette on her roof, hear about her night with Levi, tell her about sleeping in Ian's bed, make fun of Lazy Tracey, and laugh until Dot calls and we have to flick the cigarette and pretend we have no idea why we smell like smoke and then laugh.

That's the way it should be.

And the way it will be, at least for Keller. I promise myself this as I take my seat in the classroom.

CHAPTER TWENTY-EIGHT

The next morning, I leave the house before the sun is up. I stop by The Triple S to rotate the stock in the refrigeration units, because it has to be done properly and only I can do that. Nora almost laughs at me because she knows I can't stop myself from being meticulous and careful. I tell her it makes me feel like there is some order in the world even when there is no order, where one day you're clocking into work and the next day your boss is dead.

When I'm at school, I'm on autopilot. Sitting in math, then science, then history, and at lunch and walking down the halls, and then in French and computer science, and then at my locker shoving everything inside because I'm not doing homework tonight, I think about the things I have told to Dana Blakely a.k.a. Daryl Romansky and the things I have told to Agent Zellman and the things that Barry knows about me, like the fact that I hold the key to finding the money.

I don't exactly have the whole afternoon figured out. I know my mom will be at the hair salon getting blonder, which takes three hours. The house will be empty. I know Dusty and my brothers will be at The Kids' Cabin because Dusty paid for one more night and they don't offer refunds, so even if Dusty was turning into a shriveled prune from the water park, he would not come back and lose his deposit on the room.

I know I've done everything I can possibly do to make it out of this situation.

And still, my heart is bursting, my head is burning, and I feel like the person they are going to expect me to be. A girl who's good for nothing except math and making sandwiches.

Yesterday, Dana Blakely gave me the address for an office on the far end of the downtown strip. It's called Sawyer Executive Suites. It's a brand-new building, and it even has a bike rack, where I park my bike and let my backpack slide off one shoulder. She says her firm rents one office there in some kind of time-share agreement, and I don't question her because I know she's probably lying. *Rule Number Zero. The Golden Rule. Trust No One.*

There are signs for a real estate broker outside, the kind with the giant head of the agent with bright-white teeth and a friendly smile and a colorful scarf. Always the scarf, because it makes the agent look professional but nonthreatening. No one has ever been intimidated by a woman in a scarf. No one has ever wanted to have sex with a woman wearing a scarf either. She feels like a safe choice for clients of all genders and ages. I think about this as I walk to the entrance of the building, even though I should be thinking about the fact that I did not see a van or a black SUV or anything out on the street that looked like it could be Agent Zellman to keep watch over me. But there's no turning back.

The parking lot has just two cars. One of them is a red Subaru, and the other is the white Mercedes sedan that Dana Blakely was driving the day she was waiting at The Triple S. The day she made me trust her and believe she wanted to help me, and got me to tell her about the cell phone and the money and Agent Zellman.

The back of the building is thick with woods and then a stream, so I doubt Agent Zellman is parked there. But I can't stop now. I am prepared to do what needs to be done, which is to lie to this liar with the pantsuit and black pumps and tight bun to get what I need.

The offices in the building are mostly empty. I open the door and check the board that lists the businesses. There are eight of them, from physical therapists to shrinks to a Pilates studio. Individual companies. And yet no one is in the lobby.

I think about the real estate agent with the scarf, and I wonder if she made up all of these businesses herself so that when people see the sign, they don't know that the building is empty and then think that maybe it's a shitty building.

Dana Blakely said she was using office 2C, which is on the second floor, so I stand in front of the elevator bank and push the button.

It dings. I get inside. I hit the number two, and the doors close, and then up I go, one flight.

The doors open to a floor that is just as quiet as the first, except that the hum from the traffic is even softer here. I see just three offices. Two doors are closed and have no names on them. The third is slightly open, and when I walk over, I see a gold sign that reads 2C, and I remind myself not to be fooled when I see her. She is not who she says she is. She is Daryl Romansky. And she wants to trick me into giving her the cell phone.

I knock on the door, and this makes it swing open slowly, softly. No hint of a squeak because it's brand new but also hollow—as nice as everything looks in this building, it is cheaply made. Even the elevator jiggled like something that could break at any moment.

The door opens to a gray-speckled carpet and a light wood desk with a huge paper calendar and a phone, an actual phone with a cord that runs down to the wall, and a chair behind the desk that is some kind of black vinyl and looks like it might swivel. A leather bag sits on the vinyl chair, and I recognize it from that day at the police station.

I stand there and look inside and wonder now if maybe she's gone to the ladies' room, which I saw down the hall. Or maybe this is all a trick.

I step inside and check behind the open door. Nothing, just a file cabinet and a fake plant that sits on top of it.

My heart settles because the office is empty, and then I realize that this is my chance to see whatever's inside the leather bag. I decide to leave the door open, because then I will hear her when she comes out of the ladies' room or out of the elevator or even from the stairwell. You could hear a pin drop in here.

I step closer to the desk and place my backpack on one of the chairs. My eyes go first to the bag, but then I see something else, which is so strange it takes a very long moment to register.

Blood.

First I think it's a design on the gray carpet, and then a stain from a leak somewhere, but then what could be leaking that looks like ketchup? And then it hits me, and I freeze.

I walk around the desk, slowly. The large file cabinet is in front of the stain, between me and the window that looks out at the woods. My heart is in my throat. That's a dumb expression, but there's a reason for it, which I now understand. Every vein in my body is opening up to allow adrenaline to race through so I can protect myself like an animal in the wild facing a predator. Only I am not the one facing anything, except what waits for me behind this file cabinet in this empty room.

The blood forms a circle on the gray carpet. And right in the middle of the circle is a black high-heel pump.

CHAPTER TWENTY-NINE

I don't remember taking my eyes off of the shoe. I don't remember picking up my backpack from the chair on the other side of the desk or running from the office or down the stairs or out the front door to my bike.

But I do all of those things, because suddenly I am in front of the convenience store where there are people and cars driving by. I call Agent Zellman and tell him what happened and ask where the hell was he? He was supposed to be close by watching with a team from the FBI, and then he was supposed to come in if there was any trouble, which, I think, this would qualify.

"Calm down, Charlie. Tell me what's happened."

I have trouble finding the breath to say the words.

"There was blood! And her shoe! I think someone killed her!"

He is shocked. He tells me that his team is at a different address, another building owned by the same company and with the exact same name: *Sawyer Executive Suites*. They have more than one location and I didn't know. I didn't bother to check.

"Charlie, we thought you didn't show . . ."

I must be panting into the phone, because Agent Zellman tells me to "calm down, take a deep breath," and then I manage to give him the address of the building where I've just found Dana Blakely's blood and shoe, and he tells me two things.

First, he says, "We're on our way now."

Second, he says, "We need to take you in. You're not safe."

He tells me to get home and lock the doors, and I say, "Won't I be safer out in public?" and he says, "No, that's not true at all. That's a myth, something on TV. Go home and lock the doors." He says he'll meet me there as soon as he checks out the scene at the other office.

I agree to go back to my house. But I don't leave right away. First, I call Ian. He doesn't pick up, so I just leave a crazy message about a dead lawyer and an empty office building and the FBI. I hold the phone in my hand, thinking what else can I do? Who else can I call for help, and I run through the list of everyone from my mom to Nora to Janice and even to Dusty.

My fingers hit buttons, then stop. They do this again and again and again until I finally accept what I have to do now.

Think. I have to think. I have to think about numbers and rules. Numbers and rules. Numbers and rules.

I think while I ride my bike. I let part of my brain count the pedals. I make them into a pattern. *Three fast, two slow. Two fast, three slow.* It wakes up the other side, the analytical side, which needs to get to work.

I go through my rules. Number Ten about impulsive behavior. Number Eleven about emotions and rational decisions. Number Four about feelings and brain chemicals. And I come to the conclusion that I have to calm my brain so I can stop feeling scared. Stop being emotional.

Think don't feel. Think don't feel.

I make a new calculation in my mind. I list facts in one column— only things I know to be true. Things I have seen with my eyes and heard with my ears and that cannot be untrue. There aren't many of those. Some of the ones I begin to put there I have to take away when I ask myself the question—*could* this be untrue, and if so, how? And if so, why? The column grows longer as my brain allows memories to re-surface. Small things. Things I didn't even think to hold on to but for some reason did.

In the next column are facts that don't add up. That have been contradicted by other things in the first column.

Two fast. Three slow. *Agent Zellman's car keys.*

Three fast, two slow. *Sandwiches and inventory. Real and fake.*

All fast now, faster and faster and faster as I see the number from Coop's phone and the number written on that piece of paper and then all of the street signs I ride past. Regina Cooper knows the code. She has to. There is no chance she would make heads or tails of this number unless she knew how to decode it. She thinks the government is going to steal her money. She has no idea where Coop keeps records. These are not the kind of things she's ever had to think about. Coop would make sure she had instructions.

The calculation is nearly finished when I get back to Dusty's house, and I run out of time. It will have to be enough, what I have sorted out. It just will.

I wait now, in Dusty's house, in the dining room, by the window where I can see the street but the street can't see me because of where I'm standing. The doors are all locked, and the alarm is turned on.

I call the hair salon and make sure my mom is there, and they tell me that she just sat down at the sink, which means they haven't even started, and it takes three hours to do all the things she has to have done. I call the police station and ask to speak to Ian, but they tell me he's in an all-day training program, which explains why he hasn't called me back. I think that this is not good, and I ask them to tell him to check his messages from me, it's important.

Dusty has a grandfather clock, and it sits in the corner of the dining room and makes a tick-tock sound with every second that passes and a ding with every minute and a chime with every hour. It tick-tocks and dings and tick-tocks and dings, and I feel like I might take one of the candlesticks from the center of the table and just go and smash it to pieces.

I am not in a good state of mind.

It has only been five days. Five days since everything changed. When my simple plan to get out of here and go to college was derailed by one man and a chain of events that I still cannot believe.

I think about this while I wait. Watching for Agent Zellman's SUV. Waiting for Ian to call.

I think about every action I've taken since I got that first text from Keller at 8:52 Friday night. Everything I haven't told a soul and never, ever will. I think through it all, making sure I haven't missed anything in my calculations. No mistakes. No mistakes. *No mistakes.*

CHAPTER THIRTY
THE NIGHT OF THE MURDER

I was at The Triple S working the dinner shift until close. We close at ten every night except Sunday.

I was in the back at the sink, filling the mop bucket. The night was slow, just a few trickles of customers, and Tracey was handling those while I started the cleaning, because I'm much better at the cleaning than he is. The bucket fits in the sink, but if you fill it more than halfway, it's too heavy to get out, so I did that—I filled it halfway and then turned off the water. That's when I heard the *ping* on my phone.

> Need u

It was from Keller.
That's all it said. But then another came.

> Now

> Pls come now

> When r u coming

I dried my hands and texted back.

OMW.

It was just me and Tracey, and he didn't know how to close the store. I texted Nora and asked if we could stay open until eleven. I asked Tracey if he could stay until then, in case I needed more time with Keller. I told him if he did, I would cover his Saturday-night shift that he'd been complaining about all week—two weekend dinner shifts on the same weekend was more than he could tolerate because he was missing all the fun smoking weed with his loser friends.

I told him I might even get back faster if I could borrow his car. That was a bigger problem, but he still agreed. He gave me his keys, and I left.

Just like that—with the bucket in the sink, my apron on the counter, and the back door open.

Keller lives about ten minutes from The Triple S, and I got there in eight. I could hear the screaming when I pulled up to the curb and turned off the engine.

Levi's car was not on the street or in the driveway. Keller's car was parked under the covered carport. Lights were on upstairs and downstairs and everywhere throughout the house. I ran to the front door, and it opened right up.

The screaming was coming from the back, from the kitchen. It was the screaming of girls, women, fighting.

The words were familiar.

"You're a whore!"

"Stop it, Dottie! Stop!"

"Whore, whore, whore!"

I ran toward the voices. They were coming from the kitchen, and they did not stop when I got there. When Keller and Dot saw me.

Instead, they pulled me in.

"She's a whore!" Dot said to me, though her eyes were glued to Keller. She held a small cast-iron pan in her right hand. Keller was in the corner, pinned to the wall by Dot's left hand, which was around her throat. The old woman's walker was on the ground, the oxygen tank had rolled away into the corner, and she'd pulled off the attachment that usually fits beneath her nose. She could barely stand, but that didn't stop her.

Keller is smaller than Dot, but twice as strong. She could have blown Dot off of her with one breath. Still, she wasn't doing anything to protect herself.

I had witnessed this before, the fighting, when Dot lost her senses and thought Keller was her mother. But I had never seen Dot lay a hand on Keller.

"Dottie, this is Keller, remember? And I'm Charlie," I said, trying to pull her back.

But she hadn't gone anywhere. Not this time.

"I know exactly who this is, and she's a whore just like her mother was a whore. All whores!"

Keller was wearing going-out clothes. High heels, a short tube dress with a low V-neck. And her mascara was running down her cheeks just like my mom's the night we ran from that house. The house where another old woman was screaming that word at us. *Whore!*

Dot raised her left hand, the one with the frying pan, and bashed it against Keller's thigh, and I knew right then who'd been hurting Keller all along. Not Levi. Not Clay Cooper.

Dot, her grandmother, the frail old woman with the failing memory and foul mouth and hatred for her own dead daughter. And Keller did nothing to protect herself.

"Stop it!" I yelled, rushing toward the old woman, grabbing the frying pan. I pulled her off Keller and saw the damage she'd already done, to her face and her neck and the other leg.

She came away easily, like a rag doll. And I wondered why Keller hadn't pushed her, even a little, to get away. Why she let Dot beat her and hold her throat and call her a whore. Why she'd been letting her do this for years, causing bruises so bad and so often that Janice had called the police to report the abuse.

With Dot in my arms now, the frying pan on the floor, and Keller huddled in the corner, I almost asked her, because it was that kind of question. The kind that is so big you can't hold it inside.

But then, somehow, I knew. This was how Keller lived with herself and the way she let Coop look at her and touch her and ogle her so she could keep her job. This was her penance. The thing she had to allow to balance the seesaw in *her* brain, and the one side that hated itself for what it tolerated from Coop.

"Let's get you a pill and get you to bed," I told Dot. And I coaxed her upstairs, got her a pill, and brought her to the bathroom so she could pee and wash her hands and put on a clean diaper. Then I tucked her into her bed the way Keller always did, with the tight covers and the bed rails.

Dot never stopped saying the words, but I had stopped caring. "Whore, whore, whore." Because she was an old, senile woman, and if she understood what Keller did for her, what she'd had to do so Dot wasn't shoved into a state hospital and given the wrong medication that made her want to kill herself, maybe she would shut up about the whore business. Maybe she would just shut the hell up, period.

I found Keller downstairs, still in the kitchen, a glass of something brown in her hand. Jack Daniels, it turned out.

"Something horrible happened" was how she began her story, then she lit a cigarette.

Keller never smoked in the house, but tonight, as I would soon learn, had called for breaking all the rules.

Every last one.

CHAPTER THIRTY-ONE
NOW

I'm lost in these thoughts when I hear the creak of a floorboard. I know every sound in this house after eight years of living in it, so I know it's not just the wood settling from a change of temperature. It's the creak the floor makes when a person has stepped on it.

But I haven't heard the alarm. I haven't heard the locks turn or the garage door open.

I get up from the table and walk slowly to the wall by the clock, and I hide behind it. I don't make a sound—I know how to walk in this house undetected.

The floor creaks again. Then a pause. Then again, my heart is in my throat.

I am not prepared for a sneak attack.

Another creak and then another, until I see a shadow and then a shoulder and then a body, enter the room.

I step out from behind the clock, because it doesn't hide me well enough. I've been seen. I stand straight and pretend to be unshaken when I hear someone say, "Hello, Charlie."

CHAPTER THIRTY-TWO
THE NIGHT OF THE MURDER

I wanted a drink. I wanted a cigarette. But I wanted to help Keller more, so I sat down and told her to sit down too, but she couldn't. She was wired like I had never seen her before.

So I got up and walked to the sink and wet a dish towel and then went to where she was, leaning against the counter, and began to wipe the tears and blood and mascara from her face.

"Tell me," I said.

She was shaking head to toe, her nerves unable to settle.

"You have to find Levi," she cried. "Right now—find him and stop him!"

I asked her "Why?" and "Where is he?" and "What is he about to do?" and she said there wasn't time, that I needed to call Ian and ask him to find Levi before he killed Coop.

"Why does Levi want to kill Coop?" I asked her.

But she walked away from me and started to pace and then beg and plead, "Just call Ian! Right now! Please, Charlie! He'll do it for you. I know he will."

I took out my phone and called Ian and told him I didn't know what was going on but could he start looking in all the places Levi might go to find Clay Cooper—his stores, his house, the warehouse where he holds his illegal poker games.

"Just look for his car. And look for Levi's car. And keep calling Levi until he answers."

Ian agreed, just like Keller said he would.

"Okay?" I said to Keller, coaxing her to the table with her drink and her cigarette. I got some ice from the freezer and put it in the towel and made her hold it against her face, which was starting to swell.

"Can you tell me what happened?" I asked her, then she took a long, shaky breath, then a drink, then a drag.

"You know about what Coop does, right? How he tries to date us, the girls who work for him, and if we do, we get better hours and bonuses, and if we don't we get fewer hours and the worst shifts—enough to hurt us but not enough to get him in real trouble."

I nodded. I didn't tell her how I knew, how I'd seen Coop at the Marriott Hotel with the girl from the diner.

Keller went on, her body seeming to calm as she reconstructed the story piece by piece so it became a clear picture, not just an emotional tornado that I saw spinning behind her eyes.

"He started asking me the day I turned eighteen, and I told him no. And not just once. Over and over. He never stopped asking. And you saw how he cut back my shifts, or made them all conflict so I had to choose between the diner and The Triple S. I told him no over and over, even though I couldn't stop him from looking and touching, and it made me sick."

"I know, Keller, I know."

"And then today he told me he had a new job for me. He said his friend who managed the Marriott was looking for a hostess at the restaurant and that I should go for an interview and wear something *grown-up* so I looked attractive for all the businessmen who stay there from out of town. He sounded sincere, like he really wanted to help me. He sounded nice for a change. And I believed him! I'm so stupid, Charlie! So stupid!"

She stopped herself from crying again with a drink and a drag and then looked at the burning cigarette and the long piece of ash that hung on its edge.

"I waited a long time for the manager. Over an hour. I sat at the bar with a Shirley Temple because that's all they could serve me, and they were nice to even let me sit there at all, and then all of a sudden I heard his voice say hello."

"The manager?" I asked, because I was still a stupid idiot.

"No," she said, shaking her head. "Not the manager."

Suddenly, I got it. The whole scene. The whole picture. It had all been a setup.

"Oh!"

Keller nodded. "It was Coop. And he sat down and ordered a drink. I asked him what was going on and where was the manager? Was he meeting us later? Was Coop going to introduce us? And you know what he did?"

I did know, but I let her tell it.

"He laughed. That horrible laugh he makes when he wants to humiliate us. The way he laughed when he called Janice's son *half-pint*. That kind of laugh. And he said, 'Why do you need another job when you already have two jobs working for me?' And I said, 'Because you keep cutting back my hours, and I can't pay the rent and take care of my grandmother,' and he made this . . . this fake pity face, and I wanted to punch him right on his nose!"

"What did you do?" My heart was pounding with sheer hatred.

"I swallowed it all down. And then I asked him why I was here, and he said, 'So I can show you that it's really not so bad to go out with me. See?' He said, 'Look how nice this place is. And they have good food, and I can even sneak you a cocktail if we sit at a table. And all we have to do is have dinner. That's all. Just dinner, you see? Is it really so bad?'"

Another sip and another drag and then she started to cry, and I was suddenly hoping Ian wouldn't find Levi in time and that Levi would pound Coop's face right into the ground.

"So what did you do?" I asked.

She started to laugh, but it wasn't a normal laugh. It was a laugh that people make when they can't cry anymore.

"I lost my shit, Charlie. I ran out of the restaurant and even took off my shoes because they were slowing me down, and I kept running, barefoot, through the lobby and out to the parking lot and got in my car and locked the doors and drove a few miles down the road until I realized I was in no shape to drive. So I pulled over, and then I did something even more stupid than anything else that night. I called Levi."

Keller said that he calmed her down and then talked to her the whole time she drove home. He didn't want her to wait for him to get to her, because what if Coop drove past her on the interstate? Or some other creep? She had to keep moving.

And while she was driving home, Levi went to her house. Dot let him in, and she was lucid and watching her shows on the TV. Soaps all day. Game shows all night. The usual. Keller recorded them on the DVR. She had to make sure they were new episodes because Dot wouldn't watch anything twice. Even when she couldn't remember that Keller was Keller and not her mother, she could remember whether she'd seen an episode of one of her shows, and it would send her into a rage. I had no idea before tonight what those rages really looked like. That those rages had been causing all the bruises.

But Levi did.

So when he got there, he went inside and made sure Dot was lucid and calm while he waited for Keller, and when he saw her car pull in the driveway, he ran outside and met her at the door, and she fell into his arms.

"He picked me up, Charlie, just like I was a little girl, like I weighed nothing. He picked me up and carried me into the house and put me down on the sofa next to Dot's chair, and they both looked at me, and they both thought things because of the way I was dressed and my hair and the makeup that was running down my face. And because I wasn't wearing any shoes."

I could picture it as I sat there looking at Keller's face and her bare legs that were crossed in the chair because the tube dress was so short and so tight. And even after I'd cleaned off what I could with the towel from the sink, the mascara was smeared all around her eyes.

"Something went off inside Dot, and she started screaming at me, about being a whore, but not because she thought I was my mom, but because she thought I was a whore. The real me. Even if all I'd done was try to get a new job where men like to look at you while you walk them to their table."

She sighed and I waited. And then she continued.

"Levi started pacing around the room like a wild animal, asking me all kinds of questions. Was there even a job? Was it all a setup and did I consider it? Did I think about having dinner with Coop to get more hours at the diner and The Triple S? He was getting louder and crazier. So loud and crazy that Dot shut up and sat perfectly still in her chair because we both felt it, how Levi was about to explode. I tried to tell him that of course I didn't stay, that I left, and Levi said it didn't matter. It was still wrong. Still a betrayal, because I didn't tell him I was going there in the first place."

Levi finally did explode. He didn't stay to comfort Keller. He didn't stay to make sure she was safe from Dot.

"He just stared at me like I had mortally wounded him because of something Coop had done! Like maybe *I* was responsible for him getting the idea in his head. Maybe *I* had led him on, and look at my clothes and makeup—what was Coop supposed to think? So when he turned and left and his car peeled away from the curb, I knew where he was going and what he was planning to do. Before he left, Charlie, right before, he said he never wanted to see me ever again."

She broke down after she told me this. Head in her hands, hands between her knees. Sobs and heaves of breath and just wrenching despair that I could not stand for. Not in Keller. This was not how her story would end.

"Come on," I told her. "Let's get you changed. I'll take care of Levi."

I grabbed the phone again, and this time I didn't just check it to see if Ian had found Levi. I had the power to do something. I had the ability to stop this.

I dialed and waited just two rings before Coop picked up.

CHAPTER THIRTY-THREE
NOW

Hello, Charlie.

It's Agent Zellman.

"How did you get in here?" I ask him. He tells me the door was open, but I know I locked it behind me. And I turned on the alarm.

"You must have forgotten," he says. "You're in a panic, Charlie. Sometimes when that happens, we don't remember things. Short-term memory is lost. But it's okay, because I'm here now. You're safe."

I remember about the office and the blood. He was going to send his team to check on Daryl Romansky a.k.a. Dana Blakely.

"Did you find the office? With the blood? Did you find the dead lawyer?"

Agent Zellman nods calmly. "We saw the office with the blood. And, yes, Charlie. We did find Daryl Romansky. I'm so sorry to have to tell you this. Please try not to get too upset. But we found her body. It was in the dumpster behind the building. They shot her."

"Oh my God! I knew it! I knew they killed her!"

He tries to calm me down but that's impossible. That woman is dead.

"But why? I don't understand. Wasn't she working for them? To trick me into giving her the things from the safe?"

Agent Zellman shrugs and holds his palms to the sky. "These people, it's like I said about dog-eat-dog. Loyalty breaking down. Anything could have happened—a fight over how to split the money once they found it, or maybe she was double-crossing them. We'll probably never untangle it all."

"But now they have no way of getting the money. It doesn't make sense."

Agent Zellman agrees with me but that's not important now.

"What we do know is that you have what they want, and they know how to get to you, with or without that woman pretending to be your lawyer. Which means you are in terrible danger. We need to bring you in. Right now."

He goes on about how I need to give them everything I have to use against them—the cell phone, what was in the safe, and anything I know about the inventory and sales numbers.

"We have to build a case to put them in jail where they can't hurt you or the people you care about."

Now I'm worried that what I have isn't enough. "What if all of that evidence isn't evidence of anything, just money hidden somewhere. The money on its own doesn't prove a crime was committed. Money is just paper."

He tells me they're good at building cases and I shouldn't worry about any of that.

"This is what we do—and believe me, we have plenty of evidence already in place to arrest Barry and his team. And now we have a murder—maybe two murders if they killed Clay Cooper and we can prove it. I just need you to give me what you have and let me bring you in so I can keep you safe. We don't have much time."

I can't think but I have to do just that. I have to think!

"Where's your team?" I ask him. I haven't even seen him with a partner.

"They're outside, Charlie. I thought it would be intimidating for you to be bombarded with agents. But they're right outside, waiting to take you in—to safety . . ."

Just then, the house alarm goes off. I knew I'd set it.

Agent Zellman is worried. "What's that?"

"I told you I locked the door and turned on the alarm . . ."

"Who has a key to get in?"

I know who it is. The only person it could be. We hear her voice call out as she punches in the code to turn off the alarm before it sends a signal to the police.

"Charlie?" my mom calls out. "What's going on?"

Agent Zellman holds his finger to his lips like I'm supposed to stay quiet now and not even answer her. But she calls out again.

"Charlie?"

I step out of the dining room where she can see me. "Mom, why are you back so early?"

She walks toward me, her eyes on her keys which she slides into her bag.

"You wouldn't believe it! The girl who does my color was out today, and the others don't know what they're doing, so I just got up and left, my hair soaking wet and . . ."

Now she looks up and sees Agent Zellman standing behind me.

"Who is this man in my house?

"Mom, don't . . ." I try to warn her.

And then she says the strangest thing.

"Is that you? After all these years? I'll be damned. Ward Harlow, is that really you?"

CHAPTER THIRTY-FOUR
THE NIGHT OF THE MURDER

Coop was easy to lure in. He picked up on the second ring, and when I told him that I needed to see him right then, that night, he was curious in a disgusting way, because it meant I needed something from him. And when you needed something from Coop, that's when he could make you give him something in return, even if that something was nothing more than your dignity. His two hands, one giving and the other taking. Rule Three about people being predictable. Rule Twenty-Four about good and evil.

It was no surprise that Coop said he would meet me at The Triple S in half an hour.

Levi had been chasing his tail, stopping at all the same places, but missing Coop here and there, which is why they say to children, if you ever get lost, stand still and someone will find you.

I still had Tracey's car, and he was stuck at the store, already past closing and pissed off at me because he had a party to get to.

When I pulled into the parking lot, Coop wasn't there yet. It was just Tracey, so I parked, went inside, quickly helped Tracey close up, and rode off on my bike before him, so he saw I was leaving. I didn't want anyone to know I was meeting Coop, alone, after hours, because rumors would start, and then they would spread, and I needed to just go to college and not become the talk of the town.

I circled back around the shop and waited for Coop. He got there just past ten thirty. He drives a silver pickup truck with a special container in the back to hold animals he kills when he goes hunting. And he has a rack for his shotgun, which he sometimes keeps there and sometimes doesn't, because he's always afraid someone will break in, steal the shotgun, and kill someone, and then he would somehow get framed for the murder, because that's the kind of world we live in.

I watched him pull in and park. I watched the lights go on in the store. I checked my phone one last time and even tried to call Ian, but he didn't answer.

I almost texted Ian about where I was, but I really, really didn't want anyone to know where I was and who I was with. The whole idea of it made me sick, and I hadn't even gotten off my bike yet.

The back door was open, and I went inside. Coop was in the office sitting at his desk. He was agitated, and that was not a good thing.

"Charlie Hudson," he said, seeing me there, still in my jeans and Triple S T-shirt from the dinner shift.

He slid out of his chair and walked to where I was standing in the prep room, between the two metal tables.

He stood too close, which was something he liked to do, but it felt even worse when we were alone, and I realized that in all the years I had worked for Clay Cooper, I had never been with him like this. Alone.

He tilted his head and smiled.

He said nothing about Keller, because he had no idea she was my best friend and had probably told me what had happened at the Marriott. He knew next to nothing about any of us, even though he saw us every day, because nothing mattered beyond what he wanted from us. He didn't care about Keller's grandmother or the bruises or about me wanting to go to college or about my spreadsheets and how I kept the inventory and stocked the refrigeration units and that I was good with numbers. Very good.

"So what's going on, huh? Where's the fire?"

I had the story worked out in my head. What I needed to say to make Coop interested and engaged so he would stay here long enough for Ian to find Levi. I had my phone on vibrate inside my back pocket so I would know if he texted or called and I could get the hell out of there and away from Coop.

It would have been far easier to tell him the truth—that Levi wanted to beat him to a dead, bloody pulp, but then he might have welcomed that challenge. He might have found Levi himself and asked for the fight and then gotten Levi arrested. Nothing would have made him happier, and he would have taken a beating to see that happen.

So I lied.

"I've been saving money for college."

Coop leaned against one of the prep tables and crossed his arms. A creepy smile began to form in one corner of his mouth when he nodded.

"Well," I continued, "I'm already working as many hours as I can here without missing school."

Coop let out a little moan, like an *aha-I'm-starting-to-understand* sort of thing.

"I can get some money in federal loans," I tell him, killing time. "But for other loans, I need a co-signer, and my mom can't do it because she doesn't have anything in her name, and my stepfather, Dusty, well . . ."

Coop jumped in at the mention of Dusty's name.

"He's a cheap prick, right? I always knew it. Lawyers. They're all the same. Every last one of them. So . . . Go on . . ."

I told him that if he co-signed a loan for one year, I would promise to come back and work every summer and that I would use that money to pay down the loan and *blah, blah, blah*. I went on and on because none of this was real. I would never ask Clay Cooper for a favor. *Never.*

Coop looked me up and down, then shook his head. "Follow me," he said.

He led us into the office and bent over to where the safe is kept under the desk, and he opened it.

His breathing was heavy with agitation. I'd seen him like that before. Once when a customer complained about his sandwich and wanted a refund. Once when he caught Levi and Keller making out in the parking lot on her break. Once when Nora showed him the Excel models. The list was actually pretty long, so I stopped thinking about it.

When he stood up and faced me, he was holding a large handful of bills.

"You need money for college, Charlie? Money like this?"

He shoved the pile of bills right up to my nose.

"Smell that, Charlie. That's what money smells like. Real money. Cash money."

It smelled disgusting, like must in an old, grimy closet, but I kept a straight face.

When I turned my head to the side, he yelled at me to "smell it! Smell it, Charlie!"

So I sniffed in the smell of the bills and winced.

"That's right. It smells bad, doesn't it? It's dirty and it smells dirty. Because thousands, maybe even millions, of human hands have touched it and handled it, and human hands are filthy dirty. Everyone talks about crisp, clean bills, but money isn't like that for men like me. Maybe for a banker who gets his money right off the press. But for the rest of us, it's like this. It's filthy. But it doesn't matter. Because my filthy dollar is just as valuable as that asshole banker's crisp, new dollar, so screw him."

He took the money away from my face and looked at it while he went on and on about how you had to be smart and avoid taxes. Taxes and taxes and taxes. Payroll taxes. Social Security taxes. Unemployment Insurance taxes. Medicaid taxes. Every one of those filthy dollars would be cut in half. But he was smarter than that.

He stepped closer to me, his face again becoming playful but aggressive.

"You're still a girl, aren't you, Charlie?" His eyes traveled to right smack between my legs. "You are, aren't you?"

I felt my face turn bright red with embarrassment, and then the heat came.

"It's important to know what your assets are, Charlie. And how you can monetize them. Do you know what that means? It means to get money for something. Money for the things you have that people want."

I didn't answer. I knew about monetization from my economics class. Duh.

But then he went on, telling me about what men paid for nice girls like me.

"You need money for college? All you have to do is go on the Internet, with that innocent face of yours, and name your price. I bet you'll get two years tuition for one go."

It took me a second to realize what he was saying, and when I did, I looked at him with disgust because Coop had never looked as dirty as he did right then.

I didn't say a word as I backed away from him.

Coop followed me, his face beaming with agitation and the sweat running from the bald spot down the sides of his face.

"Girls give it up for a smile in gym class. For a date to the prom. For a moment of feeling important. Such a waste. Some schmuck would pay your college tuition, Charlie. For one night. And you girls all complain about not having any power."

This was one of those times when it was good to be a girl people don't understand, because I forced the disgust off my face and replaced it with a smile and said I needed to use the bathroom, and then I walked and didn't run even though I felt like running. I had never been afraid of Coop. Not really. But tonight he was agitated and talking about men paying me for *one go*, and I started to wonder if it really was good to be a girl like me right then, because who would ever believe me if Coop suddenly lost his shit and decided to take from me what Keller wouldn't give him?

I went into the bathroom and locked the door. I needed time. I needed to know what was going on with Levi. I needed to know if I could leave, and then I needed a plan to get out.

I ran cold water and cupped my hands to catch it and pressed it into my face. I took a long, deep breath and told myself it was almost over. I just had to make sure Levi was safe and then make it out that back door.

I had no idea that this was just the beginning.

CHAPTER THIRTY-FIVE
NOW

Ward Harlow? Is that you?

My mom seems surprised, like she's just run into an old friend at the mall.

"What are you doing here?"

But then it hits her and everything changes.

"Hey—what are you doing in my house . . . with my daughter?!"

I'm so confused. But also, worried. She's about to make everything worse.

"What are you talking about, Mom? This is Agent Zellman. With the FBI. He was asking me about Coop's murder. That's all."

She's not buying it. "Zellman? FBI? That's Ward Harlow, from Sawyer High! He was in the same class with Coop and Cullen Maguire. He moved away the summer after graduation . . ."

I don't give up. "But he's with the FBI. I saw his badge, and Ian checked it out and . . ."

"That can't be right! Ward . . ."

Agent Zellman is tongue-tied. He hems and haws, which is what Janice calls it when someone stalls for time. "Uh . . ." is all he manages to say.

I use the time to manage the situation. "Mom—listen to me! Coop was involved in some bad things, and Agent Zellman has been trying to find out what his employees saw. Isn't that right?"

Agent Zellman gets on board. "That's right. Who is this man you think I look like?"

"His name is Ward Harlow," my mother says now, her voice wary and tentative like she's not sure what to believe. "I haven't seen him since high school, but still . . . the resemblance is uncanny . . ."

Agent Zellman latches on to this. "Well, they say we all have doppelgangers out there."

My mom tries to walk the thin line that she sees before her. "I hope this doesn't sound rude, but I'm not really comfortable with any of this. You shouldn't be in my home, alone, with my daughter. I don't care who you are. She has a lawyer, you know. And how do I even know that you are who you say you are? I'm going to call Dusty and have his office verify your credentials. And then I'm calling Charlie's lawyer. It won't take long—we can go in the kitchen and have some coffee if you want . . ."

She doesn't realize she's just crossed it.

"Eileen—put down the phone."

Agent Zellman has drawn a gun from his waistband and points it at my mom.

"Are you seriously pointing a gun at me in my own home? Charlie? What's going on?"

I don't have time to explain. "Mom—just do what he says. Please. I was trying to warn you."

She studies his gun and sees what I see—a silencer. It's unmistakable if you've ever seen one on TV. It's long and sticks out from the barrel.

"Cops don't use those," she says, pointing at the weapon. "FBI agents don't use those . . ."

Now my phone rings and everything stops cold.

Agent Zellman looks at me and suddenly he's not Agent Zellman. He's Ward Harlow from my mom's high school. "Don't get that, Charlie. And, Eileen, same goes for you. No one touches a phone."

"But it's probably Ian, because I left him a message earlier and . . ."

My mom chimes in, cutting me off. "And if she doesn't pick up, he'll know something's wrong, and he'll be here in a split second. In fact, he's probably here right now, outside this house, with the entire police squad!"

Ward isn't buying it. "Both of you—slide the phones over to me. Across the floor."

We both do what we're told, which is a bad sign. Especially for my mom.

"Okay then," Ward says. "That wasn't so hard, was it? And I don't see any cop cars out there, Eileen. You know, you used to be smart. A little naïve maybe, letting that teacher get his way with you, but smart. That's what happens in Sawyer. Nowhere to go but down. Now—Charlie. Let's get back to what we were discussing. You were about to give me the cell phone and the things from Coop's safe, remember?"

I nod. I need to get him away from my mom. She's what people call a loose cannon.

"They're upstairs. In my room," I tell him.

We start to move but my mom isn't having it.

"Charlie, don't you move. You're not going anywhere with this piece of garbage."

"I'm sorry you feel that way," Ward says.

And in a split second, she lunges toward him and he fires. The shot hardly makes a sound.

"Mom!" I yell as I watch her fall back against the wall and slide to the ground.

I start to go to her, but Ward points the gun at me and says,

"She has about fifteen minutes before she bleeds out. Better get moving."

CHAPTER THIRTY-SIX
THE NIGHT OF THE MURDER

I was about to give up on finding Levi. I was about to leave the bathroom and make my escape past Coop and his wad of cash when I felt my phone vibrate in my back pocket. It was Ian calling.

"Do you have him?" I asked. "Did you find Levi?"

"Charlie . . ." Ian could hardly speak. He was driving, that much I could tell, but his voice was shaking. He might have even been crying.

"What? What happened?" I leaned against the edge of the sink, staring at the tiles on the floor, which were dirty because Lazy Tracey could never do a damned thing he was told.

"I found it. I found the car."

"Levi's car?"

"No, no . . . the car . . . the orange car. The orange Buick LeSabre. The car that killed my father!"

"What? Where is it? Where are you right now?"

"Coop has it, Charlie! Which means Coop was driving it and has hidden it all these years, right here! Right under our noses!"

I was speechless then, staring at the dirty tiles, my butt against the sink.

"How . . . where?"

I heard Ian draw a long, deep breath so he could tell me what had happened.

"I went out to the warehouse where Coop has those poker games. I was looking for Levi like you asked. There were no cars, and it was dark, but I got out to make sure, in case Levi had come and gone. I walked the perimeter, checked inside through the windows. But there was nothing. No one. And then . . . then as I was heading back, I noticed this old garage through some trees with a small access road. So I thought maybe that's where he holds the games, or maybe something else, I don't know. I went back there, flashed my light through a small window on the side. And there it was, Charlie! After all these years— there was the orange Buick! The car that killed my father!"

I didn't know what to say. So I said the dumbest, most obvious thing. "Are you sure?"

"Tell me the VIN number. I wrote it down. Tell me! Do you have the one from the car that was stolen?"

"Hold on." I open the notes app on my phone where I keep important things. Like this. "XPG749TYW8643PL97," I tell him.

"That's it! That's the one on the car in Coop's garage. And there was a dent along the hood, and scraped paint—and . . . there's something else, Charlie."

"What is it?"

"I couldn't be sure, but it looked like he hit my father dead on, not from the side, not like he was trying to swerve to miss him. But head on, like . . . like he wanted to kill him!"

My heart was back in my throat. I heard Coop calling for me. Then I heard a car pulling into the lot, and I peeked out the door in time to see the flash of red, the taillights passing.

"Where's Levi?" I asked Ian, stepping back into the bathroom so Coop couldn't hear me.

But there was no answer.

"Ian?" I said his name over and over, louder and louder. "Ian!"

There was no answer. The call was disconnected. And now someone was here, after closing. Levi was missing, on a quest to find Coop. Maybe even to kill him. Coop was in the back of the store with the door unlocked. And I was here, in the bathroom like a scared little mouse.

Time passed. I can't say how long because I was frozen, staring at my phone. Willing it to ring. I needed to hear the end of Ian's story. But then I remembered about Coop waiting and being agitated, and I knew I had to just get out of there any way I could and worry about Ian and Levi later. I devised a plan using Rule Number Six. *People are easily distracted.* I would distract Coop by talking about Keller as I moved slowly around him toward the exit.

I opened the bathroom door and began to walk back toward the service area. And that's when I heard the sound that had me scrambling to hide beneath the counter.

I hid there and listened to the fighting. Fists punching and things crashing from shelves and then the sound of a metal tomato slicer on a skull, which I would only identify later, when I saw it.

It was the sharp corner that hit Coop's head, crushing it, smashing it in deep, and with such force that Coop fell over onto the metal table and began to bleed until he was dead.

CHAPTER THIRTY-SEVEN
NOW

"Mom! Mommy!"

I scream and lunge toward them, Ward with his gun still pointed down and my mom lying on the ground. Not moving.

I haven't called her *Mommy* since I was a little girl. Since before we ran from that house in the middle of the night. But that is the word that leaves my mouth in this moment.

Ward turns the gun at me.

"Fifteen minutes before she dies. What are you gonna do, Charlie?"

It was in that moment that I understood myself more than ever before. I could feel emotions taking over, my hot head making me freeze like I did in the car that night when Agent Zellman surprised me, shocked me.

The analytical part was retreating, shrinking back, away from the heat.

I look at my mom lying on the floor, bleeding, dying, because of me. Because I brought Ward here, and because she tried to save my life.

I'd put it all together on the way back from the pool of blood at my fake lawyer's office. As I was pedaling faster and faster to get to this house and finish what I started.

Rule Number Zero. The Golden Rule: Trust No One.

I went through the list of things that didn't add up. Things I could use to prove Zellman couldn't be trusted.

First, his car keys hung on a Budget-Rent-a-Car chain. What kind of FBI agent rents a car from Budget?

Second, he smells of cigarettes and alcohol, and what kind of FBI agent smells like that? Especially on duty?

Third, he doesn't have a partner, and he only has one set of clothes.

Fourth, his story doesn't add up. Coop didn't pretend to sell *more* sandwiches and cigarettes. He didn't pretend to order *more* inventory. And he didn't pretend to rent *more* apartments. Agent Zellman told me that Coop inflated all of those things to clean the cash Barry gave him. Barry, this criminal from the city. But Coop didn't inflate those things. He *deflated* them.

I know exactly how many sandwiches we sell and how much inventory we buy because Nora and I keep track and we put it into the spreadsheets that she keeps on her thumb drive, so that we can be efficient, in spite of Coop's refusal to keep any records. I remember enough. The ledgers Coop wrote down and the actual numbers from the register and the invoices for food. It was on Nora's thumb drive, but it was all in my head too.

Coop wasn't involved in any money-laundering scheme. He was selling sandwiches and tobacco and food at his diner for cash, and renting apartments for cash, so he could take the cash and put it somewhere safe where he would never have to pay taxes on it, or risk having it in a bank or the stock market or have anything to do with the government in any way.

Numbers don't lie. People do.

And I know I locked the door. I know I turned on the alarm. Which means Zellman was in this house before I came in. He was lying about being "in the field."

Finally, Agent Zellman was lying about his identity.

Pretending not to be "Barry," but the man trying to catch him.

And now I know that "Barry" is actually Ward Harlow—the fourth boy on that ledge when Rudi Benton fell to his death. I don't know much more beyond that, but that's still a lot.

It was a visceral reaction that became the most important part of my analysis. Yes, it came from years of watching my shows and studying behavior, but also from my mom's theories about men and women and from watching her theories play out around me every day. And it boiled down to this: Why would an FBI agent enlist a teenage girl with a lop-sided seesaw to help catch a low-life crime lord? A real FBI agent would never do that. No one would.

Now I know exactly who Ward is. I know what he wants and what he thinks of me. But I'm in control and I have to survive.

I make the decisions I had planned to make before my mom came home early from her appointment.

"I told you—they're upstairs," I tell Ward. I make sure my voice is shaky. I make sure to tremble, to look weak.

And then I say the things that he's expecting me to say as I walk up and he follows behind me, the gun pointed at my back.

"Please don't kill me . . . I'll give you everything . . . And I won't tell anyone. I promise. I'll never tell a living soul."

Ward doesn't say a word as we reach the top step and walk to the left and open the door to my bedroom.

"No tricks," he says when I lead him inside.

I think of that moment when we drove away from that house where my grandparents were left standing on that lawn. We drove away so they couldn't hurt us anymore, and it didn't matter what came next. Some-times, it all comes down to one choice. And I realize that my mom has been preparing me for this moment my entire life, even if I didn't know it.

I open my closet door, but then I turn back to look at him.

"Promise you won't kill me . . ." I say again.

Ward's face softens. "I don't want to hurt you. I just want my things, and then I'll be on my way." He says it again. "I won't hurt you if you just give me what I want."

And I remember the first rule I ever made, which is Rule Number One. *If someone says the same thing over and over again, that means they don't believe it.*

He holds the gun and stands a few feet back. I reach for my teddy bear and pull it from the shelf. I open the back compartment where I hid Coop's cell phone. But this time, I pull out a folded piece of paper with the number written on it, which I had put in the teddy bear as soon as I came home after finding Daryl Romansky dead.

"This is what I found in the safe," I tell him.

I hand that to him, and I can see that he is hopeful now. That he will get the number and then he can kill me and then blow out of this crumbling, shitty town and find another shitty town and no one will ever know he was even here.

Then I turn back to the closet and reach into the pocket of a ski parka hanging way in the back. I pull out a cell phone that looks just like Coop's. But it's not. It's one I bought at a convenience store the day I hid the real one.

I hand it to Ward and watch as he tucks his gun under his right arm.

He needs both hands to check the phone.

Ward stands behind me, with his gun under his arm while he flips it open. He checks to make sure it has the number he wants, the one that isn't a phone number and that will somehow lead him to Coop's hiding place. He wants to check it against the paper I gave him from the safe. Of course he does. *Trust no one . . . people are easily distracted . . .*

And while Ward flips open the phone and powers it on and begins to scroll through the contacts and notes and other apps to see where the number might be, I reach back into the closet.

"There was also money in the safe. It's here," I tell him.

But there's no money in my closet.

Just Dusty's old pistol, which I pull out with my right hand just as Ward begins to smile, because he sees the number in the memo app.

I flip off the safety with my thumb. I've practiced this a hundred times, so I do it easily. Quickly. I turn. I point.

Ward looks up because one part of his brain has captured the image of me standing there, not with the money or a bag that could be holding it, but with a gun, and it sends an alarm to another part of his brain, which then causes his mouth to gape open and his hands to drop the cell phone and reach for the handle of his gun still tucked under his arm.

But all of this happens too slowly.

Because I don't hesitate for one single second before shooting Ward in the chest.

CHAPTER THIRTY-EIGHT
THE NIGHT OF THE MURDER

The sound of a skull cracking is unmistakable. I had never heard that before, and yet, as I crouched beneath the service counter in the dining area of The Triple S, I knew what it was instantly.

That was the sound that made me wince and cover my ears and that kept me from being the suspect in Coop's murder. It was that look that was just as unmistakable as the sound of the tomato slicer crushing Coop's skull.

I stayed there, under the counter, until I heard the killer go out the back door, and then saw the headlights of a car leave the parking lot and travel down Highway 65 as fast as it could possibly go.

That was when I crawled to the side of the entrance to the service area and peeked around the corner and then moved into the service area. And finally, I disappeared from the camera's sight. The camera I didn't know was there until the next day.

I didn't see Coop's body until I was clear of the center island where we make the sandwiches. It's tall, and we pile things on top of it, like the containers with the oil and vinegar and the box of gloves and other things that don't need to go in the refrigeration units for the night.

And when I did see his body, I stood in place for a long time. Maybe thirty seconds. Maybe five minutes. I have no idea. It felt long, but when you're looking at a dead body, time loses its normal calibration.

He was bent over the metal table, face to the side and looking straight at me with open eyes, his arms stretched out wide.

He looked like a robot. Like someone had unplugged him and put him away for the night. Butt in the air, arms limp across the table.

It was just the blood that gave away the fact that he was human.

And then, what to do?

I can't say what drove me to my decision. I can only say that I felt like those boys in *Lord of the Flies*, which we read in seventh grade. My plane had crashed, and I was on a desert island. No one to help me decide what to do. No rules to follow. Because, as far as I knew, no one had any idea where I was when Clay Cooper was murdered.

In that moment of truth about who I was and what I had just become when that plane crashed, these were my thoughts.

There were five people who wanted Coop dead. Keller. Levi. Janice. Nora. And now, Ian. Any one of them could have been fighting him. Any one of them could have swung that tomato slicer at his head. Maybe in self-defense. Maybe it was an accident. Maybe it was deliberate. But none of that mattered to me. What mattered was that I cared about all five of those people. I cared about them more than I cared about right and wrong. More than justice. More than the trouble I could get in for cleaning up after them.

Each of them would be a suspect, and I ran through the evidence in my mind:

Keller—with the bruises and all the times people saw Coop leering at her and rubbing up against her and brushing his hand across her butt when he had more than enough room to pass by her. And she was with him that very night at the Marriott, upset, running away with no shoes. Her alibi: she was alone with her grandmother. Her senile grandmother.

Janice—a lot of people around town knew about him calling her son half-pint and her husband, Shane, getting in a fight with him and getting fired, and then Janice having to beg to get the job back because they couldn't survive without it. And then there was that huge fight earlier that night. And what about Shane? He'd already taken a swing at Coop before, lost his pride and then his dignity when his wife had to grovel on his behalf. They would be home together, each other's only alibi, and what good would that be?

Levi—Ian knew he wanted to beat Coop to a pulp, and no one knew where he was at the time of Coop's murder. He had no alibi at all. And texts between him and Keller could be even more damning.

Nora—Coop had compromised her integrity and made her lie for him every time she had to sign off on documents about the sales and inventory. Maybe she'd had enough and lost it. Picked up that slicer and smashed it against his head. I didn't know where she was that night after her potluck dinner, but I assumed she was home alone. Alone was a bad alibi if there ever was one.

Ian—Coop had killed his father, and I still had no idea where he was. Maybe he hung up because he was here, pulling into the parking lot while I was in the bathroom. Just like Levi, he had no alibi at all, not even a bad one.

And finally, me—I was here. Keller knew I was out looking for Coop. I thought about what I might have done if he'd tried to stop me from leaving. If someone hadn't killed him first and he was not in the mood for staying within the lines he'd drawn for himself. Yes. I knew. I would have killed him without a second thought.

Any and all of us could have done it if the circumstances had been right. Five people I love. Plus myself, and I wanted to get out of here.

That was when I knew. I had to protect my tribe. I had to keep them all safe. In that moment, I had to be smart and strategic and think like my life and the lives of everyone I loved depended on it. It was good to be me that night, to have my rules and memories of everything I had ever learned about people. It was strange, but I felt nothing about Coop being dead. It was not hard to detach, to make calculations, and to work the way I work every day when I arrive at the back door and say what I say as I prepare for the chaos.

Lettuce tomatoes pickles onions. Lettuce tomatoes pickles onions.

It took hours to move Coop's body and clean the store.

The details are gruesome, but I was not allowing myself to feel anything. Just thinking.

I put on a pair of gloves from the box on the shelf above the counter. I packed the hole in Coop's head with sliced steak until it stopped bleeding. I know that's disgusting, but the wound needed pressure and meat was pliable enough to shove in there. Then I wrapped it tight, round and round with the industrial-size plastic wrap that hangs from a dispenser on the wall above the table where his body lay. I was careful not to get any blood on the dispenser, because it's cardboard and it would soak in and not wash off later.

Lettuce tomatoes pickles onions.

When the bleeding was contained, I took Coop's keys from his pocket and I went to the pickup truck. I backed it right up to the door and opened the hatch to the flatbed.

He had a tarp in the back, which he used to wrap the animals he killed on his hunts before putting them into the metal container. I brought it inside and lay it on the floor, and then I pushed his body until it slid off the table and fell onto the tarp. I wrapped it up. I bound it tight with packing tape. Then I dragged it to the back door.

Trucks like Coop's that are used to help kill animals have all kinds of useful things, like a lift off the back that goes up and down with the push of a button. Flip it to *down* and push, and a metal step slowly moves to the ground. Roll the thing that's dead, in this case Coop, onto the step, flip the switch to *up*, and then press the button, and the step lifts the dead thing up to the height of the flatbed. I rolled Coop, wrapped in the tarp, into the metal container, and closed it shut.

Then I put the truck back where it was and went inside to clean. Janice was the one who told us to order the special bleach. I used the bucket and mop and sponges and towels. I didn't wipe anything down that didn't have blood, because there had to be fingerprints, and lots of them—too clean, and they'd know someone wiped the place down. All of ours and all of the delivery people and so many that they would never find the killer's, even if they tried.

Lettuce tomatoes pickles onions.

I closed the store. I put my bike in the back seat of the truck because I know there are cameras all over town, and the last thing I needed was for someone to see my bike in Coop's truck, if anyone bothered to look. As it turns out, I managed to avoid the places where the cameras are, but it's better to be safe than sorry in a situation like that.

I drove him to his street and dumped his body, then put the keys back in the ignition. I left him by the mailbox so maybe they would think someone had ambushed him right outside his home.

I took the tarp and the plastic wrap and the steak and the tomato slicer and put them in a garbage bag I'd brought from the store. We had three slicers but I doubted anyone else knew this because I do the inventory. I wiped down everything I had touched, and then I rode my bike, with the bag tied on me like a backpack, to a dump site a few miles from the edge of town and tossed the garbage bag into the pile of other bags and junk people had discarded.

Then I went home. I changed my clothes, then washed the old ones, dried them and folded them neatly and put them in the back of my closet. Next, I went to take a shower.

The same words were still playing over and over in my head as I lay down in my bed. *Lettuce tomatoes pickles onions. Lettuce tomatoes pickles onions.*

I think that's everything that happened. Everything I did and didn't do. Everything I did to keep my people safe. To survive in this new world without Coop.

Except for the cell phone and the contents of the safe—the wad of money Coop had held to my face. And one tiny slip of paper. I couldn't be sure at the time, but a second cell phone and contents of a safe seemed like safe bets for things to remove from a crime scene.

CHAPTER THIRTY-NINE
NOW

I don't hesitate for one second when I shoot Ward in his chest. That was the plan, if it came to it, if I was forced into a corner. And there I was. In that corner.

I don't think I knew I could do it until he shot my mom in our living room. But as we walked the stairs to my bedroom, I did know. It was me or Ward. Only one of us was coming out of there alive. And I still don't know why or what any of this is about. What Ward Harlow wanted with Coop or the stuff he'd hidden somewhere or even if he'd killed Coop in the prep room of The Triple S that night, because for the life of me, I thought it was one of my friends.

He looks at me as he grabs his chest with both hands, his gun falling to the ground. He looks at me with surprise, because even though I have been ruthless, finally figuring out who he is, knowing that he would never leave me alone even if I gave him the phone and the paper from the safe, and now just shooting him in the chest without a care—I am still just a teenage girl with a ponytail standing there in front of him as he falls to the ground, onto my shaggy beige carpet, and dies.

I'm shaking violently, holding the gun with both hands, pointing it at Ward even as he lies dead on the ground. It has not hit me yet that

I have done this. It has not hit me yet that this is over. And I haven't really slept for days.

I hear pounding on the front door, and then silence, and then the door breaking and feet racing up the stairs. I hear Ian's voice before I see him, calling in on his radio about a shooting at our address, back-up requested, an ambulance. He stands in my doorway and looks at me just as Ward had looked at me. But whatever he's feeling, it doesn't stop him.

"Charlie," he says softly. "Give me the gun."

I am in a trance. They have come to rescue me, and it's safe to come out now. Out of the forest where I've been a savage. I feel the fear subside. I feel a slow drip of safety enter my blood. But then I remember my mom.

"My mom . . ."

"She's okay. She's awake. She pointed to the stairs."

Relief overwhelms me as I give Ian the gun.

Then he takes my hands and rubs them on his hands to transfer some of the residue.

"Go wash them now, with soap and warm water. Dry them well. Then change your clothes. Throw those in the bottom of the hamper. Do it now, Charlie."

We both hear the sirens coming from town.

When I do as he's instructed and return to the bedroom, Ian is moving things around. He puts Ward's gun back in his right hand and then asks me for confirmation, "He's right-handed?"

I look at him, confused, but manage to nod, remembering that Ward held the gun in his right hand.

"I shot this man. I did it," Ian now says. "I came here and saw your mother shot. There was a gun on the floor beside her, the gun she tried to use to protect both of you. I picked it up then came upstairs and saw this man holding his gun on you. And I told him to stop and put the gun down, but instead he lunged toward me, and I fired, I shot him. With the gun that was in my hand from downstairs."

"But," I begin to say, thinking that a good cop would have left that first gun on the floor and drawn his own weapon as he climbed the stairs.

"I know," Ian says. "But I'm a rookie. This is my first shooting."

I was conflicted in that moment, and he could see it on my face.

"Charlie—I'll be fine, I promise. But you . . . it's not the same."

We hear the paramedics. They're with my mom, and I'm suddenly desperate to get to her.

Yes. That was the conflict. Me shooting Ward in the chest with a gun I'd hidden in my closet, even if it was in self-defense, could spin out of control a hundred different ways.

I'd already refused to tell the police what I knew about the night of Coop's death.

I'd already proven to be a strange girl with my running and my obsession with numbers and making sandwiches and getting out of Sawyer.

I could not be the girl who saved her tribe. Who figured things out and made things right. Girls who shoot men in the chest without a second thought are not brave. They are not heroes. They are either victims or villains. Or, in my case, unwanted snowflakes.

Two officers enter the room. I tell them I need to see my mom and run past them, down the stairs to the stretcher and the people gathered around her.

"She's going to be all right," one of the paramedics tells me, and I don't know if I believe her because people say all kinds of things to frantic teenage girls. But I let myself believe as I get in the back of the ambulance with them and drive away.

CHAPTER FORTY
NOW

I give my statement at the hospital while my mom is in surgery. They like it—I can tell. Every word.

What I say matches Ian's account of the events to a T, because that was our plan. And when I think about what he did, and what he risked for me, I know that I will have a lot to sort out when I finish doing what needs to be done today.

This is what we both say:

I didn't see anything the night Coop was murdered, but I began receiving threats soon after. One of the bad men must have seen me there and thought I'd seen him kill Coop, or heard them fighting. After all, it took them a long time to clean up the store and move his body.

I was then fooled by Ward Harlow pretending to be FBI Agent Zellman, right up until he came to the house to kill me, and my mom walked in, so he tried to kill us both. They checked Dusty's gun and found lots of prints—mine, my mom's, Dusty's, DJ's, Everett's, and Ian's. There was no way to disprove the story.

Ian came because I had called him earlier saying I was scared. This was mostly true. We never mentioned the pool of blood I'd found.

As it turned out, there was no dead lawyer anyway. I had a hard time believing this when Ian told me. Daryl Romansky was *not* Dana Blakely.

Daryl Romansky was, in actual fact, a young male associate from the law firm in Delaware that set up Coop's LLC. That's it. He was never involved in any of this, but I had brought up the possibility, and Agent Zellman (a.k.a. Ward Harlow) had jumped on the chance to confuse me.

There was no real Dana Blakely either. Just Ward's girlfriend, Angie, who agreed to help him work a different angle to get the cell phone and paper from the safe. She wasn't even a lawyer. She'd fooled everyone with her suit and pumps and tight bun of hair, and fake website. That's all it takes around here.

One of them was gaining my trust. The other was scaring the shit out of me. Good cop, bad cop. Fake Dana knew how to talk to me about getting out of here and going to college and all of that. She was very good at fooling us, me and my mom, because—

Rule Number Twenty-Nine: People believe what they want to believe.

And we both wanted to believe that someone was protecting us.

But that wasn't all. They had a third conspirator. The only person who knew how to decode the number Coop left behind when he died.

Regina Cooper.

She was working me from inside my tribe. Through Nora and the police, trying to scare me a different way into handing over the phone and the slip of paper from the safe, which would have gone right to Regina, who would then know what to do with it.

The police couldn't figure out exactly what crimes Ward and Coop had committed together that would make Ward so desperate to get to the things Coop had hidden. Everyone assumed it was money, and that was that.

In fact, Ward had told Regina it was money—money that Coop owed him—and threatened her and her daughter Lillian. You'd never know it by how cool Regina acted when she came into the store with that box of documents, hoping we would recognize something that could help her. She worked that angle, through me and Nora, and then she told Ward everything she knew about me so he could get his hands on that cell phone and the paper from the safe. She also told Ward every-thing she knew about Coop and his law firm. About his lawyer, Daryl

Romansky. I had the number. Regina had the instructions to decode that number to reveal the location of whatever it was Coop had hidden away. Regina must have been pretty scared. Or maybe part of her was happy. Maybe part of her also wanted whatever it was her shitty, shittyhead, shit-for-brains husband had hidden.

I couldn't have seen Regina coming. She seemed too shallow in every way to be that clever.

Rule Number Thirty-Three: People can be smart and stupid all at once.

As for the real FBI Agent Max Zellman, just like Daryl Romansky, they had borrowed his identity. He was a middle-aged desk agent who had no idea his name had been used to con a teenage girl.

The rest of the story Ian and I give to the police went like this: I bought myself time by claiming I had Coop's cell phone hidden in my room, so Ward followed me there. The cell phone I handed him was nothing, just a throw away—something I'd bought to text my friends without my mom knowing. But Ward kept asking me about it, so I figured producing some kind of phone would help me stall until the police got there.

Ian busted in, found my mom and saw Dusty's gun lying on the ground beside her, so he picked it up and came up the stairs. Dusty's gun in his hand, he shot Ward before Ward could shoot him. They asked him why he hadn't drawn his own gun as he climbed the stairs, and the truth is, he did draw his own gun, but he couldn't say that. Ward was shot with Dusty's gun, so Ian said he made a rookie mistake, just like he said he would. And that was that.

Of course, that's just the story we tell the police. A story my mother would later corroborate by claiming to have a "fuzzy memory"—because of having just been shot. When we leave the station that day, I still have no idea who had killed Coop, what Coop had hidden, or why.

CHAPTER FORTY-ONE
NOW

I wait with my mom through the night. She has surgery and wakes up, then goes back to sleep. I sleep too, in the chair by her bed, until Dusty arrives. He had to drive back from The Kids' Cabin then drop the boys at his mother's house. He gives me a very quick hug, the kind you barely feel, then waits on her other side in another chair.

The next morning, she has a lot of tests, and I really need to go to work for the lunch rush. No one questions why I need my routine. And today, even Dusty doesn't care. He offers to call me an Uber since I don't have my bike, so I take one and go to The Triple S.

There's a lot of excitement when I walk in the back door. There's a lot of explaining as well. Janice, Keller, Nora, and Helen are there. Tracey has the day off. No one can believe I have almost been killed by a criminal who also killed Coop over some business deal gone wrong.

And then, we start to prep for lunch.

I always rotate the stock of metal pans in the refrigeration units. It's my job, and people leave me to it because it's not anything exciting or fun and so who really cares?

I put my jacket on because it's cold in there. I take out what we need for the day, pulling from the front. And then I put the newly stocked pans in the back. First in, first out. That's how food stays fresh. Everyone knows that.

I do this for all the stock except the lettuce.

There are four rows of lettuce pans, and they run four deep. Normally, I would pull the whole front row, move the ones behind them forward, then put the new pans we've just shredded at the very back.

Except today, I reach first for the four pans at the back, which have not been rotated since Friday night. Not since I wrapped the money from Coop's safe in plastic and aluminum foil and then tucked it into the pans and then covered it with shredded lettuce. I take out the money from three of the pans, and Coop's cell phone from the fourth, which I put there after that incident at the library. And I place everything into a small drawstring bag, which I then tuck into my jacket.

I finish my work, return my coat and bag to the hooks in the back of the prep room, and join the team on the floor.

It is strangely joyful to make sandwiches. We have a long rush, and the team lets me take the lead, asking for orders ten at a time, laying out bread and meats and cheese and lettuce, tomatoes, pickles, onions. I slip back into my normal routine, even though I'm exhausted and even though I'm still waiting to hear about my mom. No one was worried when I left. I could tell that she was going to be okay.

We all would be okay, as it turned out.

———

The money in the safe amounted to sixty-seven thousand dollars. I had no problem keeping it and using it the way I did. The money was earned from sandwiches we made, but most of it should have gone to the government, so as far as I was concerned, it was like a ball that's slipped from the player's hands and is floating through the air. What do they call that? A fumble? Dumbass Doug probably knows.

Later that week, I would give that money to Keller. She refused at first, insisting I take the money to pay for college, but that didn't feel right to me. I was leaving. I was going to college. Keller needed it just to survive. The money would pay for one year of housing for Dot at a private nursing home in town, where they would at least give her the right medication and keep her safe. Keller would then be able to move in with Levi and live there for free, saving all of her money to pay for the next year at the home, and then the next and the next. Year by year. That's how she could take things. She just needed that little head start to get Dot taken care of. Sixty-seven thousand dollars was a great head start. When I think about how little that is, compared to other things, how little it really takes to save a life, and yet how hard it is to make sixty-seven thousand dollars in a town like Sawyer, it leaves me perplexed. I don't know how else to describe it.

The other thing I would do is pay a visit to the bus terminal on Maybury Street. It was on the ride home after seeing fake Dana's fake blood, then pedaling and pedaling until my brain cooled off and was able to think, and then when I rode past street after street, that I knew what the middle set of numbers represented. 6292879. A street name with seven letters.

I downloaded a program from the Internet that took numbers and generated the possible words they could be, based on a standard phone keypad. The seven digits in Coop's number were 6292879. It took a few hours, but I matched all of those words with a list of street names in Sawyer, and there it was—Maybury. We have a Maybury Street.

Now, Maybury Street is one of our main streets in town, and it also has one of the only public places with lockers that is not in any way owned or funded by any kind of government—federal, state, or local. A Greyhound bus station.

345—the number of the locker. 6292879—digits that contain the letters for Maybury. And finally, the first piece I had figured out, 21704—the combination for the lock.

The lock was an old-fashioned padlock—the kind that only comes off one of two ways. With the right combination, or a giant bolt cutter—but that's something people would notice. The padlock was the circular kind, and it only had digits that went up to 20, so the combination could only be one set of numbers: 2 right—17 left—4 right. Why Coop had thrown in the extra 0 before the 4 and not the 2 is anyone's guess, and I was too tired to do any more thinking. Especially thinking that included guessing. I hate guessing.

I went during the busiest time of the day—Friday at 6 p.m., a week after Coop's murder. That's when people are all going somewhere for the weekend. We don't have a train station, so unless you have your own car, the bus is the only option.

I wore a hoodie, baggy jeans, and sneakers. I bought everything at the mall, all at different stores, and I even bought them in the men's departments just to be safe. Then I covered my fingers with small Band-Aids to keep my prints from being places they shouldn't be. I carried a duffel bag filled with crumpled-up paper bags. Now that I know to look out for cameras, I spotted them right away and made sure to avoid them by walking in front of or behind people, always looking down, keeping my head covered by the hoodie. All those little details that you have to think about when you're committing a crime.

But most of all, I made sure Regina wasn't having me followed. I did that by asking Nora to invite her to the store to meet with both of us at the exact time I planned to be at the bus station. She told Regina we'd found something in her box of documents that might help her locate the thing she was looking for.

I will admit that my heart was jumpy when I found locker number 345. And jumpier still when I turned the first number on the lock, and then the second, and then the third, and then when I heard the click as I pulled straight down. I thought about what I would do if this was really my locker, and if I was just here swapping out one bag for another, like I did this all the time. I would just stare straight ahead into my locker, knowing what was there so it wouldn't cause me any hesitation or surprise.

I pulled the latch.

I opened the door.

I saw the bag.

I took the bag out and put the other one in.

And I didn't look inside. I put the lock back in place, turned the dial, and pulled it once to make sure.

And then I walked out of the station, between two very tall men, my head down, my gait casual, and I didn't stop until I was four blocks away, where I'd left my bike.

It was not easy to ride my bike with that bag.

Eight-hundred-fifty-two-thousand-seven-hundred-sixty-four dollars in assorted bills weighs a LOT.

When Regina got to The Triple S, Nora told her I had to go help with Keller's grandmother, and she didn't doubt it for a second. And then Nora gave her the paper from the safe with the number she'd gone to all that trouble to find.

It probably took her most of the night to figure out what street 6292879 was because Regina was not very good with numbers. So even though Coop had told her how to break the code—locker number, street, combination—that middle part is not easy. Each number corresponds to three or four possible letters—the ones on a dialing keypad, so it's a puzzle that requires some problem-solving.

I wonder what she thought when she went to all that trouble and then found only crumpled-up paper bags inside that duffel bag. I wonder how long she cried and whether she was kicking herself for choosing the kind of man who cheats and steals and has a bald spot that gets shiny around girls half his age.

I didn't keep that money. It wasn't mine, and besides that, I had already taken the sixty-seven thousand dollars from the safe.

Instead, I made a deal with Regina, who was facing a lot of trouble with the IRS after Nora gave them the spreadsheets that showed Coop had been cheating on his taxes. It served her right for lying about the IRS coming to her house and threatening her when really it was Ward Harlow. It served her right for scaring Nora half to death about it when the IRS had no idea what Coop had been doing all this time.

With the money from the locker, Regina then made a deal with them that allowed her to keep some of it and not go to jail. But I wouldn't just hand it over. In exchange, Nora, Janice, and Keller now own ten percent of The Triple S, which was restructured into a co-op, which means that the employees get to share in the profits as well as get their salaries. Regina probably won't make any money from it ever again, but I thought that was fair.

I couldn't go back in time and tell my mom not to let Mr. Nelson get to her, and I couldn't not be born or make my grandparents not call her a whore and give her a better life in a better place, but I could do this one thing to help my other family, and so I did it.

But there was something else in the duffle bag I found in the locker. A small cassette tape in a plastic case with one word written on it. A name. *Rudi.*

CHAPTER FORTY-TWO

It is now ten days after I shot and killed a man, and finally, I have all of the pieces to the puzzle.

First. Who didn't kill Clay Cooper. Me. Keller, who was with her grandmother and waiting for Levi to come back. Levi, who gave up soon after he went looking for Coop and went to a bar and drank six beers. Nora, who stayed late at a potluck dinner to help clean up and was actually still there at the time of Coop's death. And Janice, whose neighbor saw her take out the trash around the same time.

The tape I found in the duffel bag with the cash is a DV. I had to buy an old camcorder on eBay to see what was on it.

I watched it alone the first time, but the second time, I rode my bike to Ian's house and made him watch it with me. Once I saw it, I knew Ian was the second piece of the puzzle.

It was surreal, seeing Clay Cooper, Ward Harlow, Rudi Benton, and Cullen Maguire eighteen years ago when they were seniors in high school. They looked so young, younger than we look now, but then people never see themselves how they really are.

"What is this?" Ian asked me. I hadn't told him why I was coming or what I'd found. And of course, I hadn't forgotten what he'd said to me the night Coop was murdered—how he'd found the orange Buick in an old garage on one of Coop's properties.

"Just watch," I told him.

Clay Cooper, age seventeen, speaks as the recording plays. "Well, here we are walking through the woods . . . ooh exciting . . . is everyone excited? Rudi—hey Rudi—don't trip, moron." Then he turns the camera on himself. His stupid fat face takes up the entire screen. "In case anyone gives a shit, our teacher bailed to go swimming. Douche bag." Then it goes back to the three boys walking in front of him.

"That's my dad," Ian said.

"Yeah—your father, Rudi Benton and . . ."

"Holy shit—isn't that the guy you shot? Ward Harlow?"

I nodded as we continued watching.

The boys walk and talk trash. Ward is high strung and agitated, like he can't contain something inside him. Something powerful and ugly. He snaps twigs from trees, kicks dirt. I notice his hands swinging, patting his legs, like he doesn't know what to do with them. Until he does know. He takes one at first, his right hand, and shoves Rudi, who is directly in front of him. Rudi stumbles and falls to his knees, then gets up. He doesn't turn to defend himself. He says nothing, accepting what's happening as if it's happened before. As if he knows he will make it worse by speaking up. But Cullen Maguire, who is behind Coop and off camera, does. We hear his voice. "Cut it out, Ward." That's all he says. Ward turns around, looking past Coop to Ian's father, and tells him to "shut the hell up."

The boys keep walking. Coop keeps filming, random things now, like the treetops and the steep ledge that's off to their right. The camera is not on the boys when we hear another thud and a cry this time. Then it jerks back to Rudi on the ground again, this time not getting up. He's hurt his leg and sits, cradling it, trying not to make a scene. Coop says, "damn!" Ward laughs. Cullen moves now, in front of Coop and Ward to help Rudi. He tries to help him up. "Can you stand?" Cullen asks him. Rudi leans on Cullen and tries to put weight on his leg, but it buckles.

Cullen looks at Ward with disgust but doesn't escalate the situation.

"Let's get him down." Coop keeps filming, zooming in on what looks like a bloody kneecap. "Damn!" he says again.

"You're such a weenie, you know that?" Ward says to Rudi. Cullen tries to help Rudi walk in the other direction, past Ward. "We have to get him back down. Coop, turn that damned thing off and help me!" But Coop keeps filming. It's as if he knows this is not over.

"Are you okay?" I asked Ian as we watched. I knew what was coming.

He couldn't look away. "Just keep playing it."

As Cullen tries to walk past Ward, his hurt friend leaning against him, Ward grabs Rudi's arm and throws him to the ground. The other boys appear stunned, as Coop stops commenting on each scene and Cullen stops protesting. What happens next is beyond disturbing. The first blow is a kick, Ward's hiking boot into Rudi's stomach. The next one is to his head. The next to his chest. They happen so fast it feels choreographed. An explosion of rage and violence that lasts maybe three seconds but leaves Rudi unconscious—the last blow is Ward's spiked heel on Rudi's skull, so hard it cracks open. Just like Coop's did the night he was killed.

Ian gasped and I paused the recording.

"Play it back," he said. I hesitated long enough for him to say it again. "Play it back!"

I went back to the part where Ward grabs Rudi's arm, and this time Ian watched his father, who stands frozen, as if the suddenness of the attack has paralyzed him.

"That's normal," I told him. "It's just fight-or-flight instincts. Your father froze because his brain was trying to catch up to what was happening."

Ian didn't respond. I let it play on.

Ward steps back and watches the blood. Coop says, "Holy shit! Holy Shit!" But he doesn't stop filming. Giving him the benefit of the doubt, he was probably frozen as well, with the camera in his hand pointed at the scene. Regardless, he got it all on the tape.

Ward looks at the unconscious and bleeding boy and lets out another laugh. "Whoa," he says, as if impressed by his own strength. Then he looks around, sorting out the mess he's made. It doesn't take him long to decide. He grabs Rudi by both feet and drags him to the edge of the trail where it meets a steep cliff. Coop and Cullen don't move. Except that Coop's camera follows Ward's movements and captures him rolling Rudi off the ledge. The camera then points to the ground, but the sound of the body falling is unmistakable. The picture moves again to what appears to be inside the front pouch of Coop's sweatshirt, where there is no clear image, only sound. Then there are voices.

Ward says, "He fell. That's it. He got too close and slipped and fell." Cullen and Coop are silent. There is shuffling, like leaves and dirt being moved. "Help me cover the blood, you morons. We're all on the hook for this. Better make it look like an accident."

It's unclear if they helped, but no one says another word, except for this exchange as they appear to be rushing back down the mountain.

Ward says, "Hey, you didn't film that, did you?"

And Coop says, "No man, no. Do I look like an idiot?"

"Oh my God," Ian said when it was over. "Ward killed him. It wasn't an accident. He killed him."

"I know. Ward killed Rudi Benton, and then they all kept it quiet and pretended it was an accident. And Coop had it on tape. That's what Ward was really after. When Coop died, Ward was afraid someone would find it and everyone would see him killing Rudi Benton. Intentionally killing him."

"And there's no statute of limitations on murder."

We both sat there as I let Ian come to the same conclusion I had come to.

"You know," he said then. And I nodded.

This is when I got the second piece to the puzzle. Who did kill Coop and why.

"Coop was blackmailing Ward all these years. And Ward couldn't kill Coop until he had that tape and every copy there might be, and even then, he could never be sure. Coop probably told him there were dozens of copies, and maybe there are. Maybe this is just the original. Ward couldn't kill Coop. But when he was killed, Ward knew he had to track down the tape any way he could."

Ian repeated what he'd said a moment before. "You know."

I had my suspicions. Ian called me that night—I didn't know it at the time, but he was on his way to The Triple S to confront Coop about the orange Buick. I didn't hear who was fighting with Coop in the back room, or who had swung that tomato slicer at his head. But it wasn't Ward Harlow.

It was then Ian told me the part I didn't hear when I was in the bathroom gathering the courage to walk past Coop and his shiny bald spot and that wad of dirty money—what happened after Ian pulled into the parking lot and walked right in through the back door, which was unlocked.

"He told me, Charlie," Ian said. "When I confronted him about the car. He told me he'd been blackmailing Ward for seven years, after Ward got rich with some metalworks company in Pittsburgh. He said he offered some of it to my dad, but he refused. And then, when my dad couldn't take it anymore, when he was drinking himself to death and my mom was ready to leave him, he told Coop he wanted to go to the police.

"Coop told me he begged my father to reconsider, but he wouldn't. He said that he decided to just lie and tell him he would give him the tape. He said they had to meet on that old stretch of Highway 65 where no one would see them because Ward was always following him, trying to find out where the tape was hidden. So my dad went there. He must have gotten out of the car and stood behind it when he saw the head-lights approach."

Ian stopped for a moment, and I thought he might cry, but he didn't. He choked it back and kept telling the story of the night his father died.

"And then when Coop got close, he didn't slow down. He kept on driving until he ran right into him, killing him like a scared animal. That's what Coop called him, Charlie. He called my father a scared animal, frozen with cowardice. He mocked him. Mocked his weakness. And he told me I was just like him. And then he . . . he offered me my father's cut of the money he was getting from Ward Harlow."

"Ian . . ." I tried to comfort him, but he didn't want it. He wanted to tell this next part.

"That was when I threw the first punch, and it just got out of control. Coop had his hands around my throat, and I was able to push him off me and he fell to the ground, but then he started to get up, and he grabbed a knife from the shelf beneath the table, and I knew he was going to kill me, Charlie. Because I knew what he'd done and he knew I would tell the department and they would find the car. I saw the slicer and picked it up, and when he came at me again, I swung it, Charlie. I swung it right at his head!"

I sat beside him, and this time, I was the one to settle his hot head and stop him from shaking.

When he calmed down, he told me that he ran away from the scene. That he went to his mother's house and told her everything so that she wouldn't be shocked when he was arrested. He wanted to say goodbye to her. But she held on to him like she was drowning and he was the last life preserver in the entire ocean. She held on and begged him not to tell anyone what he'd done.

"She told me no one would believe me about being scared for my life. That Coop owned this town, and who was to say that I didn't just go there and kill Coop with intention? I couldn't prove it was self-defense. I couldn't prove he threatened me with a knife. The town would make sure I got the maximum, she said. To pay for his death."

Ian told me he promised her he wouldn't confess unless an innocent person was ever accused. He would stay silent and live with his guilt the way his father had lived with his guilt so that she wouldn't have to watch him spend his life in jail.

"I had no idea you were in trouble, Charlie. You never told me. You just said the FBI was investigating Coop, and I thought maybe that would help everyone. Maybe it would make it so no one was ever accused of his murder—that they would assume it was this criminal he was involved with. I thought maybe I would be able to keep my promise to my mom and also keep an innocent man from going to jail."

The final piece to the puzzle was confirmation by Ward Harlow's co-conspirator—his girlfriend, Angie, a.k.a. Dana Blakely a.k.a. my lawyer a.k.a. a very good liar who made me forget Rule Number

Twenty-Six which is: *If someone seems too good to be true, they are.* She had been questioned and charged with some small things in exchange for her cooperation. She confirmed that Clay Cooper had been blackmailing Ward, but she didn't know what for. Ward told her Coop had just been murdered, which meant the evidence could be found and that it would be very, very bad for him, which would be very, very bad for her.

Ward paid a visit to Regina Cooper the very next day. He threatened her just like she said, and Regina told him what she knew—that there was a number on his cell phone and in the safe that she alone could decode. She thought the number would lead to money. She also knew that I had been at the store, because she'd checked the security camera footage—she was the one who gave it to the police as well. Together, Regina and Ward devised a plan for Angie to pose as a lawyer waiting for a client in the police station, and for Regina to give us a nudge to find her, and it all worked out perfectly. They played me from three angles trying to get their hands on the things they knew I must have taken— the cell phone and the paper from the safe—or if I didn't, I probably knew who did, because of what I heard and maybe even saw.

And that's it. All the pieces.

CHAPTER FORTY-THREE

I take the last order. Chicken salad in a pita with shredded lettuce and tomato. That happens to be my favorite sandwich, and so I tell the woman who ordered it that it was a good choice, and she smiles and says thanks.

It's right after that order that Dusty calls to tell me my mom is being discharged from the hospital and he would like it very much if I could come home early. He sounds like he might even be crying. And this surprises me. It's a good surprise, because maybe it means that he really does love her beyond giving him the boys and cooking his dinner and sleeping in his bed. Or maybe that's what love is, what it gets boiled down to, just like my mom said, after the Keller-and-Levi love is gone.

Maybe that's why she stays even though I know she never loved him the way she loved Mr. Nelson, and that I am the reason she married him and had his babies and lets him sit at the pretend head of the table when she could have had her dreams. And that now she has decided it's too late for those dreams. That she is stuck in this snow globe.

I don't know what to do with these thoughts, so I decide not to think about them at all.

There will be time to think about all of that later—

After I go home and hug my mom and tell her that I love her and that I know she loves me because she saved my life.

CHAPTER FORTY-FOUR
TWO YEARS LATER

My mom picks me up at the bus station, which is ironic. I can't help but glance at locker number 345.

It's not the first time I've been home from college, but usually I catch a ride with a friend who lives somewhere along the way, or my mom comes all the way to get me. She likes coming to Boston. She likes driving her car with the MIT sticker on the back and parking on the street on the opposite side of campus as my dorm. She likes that because she likes the long walk to my dorm, which gives her the chance to be at college even if she isn't in college.

Maybe one day she'll finally go. When she realizes how much life is still ahead of her, even after she's done raising Dusty's boys.

This time, though, it's not a holiday, so the boys have school and soccer and Dusty has work and there was just no way she could make the trip.

"Charlie!" She screams my name when she sees me enter the station from the back where the buses let off the passengers. She screams it loud and proud because everyone in Sawyer has had to hear about me going to MIT a million times, and I think she imagines that the entire world can see now inside our snow globe as I re-enter its glass dome.

She gives me a giant hug and takes my duffel bag. Then she starts talking and doesn't stop until we get all the way home and she has to make dinner.

She talks about things I already know, as though she hasn't told me the exact same things on the phone every Sunday when I call her, or when she texts me every morning to wish me *a great day!*

I've come back for Keller and Levi's wedding, so she starts there. About how normally she wouldn't be happy about such a young girl getting married, but in this case, it's nothing short of a blessing, because after they put Dot in the private nursing home, Keller was able to move in with Levi and save money on rent. And since she was now a co-owner of The Triple S, she only worked one job and was sort of a business owner, which, my mom says, is pretty darn good for a girl like Keller. Levi still works at the gas station, and she rolls her eyes when she tells me this. But at least he's going to marry her, so when they have their babies—which are sure to come any time now—Levi will have some legal obligations to take care of his family.

Now she gets to Ian, and she treads lightly as we get into her car.

"She's nowhere near as pretty as you. Or as smart."

She shakes her head. "Such a shame about that boy. But you don't need to worry about any of that yet. You just keep your head down and study, and who knows where life will take you!"

I smile and nod, but my stomach turns inside out when she says his name, *Ian*, and again when she talks about my future. I suppose Ian and I have stayed friends. I see him when I come home for vacations. We go out with Keller and Levi and other people who are new to me but old to them as they live their lives here and I live mine there. As for my dreams—well, I'm not sure what they are yet, exactly. That's the thing about having a big dream like going to college. Once it comes true, you have to find a new one. I don't know why that is. I can't find an explanation, even though I study all kinds of things now. Not just math, but philosophy and history and feminist theory, which has shed so much light on my mother I can almost see her squinting her eyes as it glares down upon her.

Still, I am restless. I work on the side and in the summers to make ends meet. I study hard because MIT is a really hard school. But it's not enough. The restlessness inside isn't placated by keeping busy. It's a different kind of stirring than what my mother used to warn me about. But it's a stirring nonetheless.

Dusty is polite when I walk in the door. The boys come and give me a hug only after they're prompted, but I don't take it personally. They're boys and they're getting older. I'm a girl and that's not a good thing. Not yet.

We have dinner, and my mother keeps talking and asking me questions and I get through the night the same way I used to. With mild discomfort. It's easier now, because I know I'm here by choice and that it will be over soon, or whenever I want. Power over my life is something I have come to appreciate.

There's no bachelorette party or rehearsal dinner or anything like that. Just a wedding at the church in town and a small reception in the gathering room down in the basement where they also hold the funerals. It's depressing, if I'm being honest. Keller looks beautiful, of course. Her half-brother gives her away, though I can see her cringe as she holds his arm. Dot sits in the front pew with a nurse and Keller's half-brother's family. A wife and kids.

And then, of course, there's Ian and the woman my mother says is less than me in every way. But I don't bother to compare me to her or her to me or whatever it is my mother does when she sees them together. Because she's his fiancée, and they're going to be married in a year and raise a family in Sawyer, just as I predicted.

Only my prediction didn't include him solving his father's murder. This is what I find myself wondering as I see them in the pew across the aisle, as he turns and waves at me and mouths something about catching up after. I wonder why he didn't leave then. If it was because of his mother. Or because he became a local hero after killing Ward Harlow and solving his father's cold case. Maybe that was enough for him. Whatever it is, I feel my heart break when I see him smile.

I did love him. I know that now. And the heartache has to have something to do with the fact that he is going to spend his life with someone else. But there's something else too. I see it on his face, the weathering from his torment. It's the same torment his father carried from the moment he froze on that trail and watched his friend die to the day his other friend turned him into roadkill on the outskirts of town. Ian spent his youth trying to avenge his father's death, and in the end, that vengeance will be his undoing. Vengeance for which he will never be punished, because it would devastate his mother. Vengeance that goes against everything he stands for. I don't know how or when, if it will be slow and invisible to the naked eye or if it will end in a blaze of horror and anguish. Whatever it will be, it's already breaking my heart.

The ceremony is short and sweet and ends in a kiss. It's not as passionate as I remember, but time does that to kisses. It wears them down into something perfunctory and symbolic, but I don't pass judgment—it's this way for everyone. They are still beautiful together.

A happy reunion follows. Nora, Janice, even Helen. I try to see them when I make it home for the holidays, but sometimes I don't. Sometimes it's too hard to go to The Triple S, even though they are now part owners and I swear it's made each of them stand an inch taller. It's hard to go there and be reminded of Coop's murder and who killed him and what I did to cover it up and how all of us were so close to danger. But here, now, I give each of them a giant hug, even though I've had far too many people touching me today and there's more to come. I make myself soak it in, the feel of Janice's body and the smell of Nora's perfume, because these are the things that still make me feel the freedom that is now mine. It's good to be reminded of the time before your last dream came true. It feels important to remember.

It's not long after that Keller grabs my hand and leads me out the back door. They've cut the cake and had a dance and she's done with all of it. I talk to Keller more than I talk to my mom. We text every day. Little things about customers at The Triple S and updates on my new friends and a boy in my dorm I might like. Keller says that if we don't tell each other the little things, then eventually we'll never be able to catch up. So when she sends me a message that says *"steak and cheese guy!"* with a round red face emoji, I know the shithead from the insurance company down the road was in the store ordering his usual sandwich and being, well, shitty. Those are the things that keep our friendship alive. That's what Keller says, and I believe her because here we are, getting into her car before her wedding is even over.

We park under The Hand of God, she hands me a beer from a cooler in the back seat, and she is every bit as innocent and pure and perfect as she's ever been. We sit on the hood and stare at the stars and listen to the cars roll by on the highway. Her dress spills over, white chiffon brushing the ground. I feel a quick shudder as my shoulders dance. There are so many good memories here.

"Are you happy?" I ask her.

She shrugs and drinks her beer. But her smile is wide and her eyes light up, and I imagine she's thinking about her wedding night and maybe all the nights that she gets to lie next to Levi and feel whatever kind of love she still has for him.

I pray that her love grows into the Janice-and-Shane love and not the Nora-and-her-dead-husband love, or the Eileen-and-Dusty love. But I can't predict the future, no matter how hard I keep trying. And I do. I keep trying.

Even after everything that happened over those five days in our shitty little town, which seemed epic at the time. A tale about a battle between forces no less powerful than good and evil. A story about murder and money and sex and carnage worthy of headline news. The Pulitzer Prize. The Academy Awards. Or maybe just a true-crime podcast. But then I remember.

This is just a story about one American girl. And nobody will ever notice.

Still, every time I return, it seems that this piece of the world should have changed somehow. That this snow globe should have shattered. And yet, it all feels the same and it pulls at my ankles, just like my mom said it would. Not love for a boy, but love nonetheless. Love for these people. For the past versions of me that they will always hold. For the smell of lettuce, tomatoes, pickles, onions, and The Hand of God, and the stirring I once felt beneath it. It pulls me back, but I pull away, making a new rule as I return to my new life the next day.

Rule Number Thirty-Seven: There are no rules when it comes to love.

ACKNOWLEDGMENTS:

Writing *American Girl* was pure joy, and I had a lot of help along the way. Charlie Hudson's story began at Audible Originals, and I am deeply indebted to Lara Blackman for her insightful editing and enthusiasm, Esther Bochner and the publicity and marketing teams for being its champion, Wendy Sherman for putting the deal together, Dr. Katie Ort and Nicole D'Angelo for their professional and experiential guidance in crafting Charlie's character, Michelle Collins for her thoughtful interview, and Paige Layle for giving Charlie an unforgettable voice.

Charlie's story is now in print, thanks to Elisabeth Weed at The Book Group and the Blackstone Publishing team, including Josh Stanton, Anthony Goff, Josie Woodbridge, Addi Wright, Dan Ehrenhaft, Sarah Bonamino, and Rachel Sanders. And a very special thanks to Dan Conaway at Writers House for taking this book under his wing.

Film and television agents Michelle Weiner and Olivia Blaustein at CAA have always found homes for my work with inspiring vision and dedication, and I am truly grateful.

Much of this story is about friendship. I have so many wonderful people in my life that it's hard to name only a few. And there are no perfect words to describe all of the ways they lift me up and catch me when I fall, so I will just say *thank you*—to Pam Peterson and Cynthia Briggs for sharing my life on a daily basis, to Lynne Constantine for making me laugh and always picking up the phone, to Fiona Davis and Greg Wands for their endless support and counsel, and to Jean Kwok for the sage advice and getting me onto the dance floor. I'll guard the door for you anytime (see Chapter Fifteen).

I have dedicated this book to a woman I met when we were just thirteen years old, figure skating at a training facility in Colorado. Sharon—you hold my history in your heart and in your hands and in a way no one else could. You are a gift, both to me and to the countless girls whose dreams you've helped come true with your life's work.

To my complicated and beautiful family—I love you.

To my magnificent children, Andrew, Ben, and Christopher, endless love and gratitude—thank you for sharing your glorious journeys with me!

Finally, thank you to the legend whose song has lived in my bones for over forty years and inspired this story—the late Tom Petty.